Was Elizabeth still as fond of him as she had once been?

Travis couldn't tell.

Once, she'd imagined herself in love with him. And she'd offered him...everything.

He'd wanted to take. Heaven help him, he'd wanted very badly to take.

But he hadn't. Elizabeth Grant needed a man to love her, cherish her, marry her and give her children. Travis McCallister wasn't that man. And he'd always known it.

Years ago Liz's youth had stopped him from reaching out and grabbing for what he'd wanted, for what he knew he couldn't keep.

Such noble self-denial wouldn't be so easy now.

For Elizabeth was a child no longer, but a woman grown....

Dear Reader,

Those long days of summer sunshine are just around the corner—and Special Edition has six fabulous new books to start off the season right!

This month's THAT'S MY BABY! title is brought to you by the wonderful Janis Reams Hudson. *His Daughter's Laughter* tells the poignant tale of a widowed dad, his fragile little girl and the hope they rediscover when one extraordinary woman touches their lives.

June is the month of wedding bells—or in some cases, wedding blues. Be sure to check out the plight of a runaway bride who leaves one groom behind, only to discover another when she least expects it in *Cowboy's Lady*—the next installment in Victoria Pade's ongoing A RANCHING FAMILY miniseries. And there's more romance on the way with award-winning author Ruth Wind's *Marriage Material*—book one in THE LAST ROUNDUP, a new cross-line series with Intimate Moments about three brothers who travel the rocky road to love in a small Colorado town.

And speaking of turbulent journeys, in *Remember Me?* Jennifer Mikels tells a passionate love story about an amnesiac woman who falls for the handsome hero who rescues her from a raging rainstorm. Also in June, Shirley Larson presents *That Wild Stallion*—an emotional Western that's sure to tug your heartstrings.

Finally, *New York Times* bestselling author Ellen Tanner Marsh lives up to her reputation with *A Doctor in the House*, her second Silhouette title. It's all work and no play for this business executive until he meets his match in the form of one feisty Southern beauty in the Florida Keys!

I hope you enjoy all our summer stories this month!

Sincerely,

Tara Gavin
Senior Editor

Please address questions and book requests to:
Silhouette Reader Service
U.S.: 3010 Walden Ave., P.O. Box 1325, Buffalo, NY 14269
Canadian: P.O. Box 609, Fort Erie, Ont. L2A 5X3

SHIRLEY LARSON
THAT WILD STALLION

Published by Silhouette Books
America's Publisher of Contemporary Romance

To Tara, Lynda and all the super Silhouette gang

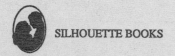

SILHOUETTE BOOKS

ISBN 0-373-24109-7

THAT WILD STALLION

Books by Shirley Larson

Silhouette Special Edition

A Cowboy Is Forever #1055
That Wild Stallion #1109

Silhouette Romance

A Slice of Paradise #369

Silhouette Desire

To Touch the Fire #131

SHIRLEY LARSON

Shirley Larson, a.k.a. Shirley Hart, read her first romance in 1976. Two years and thousands of romance novels later, she decided to try writing one. Her first novel was accepted for publication, and she's been writing ever since, loving every minute she spends spinning romantic fantasies for herself and others to enjoy.

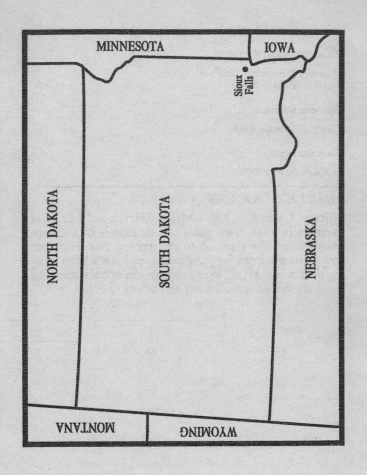

Prologue

She hadn't thought much beyond the original problem of how she would get into his bed. Normally that would have taken great stealth and planning, because her mother was the housekeeper in his house and was there all evening, preparing the supper meal. His father was there, too, his bedroom just across the hall from Travis's. But it had been easier than she'd dreamed. She'd slipped into the house like a shadow and walked down the quiet hall on quaking legs. Now, in the cool, dark night, with the prairie breeze wafting over her sensitive skin, she half sat, half lay on his big bed, her eighteen-year-old brain humming. He'd gotten his master's degree in May, and since this was the last day of August, he would be leaving soon for a job in Chicago. No longer would he be coming home from school during the summers. He was an adult now, going out into the world, leaving her behind on his father's ranch. If she didn't act now, she'd never have another chance.

Nervous as a kitten, she waited for him in the dark, feeling the rise and fall of her breasts, the tingling of every nerve in her body. Her heart pounded with fear at the enormous risk she was taking, at the danger of lying in wait for him in his own bedroom.

Eleven o'clock. Twelve o'clock. One o'clock. She was a healthy young woman who'd worked hard on the ranch that day, just as she did every day, helping with the branding, earning her keep, rounding up cattle and cutting out cows with the expertise of the male ranch hands. She'd eaten the good supper her mother had cooked. So after her first attack of nerves passed, and his bed grew softer and more inviting in the lamplight, she stretched out a little more, her head on his pillow. It was hardly surprising that she soon succumbed to sleep.

The clock chimed two, waking her. At the same moment, Travis opened his door.

He looked beautiful, as always, but his hair was tousled and his shirt was open at the throat.

Keys clinked on the dresser. She pulled at her skirt, suddenly aware that a good deal more thigh was showing than she'd meant to expose, and tried desperately to wake up her drowsing brain.

He hadn't even noticed her. He had his back to her, pulling his shirt out of his pants.

"Hi," she said.

He stopped dead, then turned.

She couldn't have known what an inviting picture she made, her hair a nimbus around her head, her eyes big and dark, like a child's after sleep. He hitched his shirt back on his shoulders.

Any other man might have pretended not to know what she was there for. Not Travis. "You little fool."

His speech had an oddly slow sound. He'd been drinking. Her heart beat like a wild thing in her chest, but she didn't get off the bed. She bent her knees and pulled her legs up, raising herself up a bit, one elbow on his pillow.

Travis wished heartily that he hadn't knocked back those last two beers with Blackie and Dick, his old high school buddies, good old high school football-playing buddies. He'd thought he could drink safely, since Susan, the cute little waitress, had promised to drive him home and he'd known he could always commandeer Jim to help him retrieve the ranch car on the morrow. Now he desperately needed all his wits about him, and where were they? Swimming in a sea of alcohol.

When Travis sat down on the bed, facing her, he knew he wasn't thinking clearly. He thought of all the things he should be saying to her; the first, most important one—to tell her to get her little butt out of there. Then he looked into her eyes.

"I wasn't—I just wanted you not to be so sad, Travis."

At that sweet declaration that was so far from anything he'd thought she'd say, his heart twisted in his breast. She didn't want him to be so sad. He didn't want to be so sad, either. That was why he'd been drinking with his old school buddies, trying to re-create the good old days, when he'd known how to laugh.

He took her in his arms and found her mouth, that sweet, soft mouth that he had admired for about a thousand years.

Travis's first words hadn't been promising to her, but this was much, much better. She'd wanted him to kiss her for so long, and now, finally, he had. She had this melting feeling, and she slid down on the bed and took him with her. His breath was strong with the scent of alcohol, but she didn't mind. He was Travis, and that was all she cared about.

He found himself sliding his hand up her thigh, her

lovely curved thigh. He found himself tasting her mouth again. He found himself wanting to make love to her. Maybe the pain would go away if he could bury himself in her…

She was yielding to him, and she was so lovely. She tasted so good, so very, very good…

He put a hand on her breast. Her flesh was firm and tender. But even as inebriated as he was, he saw the look of shock on her face, the flare of darkness in her beautiful green eyes.

"Didn't you expect this?" he asked unreasonably. "Isn't this why you're here?"

She swallowed, and it was all there for him to see, her brave attempt to control her fear, her love for him.

He muttered a soft curse and jackknifed off the bed. His head reeled with dizziness at the sudden movement, and his eyes burned. He stood next to his dresser, his hand supporting his head. He was a safe distance away from her, but it wasn't far enough. He was still close enough to have the scent of her young, succulent body eating into his brain, and his hands remembered how it had felt to touch her breast. He hadn't drunk enough alcohol to slow down the natural reaction of his body to her beauty.

She looked even lovelier, now that he knew he mustn't, couldn't, have her.

"What is it?" she asked in that low, husky feminine voice.

"Get out of here. *Get out of here now.*"

"Travis, if we could just talk—"

"You have nothing to say to me. And I have less to say to you."

"I won't go until I've said what I want to say."

"I don't want to hear it. Don't make me throw you out, Elizabeth," he said, and she knew he meant it. She stumbled a little as she slid off the bed and stood on her wobbly legs.

"Don't ever come near me again," he said.

She shook her head, and with her hand to her mouth choking back a sob, she fled.

Chapter One

You want truth? I'll give you truth. You've been lying to yourself for seven years.

Elizabeth Grant lunged out of the molded airport chair, hustled over to look at the television monitor listing arrivals and departures at the Sioux Falls airport. It said the same thing it had five minutes ago, ten minutes ago, one hour ago. Travis's flight was delayed an hour. She still had a few minutes to compose herself. Or get more edgy.

People thought airports were for going places. Not true. They were places that gave people fits of introspection. Liz could vouch for that. She wasn't nervous, not really. It must be the air-conditioning that was giving her cold chills and dancing nerves. Working on the ranch, she wasn't used to air-conditioning.

Right.

Would anything be different between them? Or would it be just the same—he cool, calm and controlled, she with butterflies everywhere? His image danced through her head, tall and lean, with his perfect body and his unmerciful face. Travis McCallister had always been disciplined. Who should know better than she? And the last few years had added to his power. She kept hearing about his successes from his sister Diana. He'd survived the company takeover. He'd been promoted to vice president. He'd assembled a team that put together a dynamite software package for use in mapping terrain and monitoring the positions of airplanes and helicopters in night flight. And, finally, he'd been promoted by the board to chief executive officer.

A company president, wined and dined and courted by men and women alike for his incisive brain, his charm and his six-figure income. As far from her existence as he could possibly be. Her world was Boyd McCallister's ranch, always had been, always would be. The world his father loved and Travis had rejected. The world Travis had walked away from—and was only now returning to in order to see Diana get married.

A flight attendant stepped out of the jetway with her navy blue suit immaculate and her sleek blond hair in a French twist. A city woman, to the tips of her pretty pale fingertips. Liz turned her head, and her tumble of auburn hair swung against her elbows. Why hadn't she run back to the little house on the ranch she shared with her mother and taken time to comb out the scent of sun-dried hay? Why hadn't she changed her clothes?

She'd been on her way to pick up Travis, that was why, and she'd been all hurry and nerves and cold chills, and all she could think of was getting here and seeing him.

She could see it all now, greeting Travis and having him pull a hay stem from her hair.

Darn it, stop this. You are who you are. You learned

*that a long time ago. Travis was the one who taught you.
You swore,* swore, *you'd never be that vulnerable to him
again, remember?*

Actually, the man should just be grateful she'd remembered to change her boots.

From behind her came the sound of a door opening. She
turned, and all her firm resolutions to stay calm scattered
like corn husk.

A tall brunette dressed in a business suit and carrying a
briefcase smiled a thousand-kilowatt smile and stepped
into a waiting rancher's arms, his jeans and flannel surrounding her city sleekness. A little boy tugged loose from
his mother's hand and went yelling at the top of his lungs
to jump into his father's arms. Two teenage girls in
T-shirts and jeans, giggling, involved with each other,
brushed by her.

A business-suited man with a ground-eating stride
whipped by. He wasn't Travis. Not nearly good-looking
enough. Two curly-topped gray-haired women were next,
looking nearly like twins in their flowered dresses and up-
to-date sneakers, followed by a quartet of businessmen,
one with his jacket off, his tie loosened. Suddenly, the
parade was over. The flight attendant reached out a graceful hand and pulled the door closed.

"Wait!" Liz cried. "Wait!"

"May I help you?" The woman's badge identified her
as Nora Winchester.

"I—I think you left a man on the plane."

Her smile was just as beautiful as she was. "I doubt that
very much. I'm very careful about leaving men on planes.
It's against company policy."

"No, I mean, I was expecting someone and he isn't
here. And he should be. He must be. He has to be."

"If you'll give me his name, I'll check the flight manifest."

"Travis McCallister. He's tall, six foot two inches, with a beautiful face, brown eyes, wide shoulders, long legs—"

Nora Winchester raised one nicely shaped eyebrow. "Believe me, if there were a man like that on my flight, I would have noticed. He must have been delayed."

"He said he would be here. Travis doesn't go back on his word."

"All those looks, and honest, too. Sounds too good to be true." The beautiful green eyes suddenly sparkled with amusement. "Really nice-looking man, is he?"

"Very. He—"

The pretty mouth was smiling now. "Tall, you say, maybe carrying a briefcase and a raincoat—"

"I don't know what he's carrying."

"Does he have a great mouth, and a square jaw that goes with meaning what he says and saying what he means?"

"Yes, that's him. You have seen him!"

"Oh, I see him, all right. And so will you, if you turn around."

"Hello, Liz."

Dark and deep, his voice washed over her. Dark and deep, that feeling of standing there looking at him curled inside her.

Nora leaned over and murmured in her ear, "You're just lucky you saw him first. Happy hunting," and walked away.

Liz opened her mouth to say her first brilliant words to dazzle and delight him. "You...look tired."

His mouth tipped into a lopsided grin, his slight bow acknowledged her superior power of observation. "Well, thank you. At least one of us looks wonderful."

First point to Travis.

"I thought you were still on the plane."

"So I heard. I was afraid you were going to arm-wrestle that lady to the ground if she didn't admit I was on that flight."

"I just...I knew you would come. You always keep your word."

Those deep brown eyes gazed at her, assessing. Eyes that undoubtedly had flicked around a boardroom and taken the measure of men ten times cleverer at disguising their feelings than she. Eyes that cut to the bone, and gave no quarter. Eyes that weren't nearly as cold as she'd thought they'd be.

"That's probably the nicest thing anybody has said to me in quite a while."

She had to move, deflect that dark gaze and what he might be seeing in her face. "Well, good. It makes up for the 'tired' bit."

"You were telling the truth as you saw it. Don't apologize for that."

She'd always wanted him to look at her, really look at her. And now he was, and now she didn't know what to do with her hands and her mouth felt dry. "You were on another flight?"

He turned, and she fell into step with him easily as they headed down the hall. He seemed to be carrying all the luggage he had, a gray suit carrier and a sleek black briefcase. "I got held up at the office, so I jumped on the company jet to save time. I wanted to get here about the same time my flight would, but we were delayed taking off from O'Hare. I didn't expect you to be the one to pick me up. Have you been waiting long?"

"A little while, but not too long."

"Exactly how long."

"An hour."

"Long time for you to be indoors."

His voice was smooth and cool, but it jolted her that he knew her that well. "I...didn't mind."

"Knowing you, I think you probably did mind. You hate being trapped indoors, but you've the good manners not to show it. Thanks for your patience."

"You're welcome."

This was how he meant to play it, then, polite, adult. She could handle that.

Outside, in an evening that was finally cooling, Travis stowed his suit carrier and briefcase in the powerful BMW that was his father's with that lithe economy of movement that Liz remembered so well. Without a word to her, he slid into the passenger's seat. Liz started the car and backed smoothly out.

"I see I'm in good hands."

"Did you doubt it for a minute?"

He frowned, looked annoyed at himself. "No. I just feel...disoriented. Like I've missed something, somewhere. Last time I looked, you were too young to know the difference between a kiss and a come-on."

That easily, he dismissed the incident that had kept her tossing in her bed in agony for years. "Well, you haven't looked for a long, long time," she said.

"Is that it? Maybe I'd better start paying attention."

"Maybe you'd better."

He put his head back on the seat and closed his eyes.

"You're off to a great start."

She got a laugh from him on that. He said, "Another point to the red-haired lady."

"I'll take any points I can get. No, don't straighten up. Stay where you are, relax."

He closed his eyes again. "You still look very...young.

You've such...a delicate bone structure. You'll look young when you're eighty."

"Good heavens. All that with your eyes shut. I wonder what you could do with them open."

"Are you fishing?"

She grinned. It felt really good, being able to hold her own with him. Of course, it helped immensely that his eyes were closed and his body was relaxed. "Absolutely."

"I wonder what you'd do if you caught something on that line of yours."

"Throw it back, probably." She glanced sideways at him, was rewarded with a lift of his lips. This was getting close to treacherous waters. It was time to divert him. "Tough day at the office?"

"Tough several days. We've been having eighteen-hour sessions, trying to get the merger completed." He was silent for a moment and then said, "Has Diana arrived from Boston?"

"She flew in the day before yesterday."

"How did you get commandeered to fetch me?"

"When Boyd looked around for somebody to come after you, there I was."

She stole another glance at him. He didn't look as relaxed as he had. Was he disappointed that Diana or his father hadn't come to pick him up?

"Boyd started a preparty show that's going on down at the corral. Harv is trying to impress the new guys by staying the standard eight seconds on a green horse your dad bought."

"A show indeed. So shall we be entertained by the rites of masculinity."

"Your dad thinks the world of you, Travis."

He sat up and smiled. It was a sensual smile that had

the pack of a mule's kick. "Always the peacemaker, eh, Liz? Don't you ever get tired of being an angel?"

"I'm not an angel, far from it. Don't decorate me with your tinsel." She stepped down a little harder on the accelerator than she intended to, whipped around the car cruising in front of her. Travis didn't flicker an eyelash at her flashy driving.

"I bet you'd look nice, all wrapped up in silver strands."

"They'd go lovely with my faded denims."

"Lovelier still with nothing at all."

The chill she'd felt fled suddenly, giving way to a heated flush. "You aren't actually flirting with me, are you, Travis McCallister?"

"Truth as *I* see it," he murmured.

"Is this the way we're going to play this, you saying anything you like and me having to watch every word I say so that I won't be accused of coming on to you?"

"Liz. I believe I owe you an apology for what happened all those years ago—"

"Darn right you do. And it's long overdue." In the silence in the car, she said, with a smile, "Sticking in your throat, is it?"

"No. I was trying to think if there were any better words, but I guess there aren't. I'm truly sorry, Liz. I was harsher with you than I needed to be. I know I hurt you. It just seemed the best way to handle things at the time."

He was glad that they'd gotten this out in the open so soon. Was she still as fond of him as she had been once? He couldn't tell. She was a woman now, strong, sure of herself. She'd imagined herself in love with him, offering him—everything. He'd wanted to take. Heaven help him, he'd wanted very badly to take. He couldn't. Liz needed a man to love, cherish and marry her. He couldn't do that, and he knew it. In the years before, her age had prevented him from reaching out and grabbing for what he wanted, what he knew he couldn't keep. Denial wouldn't be so easy now. There she sat, a child no longer, with that auburn hair flowing down her back like a molten river glinting in the sun, that plaid shirt molded against her very nice breasts, and those jeans showing off a waist and hips kept lean by riding. She looked crisp and cool and real, with her clean-scrubbed face and those big green eyes. And very, very feminine. He hadn't prepared himself for the sight of her, the way he usually did when he came home. He'd been in the business world long enough to know it didn't pay to come into a situation blind. But he hadn't known she'd be at the airport. He'd thought Boyd was fetching him, he'd thought he'd have time after he got to the ranch to brace himself for the sight of her. How long had it been since he was alone with her?

Seven years minus two months. But who was counting?

She meant too much to him. She always had. He could feel the old familiar twisting in his gut, the need to give in to the pull of attraction. He'd thought closing his eyes and leaning his head back, would help, but he could smell the clean scent of her, hear the slight movements of her body against the seat as she drove. Nothing had changed, not one thing. He was aching.

He muttered a curse inside his head. The South Dakota sunset blazed through the window, fire and light dancing. Ahead of him lay nothing but miles of prairie, shorn clean except for a few trees whose dark shadows rose in the distance like far-off stars. Desolate as the moon, this part of the prairie was. A few miles down the road, they'd go past the place where there was a monument to a tree. The tree had grown wild by an intersection, had been a landmark for years, and then had become insect-ridden and had to be cut down. A cottonwood, of course—what other tree would be crazy enough to grow wild on this prairie? Freeze in the winter, burn in the summer, flood one year, dry as hell the next. Only very determined, very fit, wild-life could survive here. And very determined, very fit, women.

"It's a beautiful sunset," she said.

He turned, saw the sleek leanness of her arms, the gold sunfire caught in her hair. She would always see beauty on the prairie, and he would always see beauty in her. "Yes. Beautiful." He wanted to touch those fiery red strands, bury his fingers, his face, in them. He couldn't remember a time when he hadn't.

Insanity. He'd never given in to the madness, and he wouldn't. Now or ever. He might burn and ache and want, but that was all he would do. Liz deserved a man who would love her and marry her and give her children, and he wasn't that man.

Despite all his good intentions, despite all his determination to keep control, he raised his hand to her hair and rearranged a strand over her shoulder. "Too good to be true," he murmured. "I've always had trouble believing in things that are too good to be true."

She felt frozen, unable to move or breathe. "What...did you say?"

He dropped his hand. "Nothing."

She must have dreamed it. He couldn't have touched her hair with such tenderness. It had happened so quickly, and been over before she could really comprehend what he said. She was only sure of the tone, low, deep, incredibly tender. She must have imagined the words, conjured them up out of her longing for him. But for the first time since that night in his room, he had touched her.

She found a way to breathe again. It wasn't as hard as

she'd thought it would be. He'd come close to her, touched her, but now he'd gone away from her, so far that it was hard to believe that her heart was still racing from the intimacy of it. His face was closed, utterly still, utterly smooth.

Foolish to feel rejected. Foolish to feel that, just for an instant, he'd given her something precious.

When she guided the big car around the curving drive, and pulled up in front of the two-story house that was the senator's pride and glory, the twilight was softer, the fire in the west gone. The air was cooler, too, almost chilly on her skin.

Down at the stable corral, the cowboys were roistering with vigorous enthusiasm, encouraging the rider on top of the horse to hang on with yells that both encouraged and mocked. Silhouetted in the soft gold light, Harv clung to the saddle, his legs clamped around the twisting horse's belly. He was game and experienced, and he held on through a sidewinder twist and a back leg buck, but just when it looked as if he were winning, he flew out of the saddle and landed on his side, hard enough to make the dust puff up around him.

Liz flinched. Not only had that fall been bad enough to have hurt, the cowboys gathered safely on the other side of the corral set up a raucous yell, giving Harv the razzing of his life.

Harv wasn't moving. The horse jerked his head and pranced on the other side of the corral, knowing enough to stay away from his would-be rider, so Harv was in no danger from that quarter, but when he lay on the ground and didn't move, Liz jumped out of the car, ran to the corral fence and vaulted over, before anybody else moved.

She knelt beside him, checking his color, reaching for his wrist to take his pulse. "Harv!"

He opened his eyes, looked rueful. "Oh, baby. You weren't supposed to see that."

"Are you okay?"

"Won't know till they do the autopsy." He gave her a grin, extended his hand. She took it, but didn't obey the invitation to pull him to his feet. "Are you sure you haven't broken anything?"

"Only my pride. But what the hell. It matches the broken heart you gave me."

"Idiot." She braced herself for his weight and helped him to his feet. He came upright and, in a smooth, practiced move wrapped his arms around her.

"Harv," she said sharply, pushing away from him. The cowboys went at it again, yelling their approval.

"I feel weak. Dizzy. You wouldn't want me to fall down and hurt myself again, would you?"

"The only thing you hurt was your ego. And that not very much." She stepped away from him.

He was looking down at her with the devil sparkling right out of those blue eyes when she heard a low, familiar voice say, "Everything all right here?"

Travis had followed her down to the corral. The cowboys stepped out of his way. He was a stranger to them. Other than Jim Eckwell, the foreman, who didn't happen to be at the corral, Harv was the only one who knew Travis.

"Well, look who's here. You're kind of far from home, aren't you?"

"You might say that."

"You boys may not realize it, but this man is the boss's son. Doesn't look much like Boyd's boy, does he, all duded up in his city clothes?"

"Harv." Liz stepped forward, laid a hand on Harv's arm. "Don't start."

"I'm not starting anything. I'm just introducing Mr. Travis McCallister to the boys, like any polite gentleman would do." Harv walked toward the corral fence, toward Travis. "You boys might just as well know that Mr. McCallister doesn't think much of a man who makes his living on the back of a horse. He went off to the big city to learn how to be a barracuda in a bigger pond, didn't you, Mr. McCallister?"

Travis didn't say anything. If he wore that face in the boardroom, he must get every vote to go his way. He might look like ice, as if Harv's derision weren't moving him, but Liz saw the tiny flicker of a muscle in his jaw. "I'm glad to see you aren't injured. If you'll excuse me—"

"Yeah, run, pretty boy. Run from anything that smacks of the ranch or horses. You're afraid, aren't you, Mr. Big Executive? Afraid the same thing might happen to you that happened to your brother."

In the silence, a cool breeze wafted across Liz's cheek, and it felt chilling indeed. An owl called.

Travis turned around. Liz held her breath, and she knew every other cowboy hanging on that corral fence was doing the same. "When you've had a little more experience with the world, Mr. Lester, you'll learn it's to your advantage not to judge men so quickly...or so imprudently."

"Talks real nice, don't he? Uses big words. Real fancy. Fancy is as fancy does, I guess. You know what horse he's really afraid to ride, don't you? The horse that made him decide the city was a safer place to be? It's the horse that killed his brother. You guys know the big white stallion. It's the one that our little Lizzy takes out for a run every morning."

Len Hollister was only seventeen. He scuffed a boot toe in the dirt and looked down at the ground. But the other men, Tom Callahan, March Huddleston, Craig Seaton, had their eyes glued on Travis's face.

"Think what you like," Travis said in a low tone. "Nothing I could do would change your mind."

"Climb up on the back of that black devil that just bucked me off and I might be inclined to think differently about you."

Harv threw the challenge out, his tanned face split in a smile that held little amusement. Liz tasted dust from the arena, felt her heart thud with tension. The cowboys didn't move. They hadn't expected this kind of show, but they were more than willing to watch it unfold.

"Harv, knock it off," Liz chided him. "Travis isn't dressed for riding, and he's had a long day traveling—"

"Excuse me." Excruciatingly polite, Travis's voice had the sound of flint struck against stone. "I may not be a macho cowboy, but I draw the line at having a woman fight my battles for me. As for you—" that laser gaze swung to Harv "—stick to your horses. You're obviously a better judge of them than you are men." And Travis turned his back and walked toward the house.

"Knew he was a coward," Harv muttered.

"You don't know anything about him," Liz said coldly. "That was cruel and unforgivable."

"Did I say anything that wasn't the truth?"

"You said a lot that wasn't the truth."

"You think he's a real hotshot, don't you? You always have."

"What I think of him is none of your business." Hair flying, Liz swung around, strode to the corral rail and hoisted herself over.

"Hey. I thought you were going to be my ministering angel."

"You don't need a ministering angel," she shot back at

him from over the top of the corral. "You need to go soak your head in a bucket."

The cowboys laughed at that. Liz caught a glimpse of the look on Harv's face, but she told herself she didn't care as she turned around and followed the path Travis had taken to the house. Harv deserved that, and worse.

The night breeze felt cool against her hot cheeks. She'd done everything wrong. She'd reacted to the knotted nerves in her stomach and the ache in her heart by giving Harv a set-down. Maybe it hadn't been fair, but she couldn't help it. He was always teasing her, trying to make her think he liked her, when she knew very well there was a lady in Rockham he kept steady company with.

She'd had such high hopes for Travis's homecoming. She'd wanted Travis to feel welcome, to forget his acrimonious leave-taking all those years ago. But because she was afraid Harv was hurt and ran to see, she'd led Travis right into a hornet's nest.

And gotten stung in the process.

She hadn't been trying to fight his battles. She'd only wanted to protect him. And she'd failed. Not only had she failed, she had somehow thrown everything into high relief. Her cheeks burned. She'd have to face the truth that, despite all her hopes that things had changed, nothing had changed, not really, and that the best way to help Travis was to stay away from him.

He would be in his bedroom by now, unpacking. The kitchen would be safe. Liz could hide there and talk to her mother and collect herself.

From years of long habit, Liz trod the path that led around the house to the kitchen. It was nearly dark now, but in the soft light, her mother's boots sat tidily inside the screened porch, just as they had for so many years. Warmth and home and tradition. This ranch was the center of her mother's life, just as it had been since they drove up to the door together that cold and snowy January day eighteen years ago. Liz hadn't known there were so many parts to the world then. She'd only known her parents' world. And that world had come apart. Liz scraped her feet on the coarse rug and pulled open the kitchen door.

Her mother was there, and so was Travis, wrapped in one of her mother's wonderful bear hugs. Liz couldn't see her mother's eyes, but she knew they were glistening with unshed tears. Rachel Grant loved Travis. His own mother had died when he was eleven, the victim of a drunken driver in a late-night car crash, and Rachel, coming to the ranch with her own grief and loss from her divorce fresh in her heart, had worked very hard to overcome Travis's initial rejection. With her spirit, grace and good humor, she'd succeeded beyond anybody's wildest dreams. Especially Travis's.

Liz turned to make her escape, and Travis moved to step out of Rachel's arms, but her mother held Travis where he was and said, "Don't you dare run off like a scared rabbit, Elizabeth. And don't you cut short this hug, Travis McCallister. I've waited long enough for it. If you aren't going to bring home any babies for me to hug, you'll have to be their substitute. So suffer."

"Yes, ma'am." Across her mother's shoulders, Travis's eyes met Liz's. He wore an odd look of indulgent humor and restrained pleasure, and she smiled back in understanding, as a fellow sufferer. He looked the way he usually did under the influence of her mother's charm...sweet. And his long-fingered hands were really pressing into Rachel's back. He wasn't just enduring the hug, he was participating in it wholeheartedly. His gentle respect for her mother ever endeared him to Liz.

How incredibly attractive those hands were. They would

be immensely tantalizing, those hands, immensely arousing on bare skin…

Rachel pushed him away just enough to bring him eye-
to-eye with her. "So when *are* you going to find a woman
who deserves you and bring home babies to me? I had
supper in town with my friend last Tuesday and she had
the cutest little brag book, all done up in cross-stitch and
eyelet lace, with the baby's name and birth date embroidered on the front. *And it had pictures in it of her grand-
daughter.* When am I going to get a book like that?"

Travis made a dramatic show of pulling his sleeve back
and looking at his watch. "You're setting new records,
Rachel. We got to my marital status in exactly one minute
and fifteen seconds. The last time I was here, you waited
for ten minutes before you got around to asking me about
my love life."

"Well, since you were here last, I've gotten older. I try
not to buy real green bananas, these days."

"You look younger than ever to me, sweetheart,"
Travis said, "and I know you'll live to be one hundred
and nine. I just hope we have the strength to keep up with
you."

"Never mind the flattery. Do you have even the slightest
prospect of getting married, Travis? Can you give me the
tiniest glimmer of hope?"

There was a little silence while Travis considered this.
Liz waited, heart stopped, breath held.

"I took some pictures of the latest company location
we've acquired through a merger. Would you like to see
those?" Travis said it with a perfectly straight face, but
Liz caught the gleam of devilment in his eyes.

"Buildings. Who wants buildings? I want a baby to
hold."

"Liz is a far better candidate to give you babies than I."

"I'll be an old woman in my wheelchair before that one reproduces," Rachel Grant said, turning to give her daughter a stern look. "She doesn't even have a steady fellow. She says she wants a man who makes her feel like turning cartwheels. Isn't that the silliest thing you've ever heard?"

"There's a certain amount of logic in it, I guess," said Travis carefully, far too diplomatic to be drawn in. "If a woman is going to live with a man for the rest of her life, she should be a little excited about it."

Liz had forgotten she'd said that. It had been five years ago, after Travis came home and left again, and she'd decided she was foolish to think he'd ever feel differently about her. She'd known then that she should give up on him, but she couldn't imagine anyone taking his place in her heart.

She still couldn't.

Liz turned away, putting him out of her sight, staring at the beige door of the refrigerator. "Mother, neither one of us will be able to get married and reproduce if we're malnourished. I haven't had my supper yet, and Travis is probably famished, too."

"You're right, sweetie. I'm being selfish, thinking of what I want, instead of what the two of you need." Liz heard a smacked kiss before she opened the refrigerator door and asked, "What would a hungry traveling man who's only been fed peanuts and strong coffee want to eat? Or does your company have peanuts on their executive jets?"

"We've replaced them with pretzels. We're cutting down on fat. In our minds, in our hearts, on our assembly lines." He put an exaggerated hand over his heart as he intoned the words. Five seconds in her mother's company and he was making jokes.

"Lord love you, my boy. You must be starved. You'd better fix that man some real food, sweetheart."

"Mom, where are you going?"

"I have to get his bed ready. You cook him a nice juicy hamburger, put some meat on his bones. He looks as if he hasn't had a good meal in days. What have you been doing to yourself, Travis?"

"Fasting in preparation for the orgy of your fantastic cooking that will be spread before us in the requisite six meals a day that I knew I'd be expected to eat out here on the prairie."

"Flatterer. You haven't changed a bit, have you?"

"And neither have you, and that's a very comforting thought."

Rachel Grant flushed. "There's some hamburger in the fridge, Elizabeth, and it's fresh, and there are some nice buns in that bag there by the stove. You fix this man some sustenance. And yourself, too."

"Thanks for the kind thought, Mother."

Rachel raised an eyebrow, but ignored her daughter's dry teasing. "How long are you going to stay with us this time, son?"

"I'll be flying out after the festivities."

"Well. We'll take what we can get of you. It's little enough to be going on with." She pressed another kiss on his cheek and swept out the door.

Liz reached for the lettuce, the dill pickles, the tomatoes, the ground beef wrapped in cellophane. Trav liked a burger with the trimmings, and so did she. She turned the meat out onto the table and set about molding it into a patty.

"If you don't want to do that, I'll do it."

"An independent man of the nineties, are you?"

"I'm used to taking care of myself."

"Me too," she said. "Still like it pink in the middle?"

"Medium rare is fine, yes. And it's not necessary to beat it into submission."

She was being teased. "Sorry." She flipped it into the pan.

"You look like a woman with something on her mind."

She lost her nerve. "I'll talk while we're eating."

Too soon, the food was ready. She scooped a burger up, split a bun and nestled it on top, her movements quick and efficient as she arranged the lettuce and tomato and garnished the plate with chips before setting it in front of him.

When she had fixed an identical one for herself and sat down across from him, he said, "Very nice. Thank you. I appreciate this," indicating the attractive food plate. "So. Tell me what's eating you while we're eating."

Despite her determination, it was hard to begin, hard to speak of that which was seldom spoken of in the Mc-Callister family. "It's…good to have you home. I've been looking forward to it."

"Have you? That probably makes you a minority of one."

"Mom was glad to see you. And Diana will be, too, when she gets home from shopping. Your dad took her."

His brown eyes softened slightly. Travis had a warm spot in his heart for his sister.

"Harv owes you an apology."

Travis's face cooled. "Are you his spokeswoman?"

"Despite the way he acts, there's nothing between Harv and me. I just didn't want your homecoming to be so…discordant."

"I appreciate the kind thought. I think I can handle a little confrontation."

"But you shouldn't have to, not here."

"Here is where I got my lessons in confrontation. But as long as we're on the subject of what happened out there—" he leaned back in his chair "—let's talk about you. You've taken that stallion and made him a pet, have you?"

"He isn't a pet. He—"

"You've got that right, at least."

"He isn't a killer, either," Liz shot back, too soon, too vehemently.

Travis merely looked at her, no emotion in his face or eyes. "I suppose Boyd condones this."

"He's glad for the stallion to get some exercise, yes."

"He probably revels in your courage."

"Courage has nothing to do with it. It's a matter of building trust. Blaze trusts me and I trust him."

"Then you're a fool. That horse killed Andrew."

"He was frightened. Haven't you ever done anything wrong when you were frightened?"

"We're not talking about me. We're talking about an animal with all the instincts of a shark."

"You don't know Blaze. You never have. Any more than you've known me or what I'm capable of—"

I know what you're capable of.

The words hung there in the silence. At the look in his eyes, she shook her head and turned away.

He said, in a very low voice, "Liz. Don't put words in my mouth that I haven't said."

She faced him, then. "All right, I won't—as long as you will agree to keep an open mind about Blaze. And about Harv, too, I guess."

"Well, you've picked a couple of beauties to champion. A troublemaking cowboy and a killer horse. I think between the two of them, I prefer the horse."

Chapter Two

"What's this about you preferring a horse, Trav?" Into the tense silence, Diana burst, like a prairie sunbeam. Liz had always thought Diana had the rare gift of brightening a room, warming it, making it a place of joy and cheer. Before Travis could rise to his feet, his sister took the liberty of leaning over him from behind and sliding her hands down his chest to rest her chin on the top of his head. "Hey, big brother, what's happening?"

While Liz watched dark head merging with dark head, Diana's long, dark hair falling forward on her cheeks, a whole panoply of emotions crossed Travis's face—forbearance, fondness, wariness. She felt almost as if she were intruding, watching him twist in his chair and turn his cheek up for his sister's kiss. He loved Diana deeply, was as vulnerable to her as he was to Rachel Grant. In other circumstances, Liz might have been jealous of Diana's place in Travis's affections, but it was impossible to be envious of such a sunny personality. Diana was too warm, too real, too generous. Liz had basked in her warmth, as everyone else had. It just seemed so unfair that every female in the house could stir his heart except her. He might flirt with Liz now, tell her she was attractive. But his heart was closed to her.

No longer hungry, Liz rose from her chair, carried her plate to the sink—and, unfortunately, brought Diana's attention zinging to her.

Those beautiful brown eyes, artfully detailed with mascara and soft beige shadow, fastened on Liz's face. "Well, this is like old times. Big brother in the kitchen feeding his face, and you leaning against the counter with flushed cheeks and furrowed brow—from cooking, of course."

"Hello to you, too, Diana," Liz said, a smile lifting her lips. She knew better than to deny anything. Diana was too sharp, too aware. "Isn't it nice to come to a place where things never change?"

Travis wanted to tell Diana to ease up, to let Liz alone. But it occurred to him as he watched Liz lean back against the counter, her body poised, her hands tucked in the pockets of her jeans, her chin brought up at that angle that held a touch of assertiveness, that Liz didn't need his defense. She was fully capable of defending herself. He was aware, suddenly, sharply, of something lost.

"Come on, big brother, smile. You can do it, I know you can." Diana leaned around and planted a noisy kiss on his cheek.

Before Travis could retaliate, Diana waltzed to Liz and threw her arms around her. "This is fantastic, all of us together again. I should get married every year."

"Heaven spare us," Travis murmured.

"Well, I don't think Bill would be too happy with the idea, either. He likes me too much."

"Got him fooled, have you?"

"Be nice, brother. I'm in a delicate condition." When he lifted one dark eyebrow, she shook her head, pleased that he'd risen to the bait so easily. "No, not that delicate condition. I mean, I'm a bride. Given to fits of emotion, tears and second thoughts."

"You've never had a second thought in your life, sweetheart. You think the whole world is your oyster."

"Right now, it is." She whirled around once, orbiting to Liz, pulling the other woman close in a bear hug and saying in a loud stage whisper, "You look fantastic. Wait until big brother catches a glimpse of you coming down the aisle in your bridesmaid dress. Maybe he'll get ideas of his own when he sees how much prettier you are than those city women he deigns to dangle on his arm if the moon is new and the planets are aligned."

"You are an unbridled brat, brat," said Travis.

"Travis, don't say that. She's the best sister you've got."

"She's the only sister I've got, a fact for which I am profoundly grateful. The mind boggles at the thought of two like her."

"Stop bad-mouthing me, or I'll tell Liz how the current CEO of Softtech Limited has to rearrange his sock drawer every Sunday night before his workweek begins or he goes spastic. It drives him crazy if his socks aren't in straight rows and color-coded."

"Diana Maureen, you're asking for it."

"She's just teasing you, Travis. It's just a joke," said Liz.

Eyes alive with glee, Diana stepped back and fixed a clear eye on Liz's face. "Well, I could always even things up by telling him how you tucked his picture in your bra and carried it around with you the entire year you were sixteen.''

"You *are* a brat, brat," Liz said, as coolly as she could manage.

"Be nice to her, Liz," Travis drawled, with evident pleasure. "She's just teasing you."

"Deny it, Elizabeth Annabell Grant," Diana teased. "Look Travis straight in the eye and tell him I'm lying."

Liz fought to stay cool, look cool. She'd run a bluff if it killed her, but she wasn't going to lie. "What does it matter what I did when I was sixteen? That was a hundred years ago."

"Well, maybe not quite a hundred," Travis murmured.

She didn't like the way he was looking at her, with that amused tolerance. Well, what the heck. It couldn't be any news to him that she'd had a crush on him. She'd told him so herself. In no uncertain terms. All she really had to do was keep him from thinking she was still smitten. "It might as well be that long ago. I hardly remember it."

Travis looked unmoved by her cool disclaimer. "I never knew your middle name was Annabell," he murmured, that wonderful smile still lifting his lips. He looked like a man who'd just received a very useful piece of information.

"You have a great deal to answer for here, Diana *Maureen*." Liz took a threatening step toward her.

"So. Just that quickly, we've moved from tolerance to violence. Strange how things change when one gets personally involved." Travis was enjoying himself far too much. "Don't hurt her, Liz. She's the nicest surrogate sister you've ever had."

"And the only one, a fact for which I am profoundly grateful," Liz said, looking straight at Travis. And they laughed together.

"Nothing like uniting against a common enemy, is there?" Diana said airily, looking extremely smug and satisfied with herself, as if she'd planned the ending exactly this way.

"I suppose you think all those years of studying for your doctorate in psychology have finally paid off." Travis leaned back in his chair and looked at Diana.

"I didn't learn how to fight with you from a college course. I learned that in my playpen. I had to. Self-defense."

"Yeah, you were a terror right from the start. Scared the heck out of me."

"The best defense is an offense. Good thing Dad always stuck up for me."

"Speaking of him, what did you do with your father?"

"You mean besides tie him up and stuff him in the closet?" It was a childhood routine that made them both smile. Whoever had been with their father was responsible for his appearance. "I sent him down to the corral to play with his horses and the big boys and stay out of my way. I wanted a chance to harass you all by myself before he started in on you."

"Thoughtful," Travis said. "Considerate."

"I learned the art of thinking ahead from you. You were always such a stand-up kind of guy."

"Is that as in 'comedian' or 'fall guy'?"

"Take your pick. Neither of you has asked when you're going to get to meet Bill. Too busy thinking how to keep from looking at each other, I guess."

"You never were good at guessing games," Travis drawled.

"When are we going to get to meet him?" Liz asked quickly.

"Tomorrow, tomorrow," Diana sang. Then she came

down to earth a little and said, "Getting married is wonderful, Travis. You should try it."

"That must be my cue that it's time for me to go unpack."

"You'll have to dance in the pig trough, you know."

That stopped Travis in midflight. "Excuse me?"

"Rachel told me. If a younger sibling gets married before an older one does, the older one has to dance in the pig trough."

"The pigs might have something to say about that—not to mention me."

"I was thinking the least we could do is throw you in the stock tank."

"The cattle might have something to say about that."

"Travis tea. Yuck."

"Look at you," Travis said in a dead-serious tone, with a dead-serious face. "You went shopping and got high on the smell of your charge card mingled with the delicate scent of new clothes."

"Yes, I did. And it feels good, too."

"I suggest immediate therapy. And required reading. Six issues of *Possum Living* magazine."

Diana shuddered delicately. "Please. Not while I'm still reveling in my successful shopping trip."

"Sweetheart, you've never had any other kind."

"Well, this is good, seeing my family all together again." Boyd McCallister stood in the doorway, surveying them all with a smile on his face, his pride evident in the sparkle in his eyes. Liz could never look at Boyd without feeling safe. And warmed. She'd never seen him in a bad temper. He was as big as South Dakota, and just as demanding. He dressed for the range—boots, jeans, belt with a turquoise buckle, red plaid western shirt. Six foot two inches tall and tanned from the sun and the wind, he had a bit of a belly these days, a testimonial to the many fund-raising dinners that had sent him to the Senate. He had Travis's strong cheekbones and chin, but his eyes were a light blue and his hair was a pale silver. There wasn't a person on the planet who could look at Boyd McCallister and not think of the West as it used to be and believe that there might be something to all those old western movies, after all. Yet, just lately there had been signs that Boyd was showing his age. Tonight there was darkness around his eyes.

"Guess I didn't tie him tight enough when I put him in the closet," Diana said, a smile on her lips.

"What are you talking about?" Boyd asked, frowning at her.

"Nothing. I've made about all the trouble I want to make in this room tonight, I think, Dad. Come and say hello to Travis. He has fed his face, thanks to Liz, so I think we can safely assume he's reasonably docile."

"Never assume facts not in evidence," Liz said.

"You know, I don't understand half the things you women say. Do you, son?" He came into the room toward Travis, held out his hand.

Travis rose to his feet. "I think we're better off not knowing." He took Boyd's hand.

"You've stayed away too long."

"Not by choice, Dad."

"Come on, my boy, let's not be so formal. It's been a long time." And he pulled Travis close and put his other arm around his son to hug him.

For the first, tense second, Travis seemed to be tolerating the embrace, rather than participating in it. Then he lifted his arms and hugged his dad.

Liz felt the sting of emotion in her eyes, in her heart. Trav's face was controlled, but she knew him too well to be fooled. He closed his eyes once, briefly, in an effort to conceal the emotion he was feeling.

Boyd might be a politician, but it wasn't his style to hide his tender feelings. He stepped back from Travis, shook his head. "I guess we can forgive the women a shopping excursion or two, if it's going to bring you home."

"Large price to pay," Travis murmured, amusement lifting his mouth.

"Whatever works. Listen, you get yourself rested up, and tomorrow we'll scout around the place a bit. I want you to see what I've done, show you through the new bunkhouse, and the addition to the barn I built for the new line of Charolais. You'll like them, son. Fine cattle. I've got this wonderful bull—can't wait to show him off to you."

"I'm sure he's a fine specimen of masculinity."

The dark beauty of Travis's face remained smooth and controlled, his mouth still, his eyes steady, but Liz wasn't fooled. It was as if she'd been watching a shimmering pond where all motion had suddenly ceased.

"I'll look forward to seeing him—and the changes you've made." Travis stayed where he was, his body echoing the stillness in his face, his smile excruciatingly polite.

Liz ached to step forward and take Travis's hand, align herself with him. He wouldn't tolerate that, not for a minute, but still, she could barely fight down the urge to go to him.

To Boyd her mind cried, *Don't do this. You're a bright man, don't be so stupid and adamant where your son is concerned. None of this matters. Don't plant your silly feet on the same side of that line you've been drawing in front of him all your life.* But she couldn't. All she could do was stand there and watch helplessly.

Boyd was frowning with displeasure. "Unless you have something more pressing—"

"I have a couple of telephone calls to make in the morning, but after that, I'm at your disposal." He sounded gracious and polite, but he didn't fool wily Boyd McCallister, not for one minute.

Men. They were so...unyielding. She hadn't wanted it to be this way. This time, *this time*, she'd wanted it to be different. A well-known ache arrowed home to its old place in her heart. Liz wanted it to stop hurting. Most of all, she wanted to stop caring. It was really none of her business if Travis and his father were estranged. She'd always been like a kid with her nose pressed to a candy shop window when it came to this family, no matter how nice they were to her and her mother, and the sooner she accepted that as a fact of life, the better off she would be.

Travis would have been the first one to agree with her. He was the one who'd made it crystal-clear that she had no place in his life.

"I'm going to see if Mom needs some help."

A spurious excuse at best, and she didn't fool Travis for a moment. Comprehension flashed in his dark eyes, and there was a tug to his mouth that made her think that even in his discomfort, he understood her need to escape.

She walked out of the kitchen with her head high. Had she disappointed him? Of course not.

But her silly conscience was bothering her as she entered Travis's bedroom. Pride. Pride had made her walk out on Travis. And the good Lord knew there was already more than enough pride in this house.

In the dark softness of the night, light pooled on the end tables beside Travis's bed. It was a masculine haven, with its brown drapes and spreads, and utterly devoid of any signs that Travis had spent his childhood there. There were no baseballs caught in an old wastebasket, no trophies, no pictures of a terribly young Travis on prom night. The mahogany chest and dresser were bare, sheened with polish, except for the elegant silver brush and comb Diana had given him five Christmases ago. It might have been a guest room. Maybe that was why she'd grown used to walking in and out without obsessing about that fatal night so long ago.

Looking at his room, seeing the loneliness, Liz felt guilty. She should have stayed with Travis, even if he didn't want her help.

The gentle illumination backlit her mother's hair as Rachel stood gathering up an armload of fluffy brown towels to take into Travis's private bathroom. "You look suitably unhappy. Come here to hide, have you?" Her succinct little arrow delivered, Rachel turned her back on Liz and went to lay the towels on the bathroom counter. Liz could see the flash of mirror, the luxury of marble and gleaming tile. Everything was spotless—she'd cleaned it herself. All the while she worked, she'd wondered if the time would come when Travis brought a woman home with him to share this sybarite luxury. She couldn't help wondering what it would be like to be Travis's woman, to strip and step into the luxurious shower with him.

Her mother reappeared with her arms empty and a look on her face like that of a canary-eating cat. "This might be a good place to hide now, but it won't do so well when Travis wants to go to bed."

"Mother, somebody should have taken you across their knee and spanked you when you were a little girl."

"Somebody did. My mother, when I told her a lie. From that day forward, I've always told the truth. You should try it. All right, all right, don't look at me like that. I'll pretend I don't know anything, and I won't say any more about it. You'll have to find your own answer." Rachel made herself very busy picking up Travis's bed pillow and stuffing it into the matching brown satin sham. "Boyd opened fire on Travis already, did he?"

Liz sighed. It was a sign of regret and agreement. "Can't you talk to Boyd?"

"I've never been very fond of holding a conversation with a brick wall. Sweetheart, when you get to be my age, you begin to understand that talking to someone to try and change their beliefs about another person, especially if that person is a family member, is about as productive as trying to get milk from a bull. Boyd will have to learn his lesson the hard way, I reckon."

"Who's going to teach him?"

Her mother's eyes met hers over that expanse of brown satin. "Why, Travis will, of course."

"I wish I had your serene confidence in a positive outcome. Boyd and Travis had been at loggerheads for years. I don't see how they're ever going to get together on anything—"

"You might be very surprised." Her mother smiled in that way she had that made her look beautiful. "Besides," Rachel said, her manner elaborately casual, "what makes you think I have any influence over Boyd? I'm just his housekeeper."

"What was that little lecture I got not a minute ago about truth-telling?" Liz smiled. "Don't you think at twenty-six I'm finally old enough to understand that you and Boyd love each other—and are lovers?"

Rachel dropped the pillow she was holding, her face flushed rosy. "Oh, sweetheart—"

Liz came around the bed and opened her arms, felt a surge of satisfaction and love as her mother stepped into them. Liz smelled vanilla and soap as her mother hugged her close, close.

Rachel said in a choked voice, "I didn't want to cause you pain or embarrassment."

"If I were still fifteen, I could understand it. But now? Come on, Mom. It's time we uncomplicated your life. All that superquiet sneaking into the house at night in the dark. And so unnecessary. Honestly, it's all right, Mother. You have a right to some happiness. You've had little enough in your life."

Her mother pushed Liz away, her eyes brilliant with tears. "I wanted to tell you when you were eighteen. But you were so quiet in August before you went away to school, almost withdrawn, and it seemed easier to keep things as they were. Then, when you graduated, I just lost my nerve. I wasn't sure you'd understand. I knew I'd really gone past a good time to tell you. How long have you known?"

"Well, only since I came home from college the first year. I mean, when I'd see this certain look on my roommate's face and come home and see that same look on yours, it didn't take an Einstein to figure it out, once I opened my eyes and stopped thinking of you as an antediluvian brontosaurus. Why haven't you married him?"

"Oh, Liz, really. Couldn't you just see me in Washington, at those fancy parties and things, me with my cowboy boots and my country ways? I'd be as out of place as a cow in a castle."

"I think you'd be marvelous," Liz said hugging her close. "A little plain speaking is just what those folks need."

"Boyd doesn't need it. He doesn't need *me*."

"I think he needs you desperately. He sure needs someone to tell him that he's a danged fool when it comes to his son.''

"Most men are danged fools," her mother said, smiling. "But we love them anyway. Don't we?" Her eyes sparkled with mischievous pleasure. "As long as we're *telling the truth*..."

She waited, with that silence that Liz knew well. "Your turn," Rachel prodded gently.

"Yes," Liz admitted quickly, knowing she'd been bested, "we just can't help ourselves. We *will* try to love the impossible creatures, regardless of how silly and hopeless it is."

"Seems," her mother amended.

"Is," insisted Liz.

"Have it your way." Her mother gave in gracefully, which was the way she did most things, somehow managing to win the argument with that wonderfully wise smile.

Filled with the rueful admiration she'd always had for her mother, Liz quit the field and cast about for a way to change the subject. She nodded at Travis's empty suitcases, spread on the caddy. "You unpacked for him? You spoil him rotten."

"That boy could do with a whole heap of spoiling. I've known that ever since I came here. Travis has always needed tender handling."

"It's a good thing you understand that, since his father never has."

"I'll never forget that first night we arrived at the ranch. You were so angry with me for snatching you away from everything that was familiar to you, and Travis stared at me with those wounded, furious eyes, as if I were the biggest interloper in the world. Andrew was nine—" her mother smiled "—but he stood there sucking his thumb, much to his father's complete chagrin. Diana wrapped her arms around her father's leg and refused to look at me. I wondered if I had taken on far more than I could handle. The next year was a rough one. Travis was hurting so badly from the death of his mother, and made ultrasensitive by his loss. He turned inward, searching for a way to cover the pain, instead of letting it out. Not like Andrew, who wasn't old enough to miss his mother the way Travis did, and simply turned to the only remaining adult in his family as the center of his world. Boyd liked being Andrew's universe, didn't see it wasn't the best thing for the boy. Diana reverted to being her sunny self. She joyously accepted you as a sister. I think she was glad to have an ally against her brothers. Travis was too serious, too responsible, to get involved in any sibling squabbles. I couldn't reach him. He brooded alone, carried his sorrow alone. I worried about him, but there seemed to be nothing I could do. It made me worry less when I saw how protective he was of Diana—and of you. After Andrew died..." Rachel shook her head. "Travis went away and grew that hard coat of city plastic over his tender heart. Wish I could say it's an improvement, but it isn't. I liked him better when his eyes shone with that sensitive shyness. That's how I remember him, all big eyes and a skinny little butt."

"Travis would love to hear that, I'm sure." A smile lifted Liz's lips. She didn't remember Travis as a child. When she and her mother first came to the ranch, she'd been too immersed in her own misery, missing her father and her play-school friends. She did remember resenting mightily that she had to share her mother with the two strange boys, wishing they'd never been born. She'd hated them and hated the ranch. Now she couldn't imagine being anywhere else.

"I keep thinking that sweet little boy still exists under the brittle hardness of that man somewhere," Rachel said, frowning in concentration.

"You're like the optimist in the story who keeps scooping out the stall full of manure, looking for the pony."

Her mother laughed. "Something like that." Rachel's long-fingered, competent hand smoothed over the brown satin coverlet on Travis's bed. "But my time for spoiling him is over. Somebody else is going to have to take over my job." Her eyes met Liz's. "Somebody who loves him."

"Well, you heard him speak on that score. Guess he can't find a woman to do that for him."

"That's because he hasn't been looking in the right place. And we both know where he *should* be looking, don't we?"

"Mom, please. Don't be wishing and hoping for something that's never going to happen. You're definitely wrong about a positive outcome here."

"We'll see."

Uttering those two maddening words that she'd always used to such good effect through Liz's childhood, Rachel went to the door and turned. "I'll see you back at the house." And then she was gone.

Liz knew she should go, too. And she would go. As soon as she'd finished her little dream, and imagined what it would be like if her mother was right, and there was a happy ending somewhere for Travis and her. Liz sat down on the bed and swept a hand across the luxurious coverlet. Darn it all, anyway. She'd wanted him to feel comfortable here, to be loved. She'd hoped, she'd dreamed, she'd ached for a happy homecoming for Travis, but it had all gone wrong, from the first moment he stepped on the place.

"Well, this is a familiar scene."

Travis leaned in the doorway, his coat off, his tie pulled down, his countenance dark and beautiful, his wonderful mouth tugged up in a half smile. It seemed to Liz that the light rushed to his face, loved the plane of his cheek, the sharp angle of his jaw.

"That was a long time ago." She stayed where she was, though it took every ounce of her courage to do so. She even leaned back on his bed, resting on the palms of her hands. A model's pose. Giving him the full treatment.

"Not so very long." He didn't like the way she was sitting there looking at him with the complete confidence of a woman. He liked even less the way her sitting there on his bed made him feel. All that long, luxuriant hair around her shoulders, that lean sleekness of her body, erotic even in jeans and a shirt. She must have the narrowest waist in the universe—and the longest legs. She looked like a woman, all right, and she was reminding him quite vividly that he was a man.

"I've forgotten it completely. As I'm sure you have."

To Travis, it seemed she hadn't even needed to breathe before she shot that arrow back at him. Now she was lifting her head and giving him one of her deal-with-that-truth-if-you-can looks. How many people did he have in his life who could look at him in quite that way? None. No one in the world could ever deliver that peculiar jolt of caring and challenge that was Liz's alone.

It made him feel…lonely. He hadn't felt lonely in years, not since his mother died. That look made him want, need, ache. He saw it all in his mind's eye. He knew her too well, knew how her eyes would flare when he touched her skin, how she would melt into his arms, under his mouth. He knew how she would sigh when he caressed her, writhe in his arms when he touched her. She'd let him absorb her, demand it, even, and he'd take it all, every sweet scent of her, the satin of her skin, the smooth curve of her breast, the feathered sweetness between her thighs. He'd drink his fill from her, take into his body all that she was and ever would be. Having once tasted her, he'd never reach the bottom of the well, never tire of her, never stop wanting her.

He could feel his body warming, lifting, readying, with the sting of desire.

"Does your determination to make me feel at home include staying here for the night? If so, you might as well strip, lie down and be comfortable. I'll use the bathroom and be with you in a minute."

"You're right," she said, her face flushed, her arms coming forward to wrap around her chest in a gesture of bodily protection. "I should be going."

"Exactly what I've been trying to tell you. Now stop looking as if I've whipped you across the face and get out of here, before I decide to take you up on the invitation you're so obviously issuing."

She slid off his bed, and the sound of satin slipping against denim resounded in his ear, a sensuous, provocative sound that made his body clench with disappointment. She stood there, her head high, her cheeks flushed. "There was no *invitation* issued or intended. I was sitting here...thinking." She hesitated, and then said, with chin outthrust, "Actually, I was feeling sorry for you."

"Sorry for me?" He lifted an eyebrow, looking terribly urbane.

She wanted to hit him. "Sorry for the reception you received. Sorry for the bareness of this room. Sorry because you and your father are at such opposite ends of the spectrum—" She flung out a hand in helpless self-consciousness. "Well, anyway. I can see now that feeling sorry for you is a colossal waste of my time."

"Yes, it certainly is. Don't squander your pity on me. Save it for your friends down at the corral."

"I know you're fully capable of taking care of yourself. I'll simply tell myself that you deserve everything you get."

"You were leaving, I believe," he said politely, his voice cool.

"Yes, I was." She went, her head high and her shoulders straight, a thoroughbred to her toes.

Travis went into the bathroom, ripped off his tie, his shirt, his pants, and stepped under the shower. He turned the water icy, and he stood there and took it, knowing it wasn't nearly cold enough to punish him adequately for his sins.

Chapter Three

A hot South Dakota night swirled around Liz, teased her nose with the aroma of roasting beef mingled with the scent of new-mown hay. Music pulsed from three different bands, one in the barn, one in the house, and one at the swimming pool. Her feet picked up the rhythm of the pool band, a steel-drum aggregation playing "Yellow Bird."

A breeze fluttered across her skin like a wispy feather. It was a night guaranteed to make a woman's hormones dance, and as she moved closer to the barn, hers were doing the rumba.

Crickets chirped with naive cheerfulness under that soft South Dakota sky, and the old moon was disgustingly full. Ripe. Like she felt. Full to bursting, aching for something to happen.

A high, wispy cloud fringed across the moon, teasing, leaving a streamer of light in its wake. That was the way her heart was, opening again. She had thought she was safe, protected, her heart completely closed.

An utter fool, that was what she was. Somehow she'd learn how to have Travis home and not feel as if her heart were aglow.

But for now she was alone, so she'd savor this moment of sweet, sensual pleasure in an evening just on the verge of tipping into darkness. She could walk in this night feeling lit from within, and hope all the people gathered at the ranch for Diana's engagement party wouldn't notice the sparkles inside her that blazed like the lanterns strung around the porch roof, and especially hope that none of the guys at the corral would see her flushed cheeks as she walked with a quick step through the yard.

Liz could keep walking to the pool, where most of Diana's girlfriends had changed into swimsuits to splash and cool off, or she could relax in the huge living room, with its vaulted ceiling, where a small jazz combo was playing and some of the older folk were enjoying the soft music and the quiet atmosphere. But she turned toward the barn, where the cement floor had been scrubbed to shining cleanliness and bales of straw were scattered about to sit on and a country-and-western band was playing "Stand by Your Man," with a female singer whose voice "cried" in all the right places, just like Tammy Wynette.

Nerves fizzing with anticipation, Liz drifted toward the fireplace, where beef sizzled on a roasting spit. The men of Diana's crowd were gathered around in a male ritual of watching the food cook, beer cans in hand. Diana's coterie had arrived throughout the day, by plane and automobile, with all the subtlety of an army invasion; in addition, there were at least a hundred people here from the community, surrounding farmers and ranchers who were friends of the family. Boyd knew everybody in the eastern half of the state, it seemed, and most of them had been invited to this party. After the wedding rehearsal tomorrow night, there would be a private dinner for the wedding party and family. Tonight was for the world.

You're a prize idiot. Travis scowled at himself in the mirror, yanked at the knot of his necktie. He didn't feel this way often, caught in a trap of his own making, and he didn't like the feeling.

He wasn't fond of parties. But he'd told himself he'd do whatever it took to please Diana. He'd done little enough for her through the years. Tonight she wanted him there to play the part of the older brother, so he'd do it with grace or die trying.

Diana had said he could dress in jeans if he wanted to, and there were a couple of old pairs hanging in his closet that he could get into easily enough, but he'd feel like a fool in ranch clothes. Worse, he'd be an impostor. So he stuck to his uniform of striped shirt, tie, and dark pants. He was what he was. Couldn't change a leopard's spots, not now, not after all these years.

It isn't the party that has you hot under the collar, it's your own stupidity.

His image made no answer, only stared back at him.

You didn't have to come down on Liz like a bucket of bricks. She might be twenty-five, but she's still young, still tenderhearted, and maybe even, heaven help us, still an optimist.

None of your business what she is.

So. Do you think you've succeeded in making her so disgusted with you that she won't come within twenty feet of you? That was your intention, wasn't it? Because you're no longer certain of your ability to stay away from her.

Maybe if he'd been able to sleep last night, he could

have put two coherent thoughts together today. But he hadn't slept more than an hour or two. Fool moon had shone in his window all night, keeping him awake, keeping him thinking. When he finally did fall into a light doze, he'd dreamed of Liz riding a white stallion racing toward a precipice. He'd come awake sweating. After that, he'd gotten up, taken a shower and gone to his laptop computer to do some work.

Later, he wandered outside. The heat of the day lingered, but there was a tease of a breeze. The faint scent of new-mown hay brought back a thousand memories. He had loved summer—once.

The sound of water splashing at the pool and women laughing reached his ears, an oddly urban sound. Not his idea of country. There hadn't been a pool at the house when he was a kid. He'd had to go to an ersatz lake to swim. It had been nothing but a pond, really, nestled in a rare hollow on the Robbins ranch, twenty miles away. There'd been cottonwood trees, and a rope swing. There'd been a gang of boys, and later a girl who invited him to assuage his raging hormones. He'd declined, but he'd been in pain for an hour afterward and wondered if he was a fool not to have taken what she was offering.

Down by the barn, a group of men stood around the barbecue pit, drinking. Come to think of it, his throat was a little dry.

The moon hung low over the barn, riding in the sky with that tiny slice out of the side, coming off full, and the stars glistened like a thousand beacons.

Did the light purposely gather in Liz's hair to torture him? She was standing in the doorway of the barn, and her auburn hair shimmered like fire. She talked to one of the men, ducking her head in that way she had of shy attention, her glorious hair falling over her shoulders. Did she know how beautiful she was? No, she didn't. She was so unaware and so genuine that it made his heart ache to look at her.

She was wearing a denim jumper thing with a white T-shirt, lots of long, bare leg showing, well-worn leather sandals on her feet. She looked comfortable—and incredibly sexy.

Travis instructed himself to stay where he was, get involved in a conversation with the guys, and stop looking at her. But she was chatting with the wet-behind-the-ears guy who'd been at the corral the night before, and Travis couldn't seem to stop watching for the faint flow of color into her cheeks, the shift of her fiery hair over her shoulders. When the puppy preened himself, tugged at his bolo tie, touched the belt buckle of his pants, and then reached out to brush Liz's hair from her face, making her head come up in surprise, Travis barely restrained himself from breaking the kid's arm. Arrogant little rooster. What did he think he was doing, anyway, coming on to Liz? He'd mistaken a woman's friendliness for interest, proving beyond a doubt that he was still more boy than man.

It was none of his business. It had nothing to do with him. But when the cowboy braced his arm in the doorway to stop Liz from walking away, and Liz got that distressed look on her face that Travis knew well, he strode over to the stock tank, reached into the icy-cold water and fished around for a cherry cola, the kind he knew Liz liked.

In an instant, he was at her side, handing her the can. "I brought you a drink."

Liz looked up, surprised. She was pleased at first. Then she remembered, and her face cooled. He thought she might refuse his peace offering, for that was what it was, and they both knew it.

"How did you know I wanted a drink?"

"You looked thirsty."

"You're very observant. Thank you." She took it, her eyes meeting his. She looked...brave. Her chin was up. He liked that. She wouldn't back down from him, ever. Why did her reaction fill him with a sharp sense of anticipation? Her eyes met his, and her lovely skin went a shade rosier. Ah, Liz... He wanted to reach out and touch her cheek, cool it with fingertips chilled by the can he'd held.

"You should have said something. I'd have gotten you a drink." The young cowboy's face was flushed. He recognized a poacher when he saw one.

The puppy sounded a wee bit petulant. Travis was pleased.

"I don't think you've met Len Hollister," said Liz.

"Howdy." The kid stuck out his hand and tried to smile, as if to show Travis there were no hard feelings. Travis grasped Len's hand, felt him squeeze hard, answered in kind. Len looked surprised, as if he hadn't expected Travis to rise to the male challenge. "Worked at the ranch long?" Travis asked, releasing the kid's hand, making him bend his fingers in relief.

"Just started this summer."

"Should keep you out of trouble till you go back to high school. How much school do you have left?"

The boy reddened to the tips of his ears. "One year."

"Make good use of it. You know what they say about education."

"What's that, sir?" He used the title deliberately, a cocky lift to his chin.

Maybe this boy would amount to something after all. "A man needs one, no matter what line of work he's in."

"I'll keep that in mind, sir."

"You do that."

"Do you feel like dancing, Travis?" Liz took hold of

his arm. Her eyes were sparkling with what he thought was a touch of irritation, but the effect on her was lovely. Flashing green eyes, heightened cheek color, pale peach under ivory, chin tilted a fraction higher. Too lovely to be let loose on the same range with a bunch of feeling-good cowboys.

He knew that it would be far safer for both of them if he refused. Better for his own peace of mind, certainly. Holding her in his arms was going to be unmitigated torture. Suddenly, he didn't like safe. He was tired of safe.

"Here's another tip, son," Travis drawled the word. "Never turn down an invitation to dance from a beautiful lady." Travis drew Liz into the barn, before Len, his face a brighter red than ever, could reply.

Travis turned Liz into his arms. She came into the circle of his body gracefully, but he could feel the resistance in her, and that touch of irritation. "I've got another piece of advice for him," said Liz. "Never let a predator within ten feet of a woman you're talking to."

"Is that what I am, a predator?"

"Len's a nice kid."

"I never said he wasn't." He could smell her hair. It was worth the suffering, just to smell her hair. "I rather liked him, actually. He's got spunk."

"But he's not in your league."

"No," he said, shifting a little to hold her closer. He could feel the restraint in her. He didn't want her to strain away from him. He wanted her to relax, to float around the floor with him the way he sensed she could if she was more at ease.

He had her in his arms, but not the way he wanted her. What would it take to make her body fluid and easy against his, the way he wanted it to be?

He shouldn't be thinking about what he wanted.

Blessedly, the band was playing a slow tune. He recognized it. "Crazy." Appropriate song. He was crazy to be holding Liz in his arms, tempting fate like this. But for some reason, he felt in the mood to tempt fate. Actually, he felt like teasing the old girl to death.

"You might have said something like 'Glad you think so,' or 'He'll get there,' or something to show you have a modicum of modesty," Liz said.

"Would you have believed me?"

"No."

"One thing I learned long ago, sweetheart. Know your audience and play to them. It's as useful in the corporate world as it is in the theater. I know you. You wouldn't tolerate anything but honesty from me. So that's what I try to give you."

Liz pushed herself away from him to look up into his face. "How accommodating you are. Do you always try to give a woman exactly what she expects from you?"

"Behave yourself," he said, but the curve of his lips lifted.

"What else can I do, out here on the dance floor?"

He'd counted on that. He'd counted on the crush of people, the laughter, the lights, the music, to dilute the potency of her pull for him. But none of it was working. He could feel her warmth, her life. He knew when she took a breath, when she was holding her breath as she seemed to do when he talked to her.

She looked up at him and smiled in that way she had, as if she couldn't do anything else when she was with him.

Travis knew he was acting like a fool. He was doing what he'd sworn not to do. He was encouraging her.

The music stopped. People drifted toward the side of the floor, a few couples remaining to see what the next tune would be. He didn't want to let go of her. He didn't want to step away and stop touching her.

He dropped his hands, broke the connection between them. "Thank you for the dance, Elizabeth Annabell." He bowed his head, trying to lighten his withdrawal with humor, but he knew she recognized his release and his stepping away for what it was: an end to their time together.

"Any time, Travis Jonathan."

His mouth lifted. She'd done her research since last night. Or maybe she'd always known.

She took his rejection the way she took most things, with spirit and a smile on her lips.

He felt like fertilizer. But he knew what he had to do, and he did it.

Liz stood watching him as Travis went to one of Diana's friends, who had come to be a bridesmaid in the wedding, and asked her to dance. Joanne Worthington was tall, blond and vivacious, and had the shapely arms of a woman who watched her fat grams and worked out. Liz tried not to like her, but Joanne was open and friendly and delighted to be on a genuine ranch, as were all of the four college friends who'd come to take part in Diana's wedding. They'd all been kind and interested in Liz when she met them earlier that day. They'd been more than kind and interested when Diana introduced them to her brother. Even Shandra, who was wearing a ring on her finger that rivaled Diana's in size, couldn't help casting her eyes over Travis.

The music began, Travis turned Joanne into his arms, and they moved onto the dance floor. They looked wonderful together, she very blond and leggy, he dark and smiling down at her.

Her hand at her stomach, Liz went to stand at the big old double doors that were opened to the night. It seemed easier to breathe, easier to block out the hurt. That moon with the slice out of its side looked down, the ranch was still dotted with lantern light. Lots of people, lots of food, lots of laughter. And none of it meant anything.

She'd thought for a little while that she and Travis might come to an understanding. It had felt wonderful, just for that small moment in time, to have him act as if he were interested in her. But once the dance ended, he'd lapsed back into the old, politely distant Travis. Thank goodness she hadn't made a fool of herself and melted into his arms as she ached to do. She was safe, her pride intact. If only her heart would accept that.

Liz stepped out of the door and began to walk, not really thinking of anything but finding relief from the confusion…and the hurt.

The stable seemed blessedly dark after the blaze of lanterns outside, earthy, warm, welcoming. A familiar harbor, an escape from the confusion in her heart. Why had Travis approached her? She could have handled Len without his help. And then, after he took her in his arms, why had he walked away? Why?

Why did he always walk away?

In the darkness, Blaze's white head shone. He whickered low in his throat—a welcome, a plea to come closer and rescue him from his boredom. She said his name once, and he poked his head over the stall door and bobbed a greeting at her.

"You're lonesome, too, aren't you?" She extended her hand, and Blaze whuffled into it. He stuck his nose in her hair, made a low, throaty sound of welcome. She did a nearly perfect imitation of the sound he made, and he bobbed his head in excitement.

"Oh, baby. I didn't mean to come and raise your hopes. This is just a friendly visit. I can't take you out."

Blaze whickered in protest, bobbed his head, snorted.

"I know, I know. Just because I got my hopes soaring out of sight doesn't mean I should do the same thing to you. I'm sorry. I wasn't thinking about you. I was thinking about me. So what's new, eh?"

Blaze touched her nose, commiserating with her.

"Yeah, you're supposed to be the big killer horse. But you understand me better than he does, don't you, big boy?"

"That *he* who doesn't understand you—that would be me, I suppose."

Travis leaned against the door of the stable with that masculine grace that came naturally to him. He'd startled her thoroughly, but if she felt vulnerable, he looked more so, with his elegant shoes half buried in straw and his shirt open at the throat, his tie untied, the two strips of dark silk dangling from under his collar.

She'd never seen him with his tie undone and his guard down. Some deep instinct cautioned her to be careful. He might deserve to be hurt, but she couldn't do it, not when he looked like this. "What is it they say—eavesdroppers seldom hear good about themselves?" Her light, chiding tone sounded just about right to her ears, casual, teasing. She prayed it had deceived him.

"Certainly applies in my case, it seems."

To Liz, it looked as if Travis were caught there in the door, in what was for him a very uncharacteristic state of indecision. He looked as if he didn't know whether he wanted to come into the stable or turn on his heel and run the other way.

"What—are you doing here?"

Again, he looked hesitant. Then he raised his head like a man deciding to take his medicine. "Joanne asked what I'd done to you. She said your face was expressive and you looked hurt when you walked out and she was wondering what I'd said to you. What did I say to you?''

She wasn't an expert at bluffing, but she'd surely have to try. "You said, 'Thank you for the dance, Elizabeth Annabell.' Nothing to·apologize for. Joanne must have a vivid imagination.''

"I don't want to hurt you," he said. "Not again. I came in here to tell you that I'm determined never to hurt you again.''

Fighting to keep her tone light, she smiled. "A noble sentiment, of which I approve.'' But it hurt her to see him standing there looking at her as if he wanted to believe her, when his good sense was telling him not to.

He lifted his shoulders, as if trying to shrug off indecisiveness—an extremely unusual gesture for Travis. Liz straightened slightly and braced herself to meet his eyes with an unguarded casualness she hoped was convincing. If she was careful enough and blasé enough, surely he would go away and she'd be safe. "Honestly, Travis, you have nothing to apologize for. I was feeling a bit…smothered by all the good cheer, and needed to escape.''

"Understandable enough, I guess.'' He looked as if he were trying the idea on for size, to see if it fit her.

"I'm used to being more solitary. All those people are a bit…overwhelming.'' She wished he would go, wished the lantern light didn't play across his face, making his eyes deeply dark and the bones of his cheeks starkly beautiful. She wished her soul didn't ache with need for him.

"You shouldn't be overwhelmed. You're as beautiful as any woman there, and as intelligent as any man.''

"Well, thank you. You can tell Joanne you have redeemed yourself completely for whatever supposed wrong you committed.''

"That's not why I said it. I said it because I believe it."

"I know," she said, her eyes clear, meeting his.

His gaze moved past her, to Blaze. "He should have been shot long ago."

"Your father wanted him to live. He said one death was enough."

"That's one way to look at it, I guess. Do you ride him...often?"

"Every day," she said, knowing she was destroying the one small, remote chance left to be his friend.

"Do you, indeed," he murmured. He looked at Blaze, and grief and regret burned in Travis's eyes.

"Travis. I'm so very, very sorry about Andrew. I know you still miss him...as much as his father does." She couldn't help herself. She reached out to touch his face, that dark face so determined not to show pain or hurt.

"Take your hand away, Liz. Now."

She looked into his eyes, and with a daring she hadn't known she had, she said, "No."

She hung on a suspended breath, wondering what he'd do. She said, "I'm not eighteen anymore."

"And far more sure of yourself. Into taming every kind of wildlife that comes into your orbit, are you? Let's see how much courage you really have."

She thought she had the courage to call his bluff, but suddenly, she didn't. If he took her into his arms for real, if he kissed her with that darkly sweet mouth, she wouldn't want to let him go. But, inevitably, he'd push her away, and then her dreams would be more tortured than ever, for she'd actually know what his mouth felt like on hers....

She dropped her hand, took a step back.

His eyes seemed to go darker in that pale light. "Not so brave after all."

She lifted her head. "What's the point? When the kiss

was over, you'd walk away from me, just as you always have."

"It isn't you," he said.

"That's a nice line. Does it work well with your city women?"

His eyes grew steely. "I'd better go."

"Yes, you'd better. You'll be missed."

Well, there was a cool dismissal. Was she as cool as she seemed? He burned to know the truth. What would she do if he disregarded her refusal, walked forward and touched her, stroked a finger over the heat of those cheeks, let his hand drift down to the hollow of her throat, traced the collarbone that stood out so prettily above her breasts? High, beautifully firm breasts.

"So will you be missed, pretty Eliza."

It took all the control she had not to tremble at the sound of his nickname for her. No one but Travis had ever called her that. "I doubt it."

Blaze gave a low, warning roll in his throat.

Travis heard the sound, saw the worry register on Liz's face. She turned to Blaze, ran a hand down his muzzle.

He wouldn't be ordered around or warned off by a horse. Especially that horse. Travis stepped forward. The straw crackled. Blaze whinnied another warning.

"You're making Blaze nervous, Travis. He doesn't know you."

"Tough."

"If you're heading back to the party, you're going the wrong way."

"Yeah."

"All the bridesmaids will be missing you. You'd better get back to them. You've made such a hit with them...."

"You think so? Then why are you standing there trembling, with your heart in your eyes?"

"I...don't want you to touch me."

"I don't want to touch you."

"No, I mean...I don't want you to touch me...and then walk away."

He reached out, picked up a strand of her hair. "The last thing in the world I want right now is to walk away." He let her hair slide through his fingers, felt her soft intake of breath.

"Not so unmoved, after all. Damn it, woman, don't you know how attractive it is to a man when a woman reacts to him with soft little breaths and goose bumps on her skin?" He ran his fingers down her arm.

Her head came up, and her eyes were bright as stars. But she didn't move back, and he liked that. She wasn't afraid of him. She wasn't afraid of letting him see how she felt.

He couldn't seem to get enough of looking at her cheeks, with their pale peach color, and the slim body, the breasts that moved as she breathed. He liked it that she was involved with him, too involved to withdraw, as she had the first time.

"I can't help the way I react to you, Travis." She reached up and touched his face. "I'm sorry you don't like it." There was no demand in her touch. There was only comfort, understanding.

"Oh, I like it all right. Too much."

Did he pull her in his arms, or did she drift into them? He didn't know. He only knew she was so close he could smell the clean scent of her, feel her breathing.

"You haven't learned anything, have you? You're still just as open as you were all those years ago. And just as giving. Don't be so giving, Liz."

"All right," she said, and all the while her hands were

sliding up his back and her supple body was yielded against his.

He burned with need, just as he had all those years ago. He felt the bones of her hips press against him, and he felt her soft breasts, and her hair against his cheek. It all had an unutterably right feeling, excruciatingly exciting and peaceful all at once, as if standing in Liz's arms were the one place in the world he belonged.

He wrapped his fingers around her hips, and holding her exactly where he wanted her, he lowered his head and found her mouth. It was as soft and supple as her body, and fit him exactly the same. And the taste of her, the scent of her!

He couldn't get enough. He urged her lips open. She allowed him inside. He tasted her again, teasing her tongue until she chased him back into his mouth. He sucked her, kept her there. His heart pounded and his brain protested, but another intelligence had taken over that would not be denied.

He slipped his hand in under her jumper, felt the soft cotton cloth of her T-shirt, the smooth muscles of her back. And he tasted her, oh, how he tasted her. When she tasted him with the same hunger, his senses went wild. He wedged a leg between hers, his body burning for more closeness, for more of her, only her, just her.

He was on the verge of losing control.

The strap of her jumper fell down over her shoulder and made him think of stripping that restricting denim off her body and the T-shirt with it. He wanted to take her there, against the wall of the stall door, down in the straw, anywhere....

Blaze whinnied—a high cry of distress. Travis felt the sound rip through him.

He drew a shuddering breath, pulled back, eased Liz's

strap into its place on her shoulder and gently brushed the hair away from her cheek.

"Maybe I've got something to thank that horse for, after all."

"Travis—" She couldn't bear the look in his eyes. That quickly, he was back in control. He'd said he was aroused by seeing his effect on her. She wasn't going to let him walk away, not this time. She wrapped her arms around him, pulled him close and took his mouth with all the ferocity of her love for him. She could feel him yielding to her, and her spirit soared in triumph.

Then, suddenly, he wrenched his mouth away from hers and she was standing alone, the look in his eyes making her skin chill, her knees shake.

"All I want to know is...why? I'm not a girl now. Is it because you think I won't fit into your world?"

"No," he said. "It's because I'm very much afraid you will."

He turned, straw crackled under his shoes. She wanted to call out to him. Even as she stood with his name lingering on her lips, Travis disappeared into the darkness.

Chapter Four

He could say that ridiculous thing to her, that he was very much afraid that she *would* fit into his world, and then walk out? He could, in one simple sentence, destroy the reason she'd given him for rejecting her all these years and then leave her as if he hadn't just opened a huge Pandora's box of questions?

Too much kept inside her for too many years. Too many tears denied, too many brave smiles delivered on demand. She was tired of keeping a stiff upper lip, being brave, hiding her feelings, being stalwart and upright like a darned Boy Scout.

She stretched out her hand. The horseshoe was hanging on a nail on a stable stud one minute, the next sailing through the air at the stable door. Metal banged against wood with a richly satisfying thud.

Blaze whickered up a sliding scale and kicked his front legs against the stable door.

Instantly contrite, Liz returned to the horse, petted his bristle-soft muzzle, soothed him with love pats and crooning. "It's all right, baby, really."

She smelled his fear and agitation as he bobbed against her and nuzzled into her shoulder, seeking for more reassurance. His nose was wet and warm against her neck. "It's okay, Blaze. I'm just being an idiot. It's contagious, you know. You catch it from those you love."

Calming Blaze brought sanity. She'd wanted to follow that horseshoe through the stable door, grab Travis's arm, pull him around, look him in the eye and say, "What do you mean by destroying the one excuse I've given you for years?"

Logical, brilliant, incisive Travis McCallister made no sense at all. Superintelligent in the workplace he might be, but he was an idiot when it came to personal relationships.

He wanted her. She knew it, could feel it, just as she had when she was eighteen. He wanted her—but he wasn't going to have her. Or let her have him. For some reason known only to himself. *Not* the one she had believed all these years, that she wasn't clever enough or smart enough to fit into his world.

A hundred years ago, the morning of Andrew's funeral, Liz had come into the stable looking for Travis. She'd found him here in front of Blaze's stall, standing in the half-light, dressed in his suit, his hair combed severely back from his forehead, his beautiful face stark with grief. He'd been twenty, almost a man to her adolescent fourteen. He'd looked like a man aged beyond his years that morning, his face so grim, his shoulders tense, his arms braced against the stable door as if he were trying to push it in and kill the stallion with his bare hands. When he heard her footsteps on the straw and whipped around to her, his eyes had been like bottomless wells of anguish and anger. Her heart had cried out to him in instant empathy and love.

When he looked at her and read the sympathy in her eyes, his face turned cold and impassive. "Get out."

The harsh words wounded her tender heart, but she stood her ground. He was hurting, and she couldn't bear it. Nor would she leave him. "Don't try to carry this alone, Travis. Please."

He had never belittled her, ever, but his beautiful brown eyes glittered with a deep, ironic anger that was aimed beyond her—or deep inside himself. "What can you do, Liz, my little angel, my little Miss Fix-It? Can you bring him back? Can you make our lives unwind like a movie reel and return us all to Saturday, so that this time I can stop Andrew from getting up on that horse?"

"It wasn't your fault," she cried out, horrified that he should be taking such a burden of guilt on his shoulders. "Boyd wanted him to ride that horse. And Andrew is an excellent rider…"

"*Was* an excellent rider, Liz. *Was.*" The ironic harshness was directed more at himself than at her.

Liz couldn't bear it. "He'd been on horses since he was three—"

"Riding a million horses wouldn't have prepared him for this one's dirty tricks. He was too trusting, too cocky. Eighteen, and full of himself. Couldn't believe that he wasn't the master of any horse. I could have told him. But I didn't."

"It was an accident. A horrible, horrible accident. Please don't blame yourself. Please…don't do this." She might have been talking to the wind.

"I was the only one there with sense enough to know what could happen. But I just stood there and let him get on the horse, because I thought…" A rare expletive exploded from his lips. Whatever he'd thought, he wasn't going to share it with her.

She said, "You mustn't do this. You mustn't torture yourself this way. You need to talk to your family, to Diana, or your father."

He made a sound. It wasn't complimentary.

"Then talk to my mother. You know how much she cares for you. Diana says we have to talk to each other at a time like this—"

"My God. Spare me from teenage women who think talking is the answer for everything. Let's spend a whole day, a whole night, talking. Let's talk until we're hoarse. What the hell good will it do? Will it bring Andrew back?"

She breathed in sharply at the vehemence of his attack. For that was what it felt like, an attack on her, everything she was, everything she thought and felt. "It might make you feel better to vent your feelings."

"The only thing I want to vent my feelings on is this horse. I'd like to see him breathing his last."

"That would make you feel better?" she said, her voice as steady as she could manage. "Two deaths, instead of one?"

"I don't know, but I'd like to try it." His eyes flicked over the horse's face, as if he were examining a specimen of a not-particularly-interesting phylum. "Go back to the house, Liz. I already had a generous portion of psychobabble from Diana. Don't make me go through the same nonsense with you. I thought you were the one person in the world who dealt in uncompromising honesty. Get out of here, and take your load of bullpucky with you."

She was not to be stampeded that easily. She'd already grown to love the stallion. "Your father doesn't want Blaze killed."

"I know that. I'm not going to hurt him. I just want the luxury of contemplating it," he said through gritted teeth. "Get out of here, Liz. You're too young to be telling me what to do—" his voice grew harsher "—or how to feel."

She'd shrugged off every other barb, but this one went too deep. The tears came, there was nothing she could do to stop them. She couldn't see, couldn't think, couldn't stand. She turned away, grabbed the wall nearest her for support.

He muttered a curse. "That was uncalled-for. I'm...sorry."

"I loved Andrew, too," she said, her back to Travis.

"I know. Unlike me, he was eminently lovable. And far too young to die." His voice was close, and then she felt his hand on her shoulder. "I'm sorry, Liz. I had no right to say those things to you."

She shook her head and fought for control, but a sob escaped her.

Gently, so gently, he turned her into his arms. She was enveloped in his warmth, in his heady, clean smell.

"Don't cry, pretty Eliza, please don't. I shouldn't have unleashed my anger on you. I keep forgetting how young you are, how sensitive. You're always such a little trouper, taking whatever anybody hands you and smiling and saying thank-you. I wish I had that gift." He ran his hand down her hair, petting her.

Her heart in her eyes for him to see, along with the tears, she lifted her face to his.

He gazed at her for a long moment. She reached out, touched his shoulder. There was a rueful twist to his mouth as he said, "One of these days, you'll be the death of me, my sweet little one."

"Oh, Travis, I can't stand to see you hurting like this. "I—I love you so much."

His face changed. "You don't even know me. And you're too young to know what love is. You're just feeling a few hormones coming to life under the stress of these days." He stepped away from her gentle touch.

"I'm not too young," she said, with all the fierce passion of her young-old heart. "And it's not hormones. I know I love you now and I'll love you always."

"You don't even know what love is."

"You could teach me."

"The only thing I could teach you about is trouble. Get out of here, Liz. Now. You don't belong in my world...and I don't belong in yours."

"Travis—" She couldn't believe that he would reject her so cruelly.

"Get out of here. Now. I don't need your sympathy. And I sure as hell don't want your love."

And he still didn't. Except that...she was a woman now, not a girl, and now she knew that while he might not want her love, he *did* want her. She'd always believed he'd rejected her because she was a country girl, had never been part of his sophisticated big-city life. But now he'd said he was afraid she *would* fit into his life. What sense did that make?

Blaze bobbed his head against her arm, acutely sensing her distress. Liz stood in that warm darkness, her heart crying out with questions. Questions for which only Travis had the answers.

The next morning, a cool breeze blew from west to east. In her room in the small house, knowing she was alone, knowing her mother had stayed at the big house last night, Liz stood in front of the mirror, plaiting her hair in a French braid and girding her soul.

In the stable, she tossed the saddle on Blaze's back and

told him from between gritted teeth that she would have
an answer to the questions she'd lain awake all night contemplating, and she'd have them soon. But for now, she
was going to let the wind blow away the cobwebs.

Mounted on Blaze, filled with a sense of freedom and
purpose, Liz kept a firm hand on Blaze's reins. He was
foxy and saucy and ready to bolt—she could feel the restrained power of him. She turned him into the south pasture, heading for Rattlesnake Hill. Named unfairly, the hill
was quiet and peaceful and redolent with clover. A creek
meandered down from the top, and a cottonwood tree
struggled to keep its place beside the stream. The hill had
been named by a crotchety old farmer who didn't want a
bunch of pesky kids coming out from town to play on the
hill.

At last, out in the sun, she loosened her tight hold on
the reins and let Blaze ease into the gallop he'd been so
desperately straining for.

"At least one of us is getting what he wants this morning," she muttered to him.

Unheeding, Blaze pounded through the clover, divots of
dirt and tufts of grass flying behind his heels. Liz threw
her head back, felt the wind singing in her ears. The stimulation of physical exercise, hot, sweet fresh air redolent
with the smell of red clover dotted with humming bees
and the warmth of the sunshine beaming down on her head
restored her natural exuberance and repaired her soul after
a night spent tossing and turning with a head echoing with
unanswerable questions.

When Blaze had run off his excess energy, she turned
him toward the north pasture. She never jumped fences
with Blaze. It was too dangerous for both of them. She
rode him south to the pasture gate, reached down and

slipped the wire noose from the wooden post to let herself through.

She combined her ride with work, checking on the water level in the stock tanks that were powered by the three windmills that dotted the ranch. There were also the salt licks to check, to see if they were getting low. The feeder cattle, rusty-red Herefords with sweet white faces, trotted up to her in curiosity.

"Hey, pretty lady."

Harv stood in the shade of a cottonwood that had sprung up next to the stock tank. Over his head, the windmill clanked away merrily. Harv had flipped the mechanism that engaged the windmill blades, and the pump was working, bringing up cool water to gush into the tank. Cattle were gathered around, drinking the fresh water. His horse, a roan gelding named Strawberry, was tied to a branch, bobbing his head, asking for water.

"Hey, yourself," she said. "Your horse wants a drink."

For a man who'd been riding most of his thirty years, Harv was a bit callous toward his horses, and Liz knew it. She wondered at the reason.

She swung a leg over Blaze's saddle, slid off his back and led him to the tank. He plunged his nose in the water and began to lap greedily. She could only begin to imagine how thirsty the roan was. It wasn't good form to interfere with another man's horse, but no animal was going to suffer around her. Deliberately she walked to the tree, untied the roan and led him to the water. He dipped his head and began to lap noisily.

"You're a soft touch, you know that?" Harv leaned against the windmill, his eyes going over her in a way that she didn't like. On the ranch, he'd seemed friendly, not threatening. She'd never encountered him alone out on the range before. She didn't like the way he was looking at her. "And too sweet to be riding that big brute. If I were foreman on this ranch, I'd never let you out of the stable...on him."

She pretended to miss the double entendre. "Then it's a good thing you're not the foreman, isn't it?"

The wind lifted her braid, and the windmill clanked away, working the pump to draw the water. Blaze swished his tail, catching her on the shoulder. He came up for air, dribbled water on her arm, deliberately, she knew, because he was as smart as a whip and twice as canny, and went back down for another drink.

The roan jerked up. He was nervous around the stallion. Liz laid her hand on the roan's neck, steadying him.

"Nice day." Harv's eyes went up to the sky, back to Liz. He had shockingly beautiful sky-blue eyes, and he knew how to use them to his advantage. A steady, sincere gaze—followed by a slow, leisurely tour of her face only. No lower. "Nice company."

"If I'd known you were here to see to things, I would have ridden on home."

"You knew I was here. On this prairie, you can see for miles." Harv's eyes gleamed.

"No, I didn't actually see you until I rode up closer. I was...thinking about something else."

"Well, now you're here and I'm here. Now what?"

She gave him a no-nonsense look, her green eyes as bright with cool honesty as his blue ones were full of seductive energy. "Now nothing, Harv."

"Liz, honey, you know you like me. Otherwise why would you come running when you thought I was hurt? Come on, you can admit it, now that we're alone."

"I'd have felt the same sympathy for any cowboy who landed on his rear in that corral dirt. I've been there myself a few times—"

"Too bad I wasn't there when it happened to you. I'd have picked you up off that hard ground...unless you decided you wanted to stay there in my arms and cuddle a bit 'cause it felt so good." He smiled lazily.

"You know something? You still need that dunking."

"You think you're big enough to try?"

Without even thinking twice, she swept her hand into the just-pumped, icy-cold water and up again.

Too surprised to move, Harv took her shot full in the face. He stood there looking stunned, his shirt wet, his nose dripping. "Why, you little—"

He grabbed up a bucket sitting next to the tank, but by the time he filled it, she'd scampered well out of range.

He came toward her. She backed away, holding up her hands defensively. "That's not fair."

"No, but it's quick." He stalked her, but she was lighter on her feet than he. She ran, he chased. She twisted and turned, and so did he, but he was hampered by the weight of the bucket and the sloshing water. By the time he did catch up with her, and had her backed against a borderline fence, there was only a half bucket of water left. She turned to take her punishment, facing him, hands up, palms out.

Growling, he wound up and tossed the water. She dodged, but not enough. The edge of the deluge caught her throat and arms.

She laughed, she couldn't help it. The water was cool against her hot skin. "I suppose I deserved that."

"Darn right you did." He was grinning, his male ego satisfied that he'd evened the score. He dropped the bucket, and his hands went to his shirtfront. Watching her closely, he pulled the snaps loose with a pop, pop, pop, and stripped off the wet garment.

His physique was nearly as spectacular as his eyes. "I'm

getting out of my wet clothes," he said, devilment in his smile. "Why don't you do the same?"

All that bare expanse of broad shoulder and rippling muscle left her unmoved. "A fast ride to the house will dry me off," she said, hoping she sounded as indifferent as she felt. She wouldn't give in to his heavy-handed teasing.

She turned and started to walk away from him, the pasture stubble crunching under her feet. His hand came down on her shoulder, and he turned her around. "Liz, I like you a lot."

"I like you, too, Harv." She said it straightforwardly, ranch hand to ranch hand—and eased her shoulder out from under his fingers.

"I'd like to kiss you. Would you slap my face if I tried?"

"Why are you doing this? You already have a girlfriend, I know you do."

He grinned with what she supposed he considered his irrepressible, boyish charm. "Yeah, but she isn't here."

"And I am?" Her mouth turned up at the corners. "You'd better get a new line, cowboy. This one stinks." She whipped around and headed for the horse in a fast power walk that was almost a run.

He fell in step beside her, but to her great relief, he didn't try to grab her again. "You really stuck on that city boy?"

She kept right on hustling. This was one conversation she wanted to terminate as soon as possible. "That's none of your business, is it?"

"I suppose not. I just don't like to see a woman get hurt, that's all."

"Oh, I can see you're all consideration when it comes

to a woman's feelings. I've just had an excellent demonstration of your thoughtfulness.'' Her voice was dry.

"So you're not a poacher?'' He sounded amused, unaffected by her crisp tone.

"No.'' She reached the stallion, grasped the reins and hoisted herself into the saddle. She hadn't thought she felt threatened by Harv's attempt to flirt with her, but up in the saddle, she felt such a sense of relief that she knew she'd been more on edge than she realized.

"I'm due back at the ranch. Mom needs my help. See you later—''

"I'll ride back with you and get a dry shirt.'' Harv caught up the roan's reins, and was mounted and trotting along beside her before she could give the stallion his head and race away from him.

Liz let the stallion pick up the pace. Harv kept up with her. She urged the stallion to a greater speed. Harv kicked the sides of the roan and gave a cowboy yell, surging past her. The stallion strained against the reins. Blaze didn't like eating another horse's dust. And neither did she.

She gave Blaze the cry that meant "Run,'' and Blaze obeyed. His powerful thighs stretched into a long, ground-eating stride that carried her ahead of the roan. The roan pounded behind her, but she was well ahead when they raced into the yard. She was so busy reining in the stallion and easing him down to a trot that she didn't notice that she and Harv had an audience.

Exultant that she had won the race, Liz drew Blaze up to a halt. In the spiral of dust curling around her and the stallion, she twisted around to Harv, ready to glory in her victory. Harv made a warning sound, and she glanced up at the ranch house. Two men stood on the porch watching them, one with his hands thrust in his pockets. Boyd and Travis.

The roan scrabbled to a halt behind Liz, close enough that Liz could hear Harv say in an undertone, "City boy has got himself all countrified."

Boyd came down the porch steps toward them, with Travis following. Travis had on old jeans that fit his hips lovingly, a light blue denim shirt, boots and an old, well-worn Stetson that Liz remembered from years ago.

The cowboy clothes should have softened the impact of his charisma. They didn't. Now he was an elemental male, stripped down to his essence, the worn-smooth jeans and work shirt accentuating the lines of his muscular strength and lean body.

Under the brim of that hat, his dark gaze roved over Liz's flushed face and the wet splotches on her blouse, then flicked to Harv's bare chest.

"Now what have you two been up to?" Boyd said, with a smile on his lips. The dark tiredness was there still in his eyes, but Boyd held his body straight and tall.

"Just inspecting the stock tank in the north pasture, sir," said Harv.

"Does that require climbing in?" Travis drawled.

"I was just… We were…" Under the steadfastness of Travis's gaze, Liz stumbled to a halt. It was evident that he'd made up his own mind about what she'd been doing. That hurt.

"Cooling off," Harv said easily, that gleam of devilment in his eyes.

Liz sat up straight in the saddle. "I told Harv he needed a dunking the other night, and the opportunity presented itself to give him what I promised him." There was heat in her cheeks, she knew there was, but it was the heat of determination, not embarrassment. She wouldn't be manipulated by these men, any of them. "Of course, he retaliated, as men always feel they must. Now if you'll excuse me—''

She clucked to Blaze and guided him toward the stable, thinking any or all of them could believe what they wanted to believe. They would, anyway. She wasn't responsible for their thoughts. Especially the thoughts of men from the city who had probably forgotten everything they'd known about ranch life.

"Fine young woman," Boyd said, looking at Harv with a speculative gleam in his eye.

"Yes, sir. Well, I better get busy hauling hay and earning my keep." Harv tipped his hat and rode in the opposite direction.

"He's a good worker. I'm thinking of making him foreman when Jim retires. Maybe then he'll be able to afford a wife. Looks like that's what he's got on his mind."

"What's on his mind is a little more basic than marriage."

"You think he'd take advantage of Elizabeth?"

"I think he'd take advantage of any woman who allowed it."

"I hear you and he had a little altercation down at the corral the other night."

Travis didn't reply.

"He was polite enough to you just now."

Travis remained silent.

"Could be he feels you're poaching on his territory. Maybe he thinks you're in a better position to take advantage of Liz than he is—grab yourself a little loving and run back to the city."

Travis turned a face to Boyd that would have frightened any man in the world but the one who had fathered him and lived through hell with him. "Liz has never had anything to fear from me, and she never will. She was raised

in the protection of your household. I won't say she's naive, but she has been very sheltered here. You're employ-
ing Mr. Lester. Has it occurred to you that you have some
responsibility toward seeing that he doesn't take advantage
of her?"

"She's a grown woman, son. Twenty-five now, twenty-
six her next birthday. One thing I've learned in politics,
you stick your nose in where it doesn't belong, you might
get it whacked off."

"Excuse me. I forgot for a moment that your policy is
expediency over responsibility."

It was a direct hit, and the arrow went home. Boyd
closed his eyes for a moment, dealing with his pain. When
he opened them again, he looked out over the ranch, at the
pastures dotted with the rusty backs of Herefords. The
grass was a deep, healthy green, fed by recent rains. This
was a prosperous ranch, and he was proud of it. There
would be no son to leave it to. "Do you think you need
to remind me? I don't need to be reminded." He turned
to Travis, and his eyes had lost their sparkle. He looked
old beyond his sixty-three years. "I often wonder. Is it me
you can't forgive—or yourself?"

Icy-cold, Travis said, "I believe we were headed out to
look at the Charolais bull you're using for crossbreeding."

On the night of Diana's wedding rehearsal, the church
sanctuary glowed with candlelight. Mahogany pews, the
varnish on their backs worn by generations of hands sliding along them, gleamed with an antique patina.

Liz admired Diana for eschewing a glossy city church
and choosing this one, where Diana had been baptized in
her mother's arms, and where she and Liz had attended
Sunday school.

Liz had dreamed of being married in this lovely old

church, too, but in her dream, the groom had always been Travis.

Diana's bridesmaids gathered in clusters to exclaim over the stained-glass windows and the tall candelabra, while Travis, utterly dark and gorgeous in his casual beige jacket, stood talking to another groomsman at the back of the sanctuary. Looking at him standing there, so tall, so dark, so real, Liz heard her dreams dancing in her head.

What a foolish woman you are. All your fantasies are soap bubbles floating onto a tree branch to burst. This is the real world. And in this world, Travis will never belong to you.

Accept the truth. Move on with your life.

And she would. As soon as Travis went back to Chicago, she would think about leaving the ranch. She would never be free of his memory as long as she stayed. She would always think of him, want him, as long as she was there where he had been.

The rehearsal began. Liz was to stand at the altar in her place in the lineup of bridesmaids, the third woman from Diana. She wouldn't walk with Travis—he was the second groomsman. She would follow him down the aisle.

Liz had nothing to do, no bouquet to accept, no train to adjust for the bride. She was there only to add to the pomp and circumstance. It was an added bonus that she could look at the back of Travis's head and ache from wanting him.

The music soared, the minister read the marriage vows, but the bride and groom did not repeat them. They would do that tomorrow, and then their lives would be bound together.

Forever, Liz thought. Hoped. Bill was tall, broad-shouldered and dark-haired, very much like Travis. Liz had liked Bill from the moment he shook her hand. Diana glowed in his presence, and Bill couldn't take his eyes off his soon-to-be wife. They laughed and teased each other constantly.

At the end of the rehearsal, Liz's mother came up to her. Rachel looked lovely in a soft, silky beige dress, utterly feminine. "Are you all right, sweet?"

"Of course."

"You look...tired." Rachel laid a hand on Liz's arm.

"I'm fine, really."

She'd have to smile more, move more, talk more. If her mother thought she looked withdrawn, then certain other people might notice her quiet mood, too. That wouldn't do.

The dinner was to be held in an elegant hotel in Sioux Falls, an hour-and-a-half ride away. She ended up in the back seat of Boyd's BMW with Joanne Worthington, Shandra Kelso, and Jane Everett, the maid of honor. Two of the groomsmen, Dennis Childs and Kevin Atkinson, jumped into the front seat next to Travis who was behind the wheel.

She would not admire the glossy sheen of Travis's hair. She would not ache to touch the tiny hairs curling at his nape. She was on a diet, a strict program of denial. She would not look, she would not desire. She was taking the cure. Starting now.

Blond-haired Kevin, whom Dennis called the original fair-haired boy, twisted around in his seat and flashed a dazzling smile at Liz. In an ebullient mood, Kevin said, "Look who's in the back seat, gentlemen. The fair Elizabeth. So quiet and gentle is she that she steals a man's heart away."

"Don't listen to him, Liz," Dennis drawled. "He has a reputation for wooing women with his bad poetry. When he gets them drawn into his web, the poetry turns erotic.

Our fair-haired boy here is incredibly underhanded and unscrupulous when it comes to women.''

Kevin was being ragged, and he knew it. He pounded Dennis on the shoulder with an easy fist. "So who was it that told the well-stacked brunette how you really admired her mind?"

Liz's cheeks might be flushed, and she might not be as experienced at sophisticated repartee as the rest of them, but she was determined to stand up for herself. "Don't worry, Dennis. I'm not quite the country bumpkin I look. I've met a man of the love-them-and-leave-them type before. I recognize the breed.''

"O-o-o... The lovely lady is not as innocent as she looks.''

"She's every bit as innocent as she looks.'' This from Travis, cool, almost...warning.

"Excuse me," said Liz, in a voice as cool and serious as his. "I may not be a sophisticated urbanite, but I draw the line at having a man fight my battles for me.''

Kevin laughed. Dennis turned to Travis to see what his reaction would be. In the rearview mirror, Travis's eyes flashed to Liz's. The look on his face told her that he remembered—and understood.

Joanne cried, "Hear, hear—a woman after my own heart," and Kevin flicked his hand back and forth, as if he'd touched something hot with his fingers. "Getting into dangerous territory here, men. Don't want the women ganging up on us, do we?''

"Behave yourself, then," said Joanne, smiling.

Liz followed her cue, and lifted her lips in a smile. Had she offended Travis? She didn't know. It didn't matter. Of course it didn't.

At the restaurant, a posh place with valet parking and blooming red petunias in window boxes under a green-

and-white-striped awning, the air was cool from air-conditioning and felt wonderful on Liz's cheeks as she entered the dining room.

Her mother had not wanted to be included in the rehearsal dinner, saying she would be out of place, but Liz was glad to see that not only had Boyd insisted Rachel accompany him, he was leading her to sit next to him at the head table, with Diana and Bill. Bill's parents, a sturdy New Hampshire couple who lived in the same house where Bill had been born, sat on the other side of the bridal couple.

The folded white place cards indicated that the attendants sat in the order they'd stood in the altar, which put Liz's escort and Jane Everett between Liz and Travis. Liz was profoundly grateful for that. She could almost pretend he wasn't there. She would put him out of her mind.

The dinner was delicious, Liz was sure it was, but she hardly tasted the cordon bleu chicken she ordered. She couldn't hear the words Travis said, but she could hear the tone of his voice, low and polite as he conversed with Jane. Kevin was playing raconteur, telling the story of an occasion when he and Diana had played a practical joke on Bill, early in the courtship. Liz listened with one ear, but she was far too conscious of Travis's hands as he reached for his coffee cup.

So much for keeping thoughts of him in abeyance.

At the end of the meal, she breathed a sigh of relief. She could go home now....

"Absolute nonsense. Of course you won't go home. The whole entourage is going out to see the sights of Sioux Falls, and you're coming with us," said Joanne, linking her arm in Liz's.

The first stop was a retro disco, with flashing lights that made Liz's head ache. Kevin asked her to dance, but she shook her head. He shrugged his shoulders and held out his hand to Jane. Too late, Liz saw that this would leave her sitting alone at the table with Travis.

Travis made a circular motion with his finger, mimicking a turn around the dance floor, in silent invitation to dance. Liz thought about stepping into his arms—and having to leave them. She couldn't do that again.

She smiled to soften her refusal. "I'm too old for this," she mouthed above the loud music, and turned away from him to face the dance floor, determined to put him out of her sight, out of her mind.

He rose, came around to her side of the table, and before she realized his intent, he gripped her elbow and brought her to her feet. But instead of heading for the dance floor, he propelled her to the door.

Outside, the air was considerably cooler. The street was brightly lit and there was a small dining area under an awning a few feet away. Travis steered her toward it, eased her down into a wrought-iron chair.

"I guess I wanted to go outside instead."

"I wanted to talk to you, and I couldn't do it in there. Why wouldn't you look at me during dinner? And why wouldn't you dance with me?"

She met his eyes as directly as she could. His face, illuminated in the soft light coming from the two lamps by the hotel door, was so darkly beautiful it made her breath catch in her chest. "Two rejections a week is my limit."

He scowled, and his hands gripped the back of the chair he stood behind. "I didn't reject you."

"I see. I wonder what you call it, then."

"I call it being sensible. I thought you understood."

"I thought I did, too. And now I find I don't at all. But it doesn't matter anymore, really. The bottom line is, you want nothing to do with me. I accept that. I could accept it a lot better if you'd stop dragging me about."

"You need dragging about," he muttered. "If you aren't interested in one of those overeducated, undersmart bozos, why did you come along tonight?"

"Didn't you notice? I'm trying to shed my country-bumpkin skin."

"And pick up a city boy in the process?"

"I don't deserve that, Travis."

"No, you don't.' He looked disturbed, as if he regretted his words more than she did.

She could almost forgive him for his high-handedness. Almost. "Stop trying to protect me from Diana's friends. They're just talking, having a good time. They're harmless."

"Yeah, like a barracuda is harmless."

"If they want to have a little fun with me and tease me, why should you care?"

"I don't want to see you get hurt."

"I'm a big girl now. I don't need your defense. I can take care of myself."

"So it seems."

"You know something, Mr. McCallister? I really do want you to give up playing the part of big brother. It's long past time. You're not my big brother anymore."

"What am I to you?"

"Well, I think you've defined that pretty well. You're nothing to me. We're nothing to each other. I can't even say that what we had is over, because we never had anything."

Chapter Five

She looked like a wind goddess, sitting there with her hair blowing in a fiery nimbus around her face, her head high, her back straight. Travis had seen her in a thousand different lights, in a thousand different attitudes, but never like this, never so sure of herself and so strong.

"We've always had something, and you know it."

A breeze caught a strand of her hair, floated the coppery strand over her shoulder. She wore a silk blouse and a longish skirt that fell in graceful folds away from her waist. She had never looked more desirable. If his words had an effect on her, he couldn't discern what it was. She said, "Then it must be time to break that connection."

"It may not be that easy."

"Yes, it is." She seemed to be entering into the spirit of the thing, as if they were playing a game. "Let me show you how it's done. I know the routine very well. I learned it from you. You simply stand up—" and she did "—and walk away." Her back to him, she clipped crisply down the sidewalk, her heels clicking on the cement.

He wanted to let her keep walking until she had to turn around and come back. He did not want to chase her.

But when she disappeared around a corner, he hustled after her, caught her arm, pulled her around. "You've made your point."

"I don't think so," she said, her hair illuminated by the streetlight, her face incredibly beautiful, incredibly dear to him. "Not yet. But I'm about to. I'm a grown woman, Travis, and I am what I am. If you don't like the way I react to other people, I'm sorry. I won't change for you. I know my own integrity. I know I'm honest, I know I'm fair. I've spent a lot of years learning about myself and other people. I know enough about life to know that I can't change to please you—or anybody else. If I do, I'll lose sight of who I am. And then I won't be worthy of anybody's love." She paused for a breath, looked as if she was trying to gather her courage. "I've accepted the fact that, for whatever reason, I feel something for you that you don't feel for me. I can accept that. I won't accept your monitoring what I say to other men—and how I live my life."

A declaration of independence, delivered with style and grace. The way she did most things. He remembered the way she'd looked pounding into the yard in that impromptu horse race, her braid flying behind her, her body bent over the back of the stallion that grown men were afraid to ride, her face young and free and joyous. He thought of how she'd looked in the rearview mirror, her face flushed from the teasing she was receiving, yet perfectly capable of quoting his own words back to him and standing up for herself. He saw her now, strong enough and honest enough to admit that she cared for him and walk away.

He'd had it all wrong. She wasn't a girl who needed his protection. Not anymore. She was a grown-up woman, with strengths he'd never realized she had—and he wanted her. Wanted her with such a need as he'd never known.

"I've never thought you lacked integrity—never. I've only thought of you as too young—too inexperienced and vulnerable to hear me say exactly what I'd like to do with you."

His mouth closed on hers. When he felt her body soften against his and her lips open to him, he deepened the kiss. He claimed her, exploring her mouth thoroughly, his hands on her hips pulling her into his body where she could feel the strength of his desire.

He established a rhythm in her mouth, felt her tremble, felt her yield. Heady, so heady, this drowning himself in her. But it wasn't enough. He wanted to bury himself in her.

His thigh between hers, his body rocking, he showed her how it would be between them.

She braced her arms on his shoulders, broke the kiss, pushed back to look into his face. "What *are* you doing?"

"If you don't know, I'm not doing it right."

A couple strolled by on their way to the hotel. Travis ignored them, closed in on Liz to recapture her mouth. She shook her head and stepped out of his reach. "Couldn't you have chosen a less public place for this revelation?"

"If we were in a private room, you wouldn't be two feet away from me now. You'd be undressed and on your back and I'd be sliding into you…"

She didn't flinch. Her eyes were clear, bright, sparkling, and her head was still high. "I might have something to say about that."

"Yeah, you would. You'd say yes."

"You've been a corporate raider for too long." She went to brush past him and return to where they'd started.

"And you've been alone too long." He caught her arm, brought her up against him again and took her mouth with all the expertise at his command, his hand sliding low on her back, cupping her buttock. It was a man's kiss, demanding, explicit. She wanted to resist that pressure on her back to press her feminine softness against his male hardness, but she couldn't. She met his aggression eagerly, with a wildness of her own, absorbing him into her body as if he were the life that she needed to exist.

"Hey, you two. What are you doing, making out in the middle of the street? Don't you know it's simply not done after midnight in Sioux Falls?"

Diana's voice. Diana and Bill, walking toward them, laughing, arm in arm. Travis loved his sister, but at this precise moment, he wished her to the ends of the earth.

"Hi." Liz pulled away from Travis's hold. "We weren't making out. We were talking."

"That's a new name for it," Travis said, just loud enough for Liz to hear.

"Nobody 'makes out' anymore," Diana said. "I wonder why."

"It's the demise of the bench seat in cars that did it," Bill said. That earned him a lifted-eyebrow look from Diana.

"Where did you come by this piece of information, education or experience?"

"I only know what I read in the newspapers," he said quickly, with a teasing grin.

"Is the party breaking up?" Liz asked.

"Well, yes and no. Some people are going to find another place to hang out, but others of us, at least that portion of us who are getting married tomorrow, want to go home to catch up on our beauty sleep." She nudged Bill. "Your cue, honey."

"My cue to what?"

"Say I don't really need any beauty sleep, I'm beautiful enough, you idiot."

"Listen, babe, you better get all the sleep tonight that you can. Because tomorrow night you're going to be a very busy lady."

"Not in front of my brother, Bill, please."

"Why? We'll be all legal by then."

"You'll make him blush."

Bill cast a quizzical glance over Liz. "Your brother doesn't look like he's blushed since he was three years old."

"Actually, I was four," Travis said blandly.

"If you're going back home now, I'd like to go with you," said Liz quickly.

"What a little coward you are," murmured Travis in a low tone that only Liz could hear.

"How about you, brother?" Diana smiled at Travis. "You ready to call it a night?"

"No," he drawled, "but I guess I'll go home if the bus is leaving."

"Dad said we could take his car if you or Liz would drive."

"Nice of him to volunteer us."

"Well, at least he gave you the chance to stay together."

"Yes," Travis murmured.

"Dad and Rachel want to go home, too. So it will be just the family." Diana beamed up at Bill.

"So much togetherness," drawled Travis.

"Why, Travis. How nice of you to say so," Diana said.

But even in the half-lit street, he could see devils of delight dancing in his sister's eyes. It was very difficult to fool Diana. She knew full well what he'd been doing with Liz, and she was enjoying his discomfort with all the fiendish delight in her crafty sibling heart. Travis gritted his teeth, grabbed Liz's elbow and said, "Come on. Let's gather the clan."

Travis stood at the altar, resisting the wave of emotion emanating from the congregation of people in the pews. What was it about a wedding that made strong men's knees tremble and women pat their eyes with bits of lace? If the truth prevailed, it should be the other way around. The men should be crying and the women shaking.

His tux shirt was too tight around the neck. It hadn't felt this tight the last time he wore it.

Rituals. Why did people have such a need for them? Jump over a broom, walk around a table three times, drink wine, crush a glass, what difference did it make?

A quick trip to the justice of the peace, sign the legal papers and out the door would be easier, safer and cheaper. And a lot less trouble for the other members of the family.

A rustling at the back of the church. Bridesmaids coming up the aisle. Great heaven! Was that Liz? She looked ethereal...and so sexy she could stop a man's breath. A misty green froth of a dress that made her seem to float, rather than walk. Her hair pulled back on one side, green and white blossoms nestled in her luxuriant auburn tresses.

She looked up, and that green-eyed gaze froze him in his place. He didn't want to feel what he was feeling. He fought it. He didn't win. He ached with need.

Diana appeared, and his father, trying not to look proud. His sister always had impeccable taste, and she certainly had done well for this special day of hers. No lace, no

furbelows. Just a cloud of white silk and a misty veil floating around her neck and shoulders, throwing her face in
shadow.

She arrived at the altar, and Kevin turned around—Travis's signal to do the same. Boyd stepped back, behind Diana.

They said their vows, Bill and Diana. Listening, Travis
clenched his hands at his sides. Why did everybody think
these words were so wonderful? They were illusions that
people wanted to believe in. No, they were worse than that.
They were lies. There was no substance to them. People
didn't love each other forever in long, happy lives, never
had, never could. They got tangled up with other people
and had affairs, or they got busy making money, or they
got bored with each other. Or they depended on other people to help them, and those people failed them and they
died.

At the end of the ceremony, he stood in the receiving
line, thinking this was another ridiculous custom. What
were people supposed to say to him? Congratulations on
standing up straight and being a great groomsman?

"Lighten up, man. You're scaring the people." This
from the fair-haired boy, Kevin, who'd served as Bill's
best man.

Travis said a barnyard word under his breath.

"If you can hold out another hour, we'll soon be where
the liquid refreshments will flow. Can you make it that
long?"

Travis caught a glimpse of Diana leaning forward for
Rachel's kiss, saw the explosion of the photographer's
flash.

"No problem," he said, thinking he'd made a promise
to his sister and he'd better start acting like he was thirty-
five instead of five.

Rachel clasped Kevin's hand, kissed his cheek. Then Travis felt her familiar scent surround him, her warm hand clasp his.

"You look like a young rooster about to go under the ax. Relax, sweetheart. It will all be over before you know it."

She'd known what he was feeling...and she'd made him smile, like she always did. "I doubt it, but thanks for the kind thought, Rachel. You look beautiful. Too young for my father."

She and Liz shared the same delicate skin, and color bloomed peach under her creamy cheeks. Her hair was a shade darker than Liz's, only faintly touched by strands of gray. She was slim and tall and he couldn't imagine his father with anyone else. And he'd never told her so.

Travis pulled Rachel more deeply into his arms and put his mouth next to her ear. "Maybe it's about time you and Dad made the long-overdue legal adjustment. You two should have married years ago. Right now, you're setting a bad example for the younger generation."

"Now you just hush." She had taken on a motherly tone, but her color deepened, and she looked flustered. "This is not the time or the place to discuss such things."

"Maybe it's exactly the time and place to discuss such things," Travis said, giving her a smile and another quick brush on the cheek before she was swept along the receiving line.

He watched her come up on her toes to give Dennis a kiss, and wondered at his audacity in speaking to her as he had. He considered marriage a joke, yet it had long bothered him that his father had not proposed matrimony to a woman he obviously loved.

It was all right for him to shun matrimony, but when it came to his parent, Travis wanted traditions observed.

Hard to believe. Maybe he just loved Rachel and wanted what was right for her. He hadn't always loved her. When she first arrived at the ranch, he'd resented her. She hadn't allowed him to stay locked in his shell. She'd hammered at the door of his heart until she made him open it. Somehow, she'd helped him come to terms with his mother's death. She'd helped him see that a lonely eleven-year-old boy's phone call to his mother on a snowy New Year's Eve, asking her to come home because his sister was crying, wasn't the thing that had killed her, it was the drunken man driving through a stop sign. As far as Travis was concerned, Rachel deserved the world. If that world was his father...so be it.

It was a first for him, thinking that there were two people in the world who ought to be married.

Actually, he supposed there were four people. Leaning against the hotel bar while he waited for the reception to begin, watching Diana stand at Bill's side and beam at people in yet another receiving line, Travis had to concede that, together, both Diana and Bill seemed...stronger.

He fingered the frosty mug in his hand. He'd only had half a beer, not enough to turn him sloppy and philosophical.

A floor shiny enough to see faces in and banks of white roses, pale pink carnations and ferns had turned the hotel into a Victorian bower. He leaned back on a mahogany bar polished to mirror-smoothness to observe the proceedings. This was the cocktail hour before the buffet dinner. The bride and groom were the focus of attention, but Travis found his gaze wandering. He told himself he wasn't looking for Elizabeth Annabell, but he was.

That bright beautiful head of auburn hair didn't seem to be anywhere in the room. Her absence made him feel...lonely.

* * *

Should she feel sorry for him, standing there at the bar, looking like a lonely guy in an old Frank Sinatra song?

No, she shouldn't. Feeling sorry for Travis was a huge mistake. Look at all the trouble it had gotten her into years ago.

The bank of ferns in the little alcove offered Liz protection from the crowd and from Travis, but she knew she'd have to face him sooner or later. Might as well be now. She gathered up her courage and started toward him, but as she emerged from the ferny glen, a jovial male voice boomed through the sound system, inviting the bridal party and everyone else to be seated at their tables for the welcoming speech by the best man.

The bridal party sat facing the guest tables, the bridesmaids on Diana's right, the groomsmen on Bill's left. Throughout the meal, Liz couldn't see Travis, but she could hear his voice and, occasionally, his low chuckle.

The food was delicious, she knew it was, yet she hardly knew what she was putting in her mouth. She felt textures, creamy, smooth, nutty, rather than taste. She kept thinking that it would be all over soon and Travis would fly away…leaving her with a very erotic memory to tuck in beside the others she had of him.

"Is that how you keep your slender figure," asked Joanne, leaning toward Liz, her eyes sparkling. "Total lack of interest in this delicious food?"

"I guess all the excitement has taken my appetite away."

"I guess." Joanne raised a nicely arched eyebrow.

There was toasting, and tinkling on glasses to ask the bride and groom to kiss. There was wine and wedding cake and coffee and laughter. There was the relief of standing and leaving the table, there was music, there was dancing with Kevin and Dennis and even with Bill, who graciously took a turn with each of the bridesmaids. And there was Travis's dark eyes on her, it seemed always. And then there was Travis scooping her into his arms for a slow tune, not saying a word to her, just holding her close and guiding her around the crowded floor with an easy expertise that disguised how inexperienced she was on the dance floor. There was Travis's body against hers, the hardness familiar now, rekindling the ache she seemed never to have lost since he held her in his arms the night before.

He said, "How do you want to play this this time?"

How subtle the change in his position and the rhythm of his body. An onlooker wouldn't have noticed a thing. Liz felt as if every nerve ending in her body were on fire, so close was he to her, almost as if she and Travis were one....

She wanted to say, "I don't know what you mean." She wanted to retreat into a safe position. But she couldn't. She had declared her independence, and it was only now that she understood that she hadn't discouraged him, freed him to go his way, as she intended to do.

She put her head back. Those darkly black eyes captured hers. She luxuriated in the joy of eating him with her eyes, of being so close to the long sweep of his lashes that she could almost feel them fan her face.

"How do *you* want to play it?" She didn't mean her words to sound challenging, but the flare in his eyes told her that was the way he'd interpreted them.

"I think you know the answer to that question." She didn't think she could get any closer to him, but Travis proved her wrong. He slipped a hand up her back to her neck and gently pushed her head into his shoulder. Her breasts were as molded against his chest as her hips were against his. "Where are you staying tonight? Here? Or at the ranch?"

"I'm driving back home."

"I have a hotel room here with a big bed. I want you in it. Now."

She trembled, he could feel it. But she wasn't saying no.

Her reaction excited and humbled him. He shouldn't be doing this. He shouldn't be taking advantage of her. But she was a grown woman, she'd told him so. She'd told him she was perfectly willing to let him walk away.

He wanted her. And she wanted him, he knew she did. Nothing could disguise the tension in her body. It matched his perfectly. He said, "How much longer do we have to stay here?"

"I should wait to leave until after Diana throws the bouquet."

"Hoping to catch it?" His voice was bland.

"No. But there will be pictures taken, and our absence would be...noticeable."

"So we'll wait."

His warm hand enclosed her fingers. She felt the strength of him—and the promise. She tried to shake her head no, but she didn't have the courage or the heart. Those dark brown eyes captured hers and held on, held on.

The music stopped. Travis tightened his grip ever so slightly, yet there was a possessiveness to his hold that sent a riptide of sexual arousal swirling through her. She felt as if a spotlight were shining on her in the middle of the floor, but no one seemed to be looking at them.

Still, after the bouquet was thrown and Travis took her arm, she was glad no one turned to watch as they walked to the elevator together.

Travis was smooth with the key in the lock of his room door, smooth opening the door, smooth stepping inside without looking at her. He yanked off his tie, popped the studs out of his shirt.

Instead of turning to her, as she thought he would, he went to the window and pulled back the curtains. The room was air-conditioned and comfortably cool, and now there was a view of Sioux Falls twinkling below. He had a suite, actually, with the bed blessedly out of sight in another room.

Trying desperately to appear nonchalant, Liz walked around the couch to gaze out the window. A safe distance from Travis, she lingered at the edge of the huge plate-glass window, her arms wrapped around her chest. The air had gone so chill.

She felt so torn, pulled toward him, pulled away from him, wanting to look as sophisticated as he appeared, yet wanting to admit to him that her stomach was alive with butterflies.

"The bathroom's just off the bedroom, if you'd like to undress in there. My robe is hanging on the back of the door."

She didn't move.

"Is something wrong?" His bland drawl was not reassuring.

"This seems a little...cold-blooded."

"Were you expecting words of love first?"

"No." Her head came up. "Not from you. Never from you, Travis."

"Well. A direct hit. The lady does have her own weapons, after all."

"This isn't a battle."

"Isn't it?"

"Why are you so determined not to belong to anyone— or let anyone belong to you?"

He turned to her, his face so darkly smooth it seemed as if there had been no emotion in him for the whole of his life. "It's...easier."

"And safer?" she shot back at him. "Safer than taking chances? You were there when Andrew got up on Blaze and you didn't yank him down, therefore it follows that you are to blame for his death, is that right?"

She was close to the truth—she knew by the look in his eyes that she was.

"When Andrew died, you hurt so much that you decided you never wanted to be responsible for anyone again. That's why you're determined not to marry. Marriage means a wife and children to worry about and loving and caring for them and feeling your heart break if anything happens to them—"

"I have the responsibility for two hundred and thirty-nine people in my company," he said coldly.

"Employees are safe. A man doesn't love his employees."

"Funny. I thought you came up here to go to bed with me, not psychoanalyze me. Or is this a new kind of foreplay I don't know about?"

"You can't frighten me with sex talk, Travis."

"Strange. You're frightening me with this sudden plunge into the depths of my soul. Maybe we should look into your soul. Maybe we should examine the motives of a woman who promises a man sex, but instead comes up to his hotel room and talks him to death."

"This isn't about sex. This is about us and how we relate to each other. We can only relate to each other the way we've been taught to relate in our families."

"I don't give a damn about what my family thinks."

"Yes, you do. You care very much for your family. If you didn't, you wouldn't have come home for Diana's wedding. And I know you care for me, Travis. If you didn't, I wouldn't be here. But if we go ahead and do this—" her cheeks flushed "—without making a commitment to each other, we're going to disappoint both our families very much."

"There can be no commitment," he said in a chilling tone.

"I know that. I've always known it."

"Then we understand each other." He moved toward her, and she wanted, oh, so desperately, to be in his arms. But she couldn't let him touch her. She saw with sudden, painful clarity that she'd made a very bad mistake. Travis's relationship with his family was so fragile. Now she was drawing it out to a gossamer thread.

"Please don't. We just...can't."

His mouth twisted. "At this point, I'm almost out of the mood, but humor me. Spell out your reason. I'm always interested in the curious workings of your mind."

She ignored the bite in his voice. Her own was low and shaky. "If we do this—" she made a gesture with her hand "—things will change."

"No," he said, his eyes dark pools that were bottomless. "Nothing will change between us. I'll go back to Chicago and you'll stay here. Our lives will go on as before."

"That's the trouble," she said, her head high. "You think everything will stay the same. But it won't. I will have robbed you of something."

Whatever he'd expected her to say, that wasn't it. "What could you possible be taking from me?"

"I'll be robbing you of your freedom to come and go at the ranch. My mother won't be able to tease you about your love life. Your father will be...disappointed in you.

You'll certainly disappoint Diana. We both will. I'll be taking away the respect your family has for you. They won't blame me. They'll blame you. And you'll stay away from your family more and more, until finally you won't come back at all. I...couldn't bear that.''

"I told myself I wouldn't grab you and throw you down on the bed the minute we got in this room. Now I see I should have followed my instincts.''

"Maybe you didn't grab me because you were hoping I'd stop you.''

He said a crisp word that expressed his opinion of that idea. "So, tell me, just out of idle curiosity. Does that mean you're going to walk out of here untouched, just to save my reputation with my family?''

"You know the answer to that question.''

"Well, I haven't had many refusals, but out of the few I've had, yours is certainly the most original.''

His deliberate reference to his sexual experience with other women hurt, as it was meant to.

He looked so cold, so composed, so very—businesslike. She'd burned her bridges completely this time. How ironic that it had happened just when she'd finally learned the truth about his long-standing resistance to her.

"How do you plan on getting home?''

As cool and unmoved as he looked, he was still thinking of her safety. What an effort it took not to go to him and take him in her arms. She wanted him desperately, never more so than now.

"I had planned to return to the ranch tonight. Len drove our car up here for me.''

"Do you have the keys?''

"Yes.''

Silence. Long, ear-ringing silence. Then he said, "There's no need for you to linger then, is there?''

She drew in a breath, a soft sound of pain. He stayed where he was, his hands clenched into fists. If she didn't move, if she didn't leave him now, he'd never let her go.

Her dress rustled as she crossed the room. The door clicked open, then shut. He was alone.

Travis told himself it was for the best. He told himself she was right, that if he'd taken her to bed, things might have changed, all right. The biggest adjustment would have been in his head. He might have been so eaten up with guilt that he would have proposed marriage. That would have been a very big mistake indeed.

He'd known he'd never marry, known it forever. Accepting the truth about himself, he'd stayed away from women like Liz. If any woman was meant to marry and live all her life with one man and make him happy every day of it, she was. His decision to stay single had nothing to do with his mother's death, or Andrew's; of course it didn't. He just wasn't the marrying kind.

He closed his eyes. He might not be the marrying kind, but he still ached with wanting her. He couldn't remember wanting a woman with such frequency and intensity.

Travis went to the cabinet bar in the room, opened it, took out a minuscule bottle of Scotch and poured it into a glass. He went to the window and, his mouth twisting in an ironic salute, he lifted his glass to the city. And to himself, the failed cowboy, the confirmed bachelor.

"You look like the morning after the night before." Diana leaned against the kitchen counter at the ranch, a coffee cup in one hand, the other around Bill's waist. "What happened, big brother?"

"Nothing," Travis said.

"Wasn't it you who used to tell me that drowning my sorrows in alcohol was a really bad idea?" She left Bill and went to Travis to put her arm around his shoulder as he hitched a chair up to the table.

"It might be a bad idea, but other alternatives weren't available."

"But I thought you and Liz went—" Diana murmured. It was the short warning shake of his new brother-in-law's head that made Diana stop in midsentence. Nice to know Travis's new brother-in-law was bringing some discretion to the family.

"Good morning." As if on cue, Liz appeared in the doorway, sleek in jeans, a blue long-sleeved shirt and stocking feet. She looked dressed for work…and nearly as worse for the night's wear as he felt. There were subtle circles under her eyes and there was a tenderness around her mouth that made him think she might have been crying. He cursed himself for his mishandling of her.

"How is everyone this morning?" Liz crossed to the coffee urn and drew a cup. She seemed to take a long time turning around, but when she did, she looked composed. And utterly beautiful.

His gut tightened.

"Miserable, from the looks of it," Diana said, her gaze on Liz's face.

"When are you leaving on your honeymoon?" Liz asked Diana.

"Our plane doesn't leave until four this afternoon. We just came back to the ranch to pick up a few things that I left behind in my absent-minded rush, and leave the gifts and my dress here with Dad. I wanted to talk to Travis this morning, too, but he'd already left the hotel by the time we got up, so he's another reason we're here. We were too lazy this morning. Getting married is hard work."

"No argument there," Bill murmured, watching his

wife as she returned to him and put out her hand for him to take. "But well worth the trouble."

Travis scraped back his chair. "What did you have on your mind? I have a plane to catch."

Diana glanced up at Bill, as if asking for reassurance. Turning, standing in front of Bill and nestling in his arms, she said, "I'm worried about Dad, Travis. He looks...tired. I talked to Rachel and she says she's worried, too. The man hasn't had a physical in five years, and he's been driving himself lately. When Jim retires, we were wondering if you could help Dad select a new foreman. Rachel and I—well, neither one of us are too keen on Harv Lester. And we think that's who Dad will pick if he's left to his own to make the decision."

Travis was silent for a moment. Then he said, "Do you know what I'd do if Dad came to Chicago and told me how to run my company? I'd tell him I didn't need his help. Which is precisely what he'll say to me if I interfere with the running of his ranch. I haven't been involved in the decision-making here for years. Dad and I both like it that way. And that's the way it's going to continue."

"Don't you care about Dad?" Diana said passionately.

The look Travis gave her might have brought a grown man to his knees, but not a sister who knew she was cherished. "Of course I care for Dad. It's precisely because I care for him that I'm going to keep my nose out of his business. You'd do well to do the same."

"It's just possible your brother is right, you know," Bill said gently, patting Diana on the shoulder.

She glanced up at him, tears in her eyes. "Oh, I shouldn't be doing this. I shouldn't be airing our dirty linen before I've even had a chance to get you alone on a Caribbean island. You might change your mind about wanting to spend the rest of your life with me."

"Never in a million years. Your family problems aren't dirty linen, sweetheart," said Bill. "These discussions are a reality of family life. One person believes one thing, one another. It's what makes families a vital living organism that grows and changes."

Diana's eye shone. She stepped into her husband's arms. "Have I told you lately how much I love you?"

"Well, not precisely lately." He looked at his watch. "Not in the last hour."

"If you'll excuse me," said Travis, "I need to go and pack. All the best to you, sister. And to you, Bill." Travis crossed the room to shake Bill's hand. "You're a good man to take her off our hands."

"I'll do the best I can to make her happy."

Travis clapped Bill on the shoulder. "You've got your work cut out for you."

In his room, throwing things in his suitcase, Travis told himself he'd done the right thing. Why was it he could make a thousand decisions on product value, the timing of release of product on the market, manufacturing schedules, maintenance, personnel and research moneys and feel confident in his ability to do so? But now, tossing his stuff together, he felt...incompetent.

"So you're going."

Her voice stopped him cold. Liz was framed in the doorway, looking like she'd braced herself to face a firing squad.

He lifted his head, raised an eyebrow, gave her an ironic smile. "Think you're safe if you stay there?"

"I'm safe anywhere with you," she said, quickly, impatiently. She wasn't going to let him sidetrack her. "Don't you believe Diana? Couldn't you stay for just a bit and—"

"No, I couldn't. I have to go. I have no choice."

"We all have choices, Travis."

He straightened away from his packing, gave her his full attention. "You should be delighted that your good friend Lester is in line for a promotion. Dad thinks Lester's getting ready to get married, and he's picked you as his future wife."

"If he is, Mary Louise Thompson might have something to say to him on the subject. She's been...keeping company with him for about a year."

Travis smiled. "I see."

"I wonder if you do." She seemed to brace herself a little more. "Harv won't make a good foreman. He's too...volatile."

Travis's lips lifted. "There's a good word. He seemed...competent enough when you and he came racing in the yard the other day."

He couldn't be jealous. Not Travis. She couldn't believe it. "That was just nonsense, joking around. It wasn't... man-and-woman stuff."

"The way he was looking at you wasn't a joke."

Travis was obstinate and obdurate and he was driving her crazy. She forgot herself and took a step into the room. "So you're going to pack your smart city bag and you're going to fly away, unscathed, unharmed, uninvolved."

Full height, brown eyes dark, he was an awesome sight. One who wouldn't want to face across the table of a boardroom. He said, "What do you want from me?"

"Some small sign that you care enough for somebody on this ranch to change your priorities," she cried. She took a breath, stepped off the precipice. "If not me, then at least your father."

"I've never found it necessary to restate the obvious. It's a waste of time."

She took a step forward. "All right, so you do care for

him. Then show it. Stay another twenty-four hours. You have your private jet that comes or goes as you command. Well, tell it to stay.''

There was a small, charged silence. Then his lips lifted. ''You mean treat it like a dog and say, 'Down, boy'?''

Oh, dear heaven, here was the charm. And the wonderful sense of humor. She had to hold her ground. ''I mean as in, for once in your life, stick your darn neck out and take a chance.''

Chapter Six

Mourning doves cooed and cottonwood tree leaves rustled outside the house. In the kitchen, her mother sang, "Don't It Make My Brown Eyes Blue." A breeze wafted in, making the sheer panel billow into Travis's room, almost touching one of his Armani-trousered legs.

The breeze bore the soft scent of his after-shave to Liz, mingled with the aroma of his crisp white shirt, the clean clothes he had tucked into his case. He'd combed his hair straight back from his forehead, city-smooth, and his jaw was shaved clean. He had a generous mouth that betrayed his thoughts to Liz more than his eyes. She had long experience reading that mouth. She couldn't read it now.

He straightened away from his suitcase and turned to her, his clothes rustling in that breath-held silence. He was beautiful, always had been, always would be. And never more so than now, when her heart told her she had failed.

He was leaving her. Heaven knew when he'd see her

again. The times in between were too long. It occurred to him that she had changed. She was a skilled, gifted woman he admired. He needed skilled, gifted people around him, all of them he could find.

"Would you like a job on my staff?"

"I... You're joking, of course."

"Not entirely. You have good negotiation skills. I can always use staff who read people accurately and know how to approach a confrontational meeting to generate a win-win situation."

"I wasn't thinking of 'win-win.' I was thinking of your father."

"But you know enough about me to know I would want a limitation on the time if I agreed to stay." He turned his attention back to his suitcase, closed it, then pulled it off the bed to face her.

"I guess we can see who the real negotiator is here," she said crisply. "You tell me what a good job I'm doing and then you do what you want to do anyway."

"That's roughly the way it works. Don't look at me that way. You had your effect, believe me. I almost considered it."

"For how long, two microseconds?"

"I think I underestimated you," he said. "You'd do very well in the business world. Tough in the clinches."

"You always have underestimated me."

Those dark eyes roved over her face. "Not always." A small, vibrating silence. He stepped toward the doorway. "You're in my way."

"You're needed here."

"I've never been needed here. Don't make me touch you, Liz."

She cocked her chin, straightened her shoulders. "Have

any of those fancy corporate people on your staff ever told you you're a big coward?''

"Not if they want to stay working for me, they don't."

That might have been a smile hovering on his lips, she wasn't sure. "I guess I wouldn't be such a good employee, after all."

"You'd be a disaster. Far too irreverent. You'd set a bad example for all those I have conveniently tucked under my thumb. Now if you'll excuse me—"

He went to walk around her, but she blocked his path.

That quick tightening of his mouth told her she was getting to him now. He was losing patience with her.

"Move out of the way, Liz."

She shook her head.

"You're pushing your luck."

That quickly, he shed his city sophistication. He was all bullheaded country male, and she remembered him this way well.

"We need you here."

"No, you don't. Move out of the way, please."

She didn't.

"Well," he said silkily. "Have you changed your mind about me since last night? Are you wishing I'd take you down on that bed and have my wicked way with you? What a pity I can't oblige you. I have neither the time or the inclination."

"Your smart sex talk isn't going to scare me, either. Travis, your father—"

"You want me to pick you up and move you bodily?"

"You wouldn't do that. You're too afraid to touch me."

Those green eyes sparkled with challenge. He'd never known her to fight for herself. But for somebody else, she was a tigress. He wondered what it would be like to have that fierce loyalty at his back, rather than in his face.

If he started thinking like that again, he'd take her twenty-four hours—and her along with it.

He dropped the suitcase on the floor, saw the flash of alarm in her eyes. He wouldn't hurt her, she had to know that. "Are you going to move?"

"No."

Impasse. She had courage, he'd give her that. He'd always been a sucker for courage. And red hair and green eyes that flashed with the fire of passionate concern.

He grabbed her around the waist, felt the slender delicacy of her body yield to his fingers. Her hands clutched his arms in startled reaction. She really hadn't expected him to grab her, he could feel that in her body, see it in her face.

Acutely aware of her, of the scent of her hair, and of the precious burden she was, he carried her out into the hallway and instantly released her, only to grab her shoulders when she wobbled on her feet.

"I—didn't expect you to do that."

"Something else you need to learn about negotiation. Always be prepared for a counterattack. Are you all right?"

That brought her chin up in the air again. "I'm fine."

"Good. Are you taking me to the airport?"

"No. Boyd asked Harv to drive you."

"He might be the lesser of two evils," he murmured. His hand came out to brush a strand of hair from her cheek. The strand was russet-red, tinged with gold from the sun. "You'd probably drive me off the road into a fence just to keep me here."

She shook her head, but she colored beautifully, as if he'd read her mind.

He loved that about her, that she was so responsive to him. There was no artifice in her, no carefully raised eyebrow, no fluttering lashes. She was an unspoiled jewel, a woman unskilled in the art of coquetry. A rare thing in his world. His hand drifted down her cheek, feather-light. "Don't be ashamed of standing up for what you believe. It's one of your most attractive traits—" his mouth lifted "—among many others." He dragged a finger over her lip. "Do us both a favor. Don't come anywhere near Chicago. If I got you out of your element and into mine, I might be tempted to take advantage of you, and to hell with what the family thought."

"I have no plans for a trip to Chicago. But if I did, my answer would still be no."

"I wonder." He dropped his hand from her cheek, felt the loss of the warmth of her skin from under his fingers. "Goodbye, Liz. Take care of yourself."

Was it the look in his eyes or the touch of his hand that made her step out of his reach? "Goodbye, Travis," she said, in a cool tone he hardly recognized. "Run back to Chicago. Stay...safe."

"Yes," he murmured, as if talking to himself. "Always be aware that your opponent can—and will—counter-attack."

He gave her an odd little salute, as if she were the victor, and left.

His step was crisp and rhythmic on the hardwood floor in the kitchen, his voice low, Rachel murmuring a reply. It was then that Liz realized the singing had stopped some time ago. Had her mother heard them talking? Had Travis meant what he said to her? Probably not. Probably he'd been trying to disconcert her with his talk of sex. Her cheeks felt as hot as Blaze's neck after a long run.

Blaze. She'd lain in wait for Travis all morning, and she'd forgotten about her old friend. She'd better go rescue him from his stall. A fast ride in a warm prairie morning would do them both good.

"Any messages?"

The air was cool in his office, precisely air-conditioned to seventy-eight degrees, the way he liked it. Hilda Moran was tall and cool, too, exactly the way he liked her. Travis's executive assistant cast a speaking look over him. He had a sneaking suspicion that she had been a kindergarten teacher in her other life. He was certain the woman could, within five nanoseconds of his arrival at the office, calculate to the moment the amount of work he had for her to do, the mood he was in, and whether he'd been out the night before. She was fifty years old, looked forty and had the constitution of a twenty-five-year-old.

"Do you want me to start with the good news or the bad news?"

"Jump in anywhere you like."

He had a walnut desk roughly the size of Montana, because it was his theory that a desk should be big enough to actually work on. It was always covered with papers and documents. Hilda had installed an in-and-out box early on, and he routinely ignored it. He set his briefcase down, tossed his jacket over the back of the chair.

All starch and vanilla, Hilda settled in beside him, like a racehorse that knew exactly why it was at the track, her long legs to one side. She was thin almost to the point of gauntness, and had the kind of features people called strong if they were kind. He liked her style. She was a no-nonsense woman, and he'd never seen her cry. She never made personal comments to him, although he suspected she admired him for his hands-on approach and his determination to park at the far end of the lot, giving the reserved places in front to the rest of his staff. She'd taken to parking her bright red Taurus next to his cream-colored Lexus. He believed she respected him, as he did her. And she'd never, in living memory, called him a coward.

"Steve called. Trouble on the manufacturing line. Needs to talk to you right away. Clyde Farris is in San Francisco, wants to know how long he should wait on that vendor out there for the computer chips you wanted. You need to set up an appointment with James Larkinson, he wants to go over the contracts with Computewell with you. Marilyn needs to set up a meeting with you for the preparation for the board of directors' meeting next month. You have a meeting with Robert at eleven o'clock, you need to go over the financial report he prepared before you talk to him. And you wanted me to remind you to reread and polish the speech you wrote to present at the Chicago Business Club tonight."

"That's it?"

"Those are the things that need your immediate attention."

"Tell Larkinson I've already gone over the contracts, and I'll messenger them with my notes to his office. Tell Clyde he's waited long enough, I'll call Claire Hendricks and see what's going on with her company. Get Steve on the phone, and have the financial report on my desk."

"It's there, along with your speech."

"Thank you, Hilda. I appreciate your keeping an eye on things while I was gone." More, he appreciated her not calling him at the ranch or on the plane. They had an understanding. No unnecessary calls to clutter his life while he was on the road.

Hilda nodded and stood up to dial.

Travis flipped over the pages of the financial report, thinking it felt very good to be out of that darned monkey-suit tuxedo and back at the helm....

A certain red-headed lady had told him he was safe here. Was that what he felt? Safe?

Elizabeth Annabell. Sweet, yet tantalizing as hell. Well, there, he'd made a little rhyme about her.

It had been a kind act of providence that made her balk when she went up to the hotel room with him. She'd said it was for his sake. He hadn't believed that. She'd gotten cold feet, pure and simple. After she left his room, he'd drunk his Scotch and tried to be angry with her, but he'd been angrier with himself. He seldom indulged in self-castigation, but he had that night.

Now he was grateful for the turn of events. If he had taken Liz to bed, it would have been difficult to come back and concentrate on his work. If he'd taken that luscious lady in his arms and tasted her delights, he might, heaven help him, be sitting here reliving his time with her like some moonstruck teenager, wishing she were there in the city with him, wondering what she was doing, wondering if she was out on that huge devil horse—worrying about her. Thank God he wasn't doing that.

A glance at his watch showed him it was one o'clock. She would already have had her ride, and be safe in the house now, helping Rachel. At least there was one sensible woman in that household. There had to be some way to get Liz off that stallion. He would give his father a call this evening, see if he could convince Boyd to take some action. Yes, he'd do that. And check on his father, as well.

On the next day, the prairie sun shining down on Liz's head and the warmth of her body from the exercise she'd gotten on Blaze's back made the cool, shadowy stillness in the stable more than welcome. Dragging her saddle off Blaze and lifting the curry brush off its nail to rub him down felt good. This was her life, the place she belonged, here where the earthy smells of animal and ranch bathed her nose with the reality of life. The sweep of her hand over Blaze's rippling side, rhythmically stroking away the sweat and dirt, was calming, familiar, ritualistic, a time she and Blaze both enjoyed.

This was where she felt safe.

She tried to imagine what it was like in the city, what Travis was doing at this moment. High-powered stuff, she supposed, meetings and papers and stress, all thought of the ranch long gone from his head. It hurt to think that she must be relegated to some corner of his mind that he wouldn't take out and look at until this Christmas, when it was time to come home again.

Blaze lipped up a bit of hay, turned his head back to Liz and dragged his mouth down her arm, slobbering on her with precision, protesting her daydreaming. He had a fey and mischievous sense of humor, and she knew he didn't like to be ignored. Liz threw an arm around his warm neck and laid her cheek against his muzzle. He was heat and life and strength, and he was the one who needed her attention just now, not Travis.

"You're a scamp, you know that? You're trying to cheer me up, aren't you? You know I'm missing that big idiot, even though I shouldn't be. Honestly, what are you males good for, anyway? You just cause trouble and heartache and then you fly off to the city and forget you've ever been here, forget the poor hapless female who loves you."

To her ears, she sounded brave, philosophical, and ever so slightly amused. She didn't fool Blaze. He gave her a consoling sloppy lip nuzzle right in her face, indiscriminately warm and wet, smelling of chewed hay.

"You big lug. Wouldn't it be nice if a certain other male showed his affection as easily as you do?"

Showed his affection. Did she believe that? Did she believe Travis really cared for her but didn't want her to notice? And worse, didn't want himself to notice, either?

"So what do you think? Should I find a daisy, to pull off the petals, as in, 'He loves me, he loves me not'?"

Blaze blew and shook his head.

"I didn't think so."

She smiled and petted him, then closed her eyes and leaned against his warm, big body, savoring his undemanding loyalty and love. "Don't worry. I won't leave *you*," she whispered. "You're my friend forever."

She got another face kiss, which she took unreservedly.

Suddenly, Blaze's skin rippled with tension. His head came up, and he trumpeted a high, warning cry.

Liz stepped back, aware that Blaze had metamorphosed from affectionate pet to powerful, aggressively alert animal. His hackles were up, and his ears were laid back against his head. He was aroused and ready to fight.

Then she heard Harv say, in a cool, low voice, "Get out of that stall, Liz."

She went cold with chilly anger, but she couldn't add to Blaze's agitation by letting him know she was upset. "I'm not in danger." She kept her voice low and controlled to calm Blaze.

"Good. Then get out. Now." Gone was the easy manner he'd had at the windmill. Under his hat, Harv's beautiful blue eyes were wintery.

All those vague feelings she'd had about Harv came clamoring to the fore. "You've no right to tell me what to do—"

"McCallister just made me foreman. And that gives me the right to do a lot of things I've been itching to do. One of them is put this white devil in restraints."

Now thoroughly alarmed, Liz slipped out of the stall

and closed the door. Blaze trumpeted again and reared. He didn't like Harv. And the horse didn't like having Harv near Liz when he was penned behind the stall door.

Liz grasped Harv by the arm and pulled him away from Blaze's stall, toward the outside door. "I'm going to speak to Boyd about this—"

Harv shook his head, a smile on his lips that had too much triumph in it for Liz's taste. "We've already talked." He looked past Liz, toward the stable door. "I guess you'll have to tell her yourself, Mr. McCallister."

Boyd stood in the doorway, casting a serious look over Liz that made her heart drop to her toes. "I assume you're talking about Blaze?" he said. "I had a conversation with Travis last night, Liz. I have agreed that we can't let you go riding that horse if there's even the slightest possibility that we're endangering your life."

"My life is not endangered ever. Not with Blaze. Surely you can't believe that he'd ever hurt me."

A look of pain crossed Boyd's face. "I never thought he'd hurt Andrew, either." He had one hand on the door frame, steadying himself, and he looked extraordinarily strained.

"Boyd, I've ridden Blaze for years and nothing has ever happened. You've always said...been glad that I..."

"Travis pointed out some things that made me reconsider my position."

"What right does Travis have to make decisions about what happens here?"

Boyd shook his head heavily. Liz knew she shouldn't argue with him. She never had before in her life. But for Blaze...

"I don't think your son is in a position to know what's best for Blaze *or* me. There is no danger to my life. Blaze needs me. And I need him—"

"Nobody needs a horse." Harv was assured, cool. "And that horse needs nobody."

"Then let me put him out in the pasture. Don't make him stay here tied up—"

"This is where he'll stay," said Harv.

She turned to the man who'd been like an indulgent father to her all her life. He couldn't let this happen. She had to make him see...

"Boyd, you know it won't work to keep Blaze in here all the time. He'll go crazy. You know he will."

"Harv doesn't want him out with the other horses."

"Harv doesn't know this horse. I do. If you won't let him out in the pasture, then...let him go out on the range. Let him have his freedom."

"That horse stays where he is." Harv said the words almost lazily, watching her.

"You're going to kill him. And you're doing it on purpose, to punish me."

"Why would I do a thing like that?" He pushed his hat back with a finger, his smile conciliatory.

"Because you're an idiot, that's why. A twenty-four-karat idiot who doesn't know a darn thing about the right way to treat a horse." Anguished, she swung back to Boyd. "You can't do this. You can't put this man in charge of this ranch."

"I'm already in charge of this ranch. You've got nothing to say about it."

"Liz—" Boyd put a hand out. All her concentration and fury had been focused on Harv, but now her eyes flashed to Boyd's face. There was a pallor on his cheeks, and his eyes looked glazed.

Instantly alarmed, she put her hand on his arm. "What's wrong?"

He shook his head. But there was perspiration on his

brow and his mouth was open, moving soundlessly. He crumpled back against a stall wall. Her heart plunging to the bottom of her chest, Liz scrambled to clutch his hand and keep him upright. His fingers were icy. The reality of his cold flesh chilled her body and numbed her mind. One thought was coherent: *Get him out, get help.* "We have to take him up to the house!" she cried. "Help me, Harv!"

Harv moved to Boyd's side. Boyd made a noise, but it wasn't an intelligible word. Every nerve clenched with fear, Liz took one side of Boyd, with Harv on the other, and they started the slow procession toward the house.

The ambulance arrived, the paramedics cool and competent and reassuring. Liz wanted to be reassured, desperately needed it. But pain, panic and guilt poured through her in such a potent mixture, she felt paralyzed. Boyd's cheeks were strangely pale, and for the first time in his life, he appeared frail and vulnerable, strapped on the stretcher. Still, he managed a smile and a quick squeeze of his left hand for Rachel.

Her mother fought the tears gallantly until Boyd was in the ambulance. But when Liz started Boyd's BMW with cold and shaking hands, and her mother slid onto the seat beside her, Rachel's eyes spilled over.

"Oh, Mother, I'm so sorry." She couldn't say it was all her fault, she couldn't admit that out loud to the woman who loved him so much.

Boyd's presence permeated the car, the tang of his daily cigar, a belt buckle tossed on top of the dash, a comb tucked in between the seats. Boyd was slightly vain about his head of thick white hair. Rachel picked up the comb and tucked it in her purse. "I forgot to pack a bag for him," she said on a half sob.

"We'll get it later." Liz reached for her mother's hand,

and Rachel grabbed Liz's fingers as if they were her lifeline.

The wait at the hospital was endless. Liz paced the length of the waiting room, while Rachel sat in a chair, her face pale and composed, her hands clasped in front of her. "I knew something was going to happen," she said for the fourth time. "I just didn't know what it was going to be. He's been pushing himself so—"

Liz knew it wasn't anything Boyd had done that had brought on illness. This was all her fault. If only she hadn't argued with Boyd. If only she'd said yes, and walked out of the stable to plan another strategy. Why, why, had she been so stupid? It was her fault that Boyd was lying in intensive care and her mother was sitting there so quietly, and she lacked the courage to tell her mother so. Oh, would she never learn to keep her impetuous mouth shut? She'd argued with Travis, but he'd simply set her aside and gone his way. Boyd was so much more vulnerable. Was there anything in the world that hurt like this horrible feeling that something you did had caused another person physical pain? Would the doctors ever come out?

The room where they waited glowed with sunshine from a skylight. Ficus trees spread green leaves over philodendrons and ivy planted in terra-cotta pots. There was a cheerful plaque on the wall, something about God hearing a prayer in a garden with keen ears, but Liz was in no mood to be comforted. She ached with pain, with regret, with guilt, with love, and the need to know that Boyd would be all right.

She sank down in the chair beside her mother. "We have to call Travis."

Rachel shook her head. "That was the one thing Boyd was adamant about. He did not want either of the children called. Not until we know that it definitely is a stroke, and what the extent of the damage is. Thank God he was still able to sign the papers when he came in. I...couldn't have done it, because I'm not his wife." Rachel teared up then. "I've been so foolish. He's asked me so many times. I kept telling him we were better off the way we were. Now I wish desperately that I had said yes. If they won't let me in to see him..."

"They'll let you in," Liz said fiercely, holding her mother's hand in a tight grasp. "Boyd will see to that."

And he did. When the doctor came out, he addressed Rachel as Mrs. McCallister and told her that her husband had stabilized, had speech and movement and was asking to see her. Rachel gave a sob of relief and went.

Liz sat down in the wicker chair, closed her eyes and said a heartfelt, exceedingly thankful prayer.

"Excuse me. I'm Hal Peterson, from the *Sioux Falls Gazette*. I understand that Senator McCallister was just brought in to the hospital. Can you tell me anything about him?"

She opened her eyes. "No. I don't know a thing." And got up to find a phone. She couldn't let Travis hear of his father's illness from a television set.

Travis wasn't in his office. No, his secretary was sorry, he couldn't be reached.

"His father has been taken ill."

She was sorry again, and she would certainly get the message to him as quickly as possible.

Her mother came out of the intensive care unit looking slightly less distressed—until the reporter who had talked to Liz caught up with her. Liz took her mother's hand, shook her head and, with an aggressive stride and a tight mouth, guided her mother out of the hospital and installed her in the car. The reporter stayed with them until Liz started the car engine and said, with a polite smile that was girded with steel, "If you don't move, Mr. Peterson, you'll be visiting the emergency ward yourself."

He moved.

Only after Liz had dosed Rachel with aspirin and cocoa did her mother fall asleep on the couch next to the phone. All through the night, Liz paced through the big house, waiting for Travis to call.

The hours ticked by, punctuated by a stillness she felt through to her bones. A cow bawled, a horse whickered. Mosquitoes hummed and, at first light of dawn, sparrows twittered in the trees. Birdsong didn't soothe the anger and anxiety flaring higher as each moment ticked by. Why didn't Travis call?

When the sun came over the horizon, its orange glory making Liz feel empty and tired, and a call to the hospital assured her that Boyd had spent a reasonably comfortable night, she made her decision. Not for a moment did she believe that Travis had ignored a message about his father. He hadn't been told about her call. It was up to her to make sure he *was* told.

Outside, the prairie air was already beginning to heat up as she strode through the dusty yard. She found Len in the corral, saddling his Appaloosa, told him Boyd had had a good night. "My mother will want to go to the hospital this morning. Here's the keys to Boyd's car. I want you to take her."

Len's eyes told her he knew what she was saying, that she didn't want Harv transporting her mother. "I'll take care of it, Liz. Don't you worry."

Back in the little house, she scrawled a note to her mother, tucked it under the red heart paperweight that sat on the little table by the door where they left messages to each other, picked up her purse and slid behind the wheel of their little Plymouth. She could be in Chicago in two

and a half hours, if there was a seat available on the first
flight out of Sioux Falls.

Liz had never been on a plane before, but her anger,
pain, and guilt worked to distract her from the strange
noises, the bumps, the grinds and, once they were aloft,
the sudden dips that left her fellow passengers totally unaffected, while she clutched the arm of her chair with a
sickening feeling that her death was as close as the next
cloud.

O'Hare was another trial by terror. Noisy confusion sur-
rounded her, amplified through her country-sensitive ears.
How did people stand all this noise? Voices asking people
to call, piped-in music that no one listened to. How did
they ignore the hordes of other people bustling about
them? And, most mysterious of all, how, when they didn't
look at each other, not once, did they keep from bumping
into each other?

When she finally found her way through the maze to an
outside door, a man with sympathetic eyes signaled a taxi
for her. The taxi driver cast a bored look over her high-
heeled boots and jeans as he waited for her to unfold the
piece of paper with the address of Travis's office building
on it.

At last her trembling fingers obeyed her will, and she
made some sense of the letters and numbers. She read off
the address and mispronounced the street name. He cor-
rected her. Undaunted, she looked him in the eye and said,
"Yes, that's right. Please hurry."

He gave her a look as if to say he knew she'd just
arrived from Venus and he was trying to be tolerant of her
but she really was stretching his goodwill to the limit.

At Travis's office building, Liz was stopped at a curving
front desk by a woman who asked if she had an appoint-

ment. She said no. She was asked for her name, she gave it. "Please, I must see Mr. McCallister. His father is ill and—"

The woman held up a hand, her eyes narrowed in suspicion. "I heard a similar story just last week about his sister and it was told by a man who thought he could worm his way into Mr. McCallister's office. You people will stop at nothing to get an interview. Just let me give your name to his secretary and we'll know soon enough whether I should allow you to go up."

While the receptionist said her name into a phone, then sat back to wait for a reply, Liz swung about and headed toward the bank of elevators, her cowboy boots clicking on the marble floor. What could they do to her, throw her in jail? At least that way she'd get to see Travis when he came to bail her out.

"Miss? Miss! Security!" In the throes of panic, for she had strict orders not to let any more women reporters masquerading as people with news about a member of Travis's family make their way into the building, the receptionist grabbed up the phone, only to hear the voice of Travis McCallister. "Yes, sir, Miss Grant is here in the building. She's on her way up. She didn't wait."

Her eyes widened. "I should call off security? Yes, sir, right away, sir." The beleaguered woman threw down the phone and frantically ran toward the bank of elevators to wave away the security guard.

Instinct took Liz to the top floor, and in through the double doors of glass. A beautiful blond woman in an aqua business suit said, "You're Elizabeth Grant? Down that hall and through the door at the end."

Before she got to the door, it swung open. Travis stood there watching her. She examined his face anxiously, wondering if she was too late and he'd already heard about his father. When a smile played over his lips, she was sure he hadn't.

Suddenly she realized how she was staring at him, and the interpretation he was putting on her avid gaze. He thought she was here because she'd changed her mind about going to bed with him. She felt like a complete idiot. To save this self-assured, classically beautiful, rich and powerful man a few moments of pain, she'd worried all night, traveled all morning and made a fool of herself many times over.

"I want you to know right now I'm not here to go to bed with you."

Too late, she could see that the door he held open led into a room filled with men and women in smart business suits seated around a polished oval table.

One of the men in the room, dressed in an impeccable suit and wearing half glasses, peered over them at her. "Young woman, what do you mean by coming up here and causing such a tasteless disruption?"

He wore a maroon silk handkerchief in his breast pocket. All Liz could think of was how worthless that bit of silk would be in case he ever had to actually do a day's work in the hot sun or, heaven forbid, caught cold.

In that endless eternity of waiting for Travis's reaction, she truly knew what it was to wish the floor would open and swallow her.

"Well, now that you've dashed my hopes completely, you might as well come in and be introduced," murmured Travis, while behind him there was smothered laughter.

"No, Travis. Please." Before, she'd only thought she was a complete idiot. Now she really *was*. She shook her head. "I have something to say to you, and I need to say it in private."

"Such discretion. A bit belated, perhaps, but still admirable." He closed the door behind him and taking her elbow, guided her through another door to her left. There was a round table in the Queen Anne style, shiny-smooth with polish, a wonderful artificial arrangement of aqua flowers with black sprays that looked snatched off a lady vaudevillian's head, and four telephones with kindergarten-large numbers at a tiny table in each corner of the room.

He indicated a chair for her to sit down in. She shook her head. She was so aware of him, and of herself and the difference between them, he confident in his own environment, wearing his glossy clothes and his polished shoes, she feeling tossed and tousled by a restless night, an anxious plane trip and the winds of the city. It struck her suddenly that she had acted foolishly and impulsively coming to see him, that she could have called him on the phone today and she would have gotten through to him eventually. She'd come because she didn't want Travis to hear about his father on the news—and because she was bearing such a heavy burden of guilt and, out of all the world, Travis was the one person who would understand.

"Who was that man?" She said hesitantly. "Is he anybody important to you?"

"No," drawled Travis. "He's only the chairman of the board. His name is Osgood Feathers. He comes from old money, went to Groton and Harvard. As if that weren't enough, he has an English cousin who's related to the royal family by marriage." He thought if he talked a bit, it would help calm her.

"Doesn't everyone?" she murmured.

He raised an eyebrow. "Don't worry about Osgood. He'll recover from your precipitate entrance. Good breeding will out, you know. Now, tell me what it is that brought you here. We do have telephones in Chicago," he said, hitching up his pant leg to sit on the table, one elegant shoe dangling.

"I tried to reach you on the phone, and I couldn't get through. I didn't have time—I had to see you before you heard it on television."

She was trembling. She'd wanted so badly to be strong, to be sophisticated, but she was trembling. She cast eloquent eyes over his face, her mind trying frantically to find a way to soften the blow for him.

He lost his lazy smile and his eyes darkened as he came to her. He reached out to her, cupping her elbows in his hands as if he knew she needed help to stay on her feet.

"What's happened?"

"Your father... We were arguing.... It was all my fault.... Harv..." She shook her head.

"Take a good breath, sweetheart, and tell me."

She searched his face and knew that any delay would only make matters worse for him. "Your father's had a stroke. Not a bad one," she added hastily. "It's really quite mild. The doctor thinks he'll regain the use of his hand and leg. His speech is... It's hard for him to marshal his thoughts, but when he docs, he can speak, if he says things slowly and doesn't get frustrated. He told us not to call you. I did, anyway, but I couldn't get through. When we didn't hear from you, I decided to come before you heard the news from the media. Oh, Travis, I'm so sorry. I wish...I wish so desperately it hadn't happened."

His eyes darkened with pain, and then a sweetness curled his mouth and he reached for her and pulled her tightly against him. "I'm sorry you couldn't reach me. It won't happen again. Ever."

She rested against him, knowing it was wrong to absorb his compassion, knowing he probably wouldn't forgive her when she told him the truth, but she was helpless to resist his comforting embrace.

He put a finger under her chin. "From the look of you, you've had a bad twenty-four hours—" that smile "—almost as bad as Dad's I'd guess. Time I shared the burden."

She wanted that so badly, wanted him to share the burden with her. But he couldn't. She'd have to carry this one alone. It hurt so much to think that not only had she harmed Boyd, she'd made Travis suffer, as well.

Guilt welled up, making her push against him to ask for release. He dropped his arms, but that sweet smile was still there on his mouth for her. "All right now?"

"Yes."

In the next few moments, while she struggled with her conscience, knowing that it would be only a matter of time before she had to tell him the truth, a flurry of activity ensued around him, such fuss and feathers as she'd ever seen. A woman running to get his briefcase, another tall lady with a face as keen as that of an intelligent horse listening to him rap out instructions that sounded like they were being spoken in Swahili. Then it was back to the elevators—this whole city would stop dead if there were no elevators—and down to the lobby and out through a door that led out into a parking area. Travis assisted her into a low-slung car the color of champagne, tossed his briefcase in the back and, with a speed that had Liz closing her eyes and holding her breath, he roared out into a street where a million other cars were all trying to do exactly the same thing he was.

Chapter Seven

Travis lived in another cloud-scraping edifice, huge and overpowering in white stone and glass, with clay pots stacked by the front door that would have held coffee for the bunkhouse boys for a year. The pots contained flag-red geraniums thriving profusely, the blossoms' color intensified by the bright Midwest sun. In the distance, Lake Michigan sparkled like a sapphire.

The plush elevator took Liz's stomach for an ascending ride that continued after she stepped out at the fourteenth floor. Travis, darn him, seemed not to be bothered by having his abdominal cavity fly up his throat. His careless dexterity as he unlocked his condo underscored his easy acceptance of an environment that felt as hostile to Liz as if she'd been plunked down in a swarm of angry bees. At least that was what she told herself. She'd concentrate on bees, or any other bizarre country image that would keep her from feeling the electrifying intimacy of following Travis to the place he slept.

So this was the kind of opulence Travis lived in, the cool, in-your-face kind of luxury, with a pale cream rug sweeping away to every corner of a sunken living room, a wall painting of a desert bloom that covered one wall with exploding eroticism, a leather couch the color of French vanilla ice cream, broken into six pieces and reassembled in an arching curve in front of a fireplace that surely must have been described in the brochures as a "symphony of glass and brass."

He was watching her look around, those dark eyes catching every nuance that crossed her face.

A mirror the size of the south pasture reflected back her image. It wasn't encouraging. After two encounters with Chicago's wind and humidity, her hair was getting curlier by the microsecond, and her blouse had been rumpled. She was as out of place in this elegant room as a common Holstein in a barn full of DNA-identified champions.

"Well, tie me up and throw me in the hog pen. This sure shoots your cowboy image right in the foot."

Her attempt to be flippant didn't fool him. He flashed her that charming, indulgent smile that he reserved for children, elderly ladies and demented young women who were nervous about coming into his condo. "I never had a cowboy image. Too much for you, is it? Actually, I didn't have anything to do with the decor, except for the couch. The place belonged to the company when I took over. It seemed easiest to move in without doing anything."

Sweeping an expansive hand toward the fireplace, she asked brightly, "Where's the bear rug?"

"On the bear."

She didn't like the way he was holding his mouth, as if he were barely able to contain that smile.

It struck her then that this place was not much different from his room on the ranch. It had nothing to do with him—or he with it. "You may not have picked out the decor, but you like this impersonal henhouse. It keeps you from entertaining thoughts of hatching out chicks."

That brought his eyes flashing to her in a swift, slicing look. "If you want to stow that line of country corn you borrowed from Rachel for a minute," he drawled, "you can come in the bedroom with me while I change. It will take Phil an hour to fuel up and file a flight plan, and more before we get clearance, so we have time to get comfortable."

He was going to get comfortable? She had a feeling that would make her very uncomfortable. "I'll wait out here."

"Spare me the maidenly-modesty routine. We used to go swimming together stripped down to our underwear. Or less."

"I was ten at the time. I didn't even have breasts."

"But I was sixteen and I had an excellent imagination."

"I'm glad I didn't know that at the time."

She tried to tug her arm away, he held her tighter. "Liz, don't be an idiot. I want to talk to you, and I don't like to shout." He towed her along with him behind the sixty-nine yards of couch. Rapidly losing ground and thoroughly rattled, she said, "Do you realize how many cows had to die to give you a place to sit?"

"I should, I paid for the idiotic thing."

He pushed, and she went. She didn't know what else to do.

His bed was the size of the north pasture, but it smelled a lot better and was draped in a black silk spread.

"Do you know how many silkworms had to die to make that cover?"

He grasped her shoulders and pushed her down gently on that selfsame bed. "Silkworms don't die. They retire and move to Florida." Watching her, he pulled his tie down slowly, making her aware of just how silly she was being. He leaned forward and kissed her on the forehead...and when she was braced to push him away, he turned his back to her and sauntered through a doorway.

There were enough pillows on the bed for every cowboy in the bunkhouse. She picked one up and tossed it at the half-open door. It missed and slid down the wall.

"Did you ever consider taking pity on your poor delivery people and getting a normal-size piece of furniture in here?"

"The rooms are big—they require big furniture. So I was told." She was relieved he was safely installed in a dressing room, or whatever the heck it was. Yes, of course she was. Not disappointed. Never.

"Could you possibly get your mind off my furniture for a moment and tell me more about Dad? You've told me the truth, his stroke was quite mild and he has a good chance of recovering full use of his legs and arms?" His voice was muffled, the scrape of a hanger on a clothes bar punctuating his question. The sound raked her already sensitive nerves.

Liz leaned back, the seductive silk smooth under her palms. Without warning, the thought popped into her head that she probably wasn't the first woman to have lounged on the bed while Travis changed. Nor would she be the last. Her hackles rose instantly, like Blaze's. Sympathy flew out the window. "No, I sat up all night and then spent all morning on a plane just so I could come out here and tell you a bunch of comforting nonsense."

Travis appeared from around the door, looking much more casual in khaki pants and a cotton long-sleeved shirt with a fine brown stripe. He smiled at her, which made Liz forget about the women who had sat on his bed. Almost.

"Will you stop clutching at that spread as if you're expecting a frontal attack? You know you're safe with me."

"Of course I am. I've always been completely safe with you. I know that." The fierce green gaze flashed over him. "I wish I could be just as sure that you're completely safe with me."

"So the country corn finally bites the dust and the lady speaks the truth." That sweet, sweet smile on his lips, he reached down for her hand, pulled her up into his arms. She felt wonderful in his arms, supple and yielding. Too wonderful. Her hands were icy in his warm ones. He could only guess at the courageous strength it had taken for her to board a plane and come to him—and then admit the truth about her feelings. "I'd say, right offhand, you're doing just fine."

"I'm not. I'm stupid and silly and scared and—"

"Sweetheart, it's all right to be scared. Everybody is scared at a time like this, and you've had more than your share of trauma."

"You don't look frightened."

"Actually, I'm terrified." He leaned forward to taste her mouth, just a little, just enough to distract her, nothing more.

It did. It made her think of the big bed behind them and how easy it would be to lie down on it with Travis and let him teach her whatever he wanted her to learn.

"Now tell me why my dad's attack is your fault."

She should have known Travis would not forget her first impulsive words. Travis never forgot anything.

She shook her head, knowing she'd rather dive straight into Lake Michigan than tell him the truth.

He smoothed her hair, gentling her like a nervous horse. His facial expression might hold tender interest, and his voice might be soft and easy, but his body wasn't. Far too lethal a combination, Travis's tenderness laced with sexual potency. She tried to push out of his arms, but he wouldn't let her go.

"No dodging, no equivocating, no escaping. Not till you tell me the truth."

She wasn't afraid to tell Travis anything. Yet it hurt terribly to think about it again. She lifted her eyes bright with unshed tears. "Harv and I were in the stable arguing. And then Boyd was there, and—"

"What were you and Harv arguing about?"

She shook her head, tried to effect her release from his arms, failed.

He had one hand on her shoulder and one on her hip, and his hold was gentle enough, but the subtle change in his body told her that he would keep her locked against him in a lover's intimate hold until she answered his question. He was a man in control of his emotions, his face smooth, but those dark eyes burned with a flash of anger and that sweet mouth had gone hard. "Was he sexually harassing you?"

"No." She looked directly into that controlled face. She was too close to those dangerous eyes. There was disbelief in them, disbelief that verged on fury. Just the tiniest spark of hope flickered in her breast—and died. To think he might be jealous was ludicrous. He felt protective of her, that was all. "No, honestly, Travis, it had nothing to do with...that. We were having a difference of opinion about—" Her words slammed to a halt. She remembered then that Boyd had said he'd had a phone conversation with Travis. Liz straightened in Travis's arms, trying to distance herself from him, an impossible task. "I'm sure you know what we were arguing about."

Comprehension cleared his face. She could feel the tension ease in his body. "They were telling you you couldn't ride the stallion."

"I wouldn't do anything to harm your father, ever. If I had known—"

He cupped her head in his hand, pulled her into his body and held her there, comforting her. She knew it was only his strong sense of feeling protective of her, but she couldn't help the rise of need and want and desire in her. Oh, she was so tired of feeling sheltered and protected and starved for him at the same time. It was wrong to feel this way, they had a plane ride ahead and a visit to the hospital, but she couldn't help it. Travis made her hungry, and he always would.

Holding Liz made Travis aware of the empty vistas in his life. He needed her. She felt so warm, so vital, so alive, and he wanted to hold her always and take her pain away and give himself to her and have her give herself to him. He wanted her happy, laughing, throwing saucy comebacks in his face again.

He wanted her, just as he always had, as he always would.

"You aren't responsible for my father's illness, you know."

She shook her head against him.

"It wasn't your fault. It was a crazy coincidence."

"If I could just take what I said to him back, do that day over—"

"Yes," Travis murmured in her ear.

She stilled in his arms, the meaning of that one word reverberating through her. She pulled back to gaze into his face, those beautiful green eyes shining with tears. "This is the way you felt after Andrew died."

He released her, his arms sliding away from her, stealing the warmth from her skin. That quickly, the barriers went up. "We're not talking about me. We're talking about you. The situation is entirely different."

She wanted to cry, "*No, it isn't!*" but that closed face warned her to hold her tongue. "So this is what you've been feeling all these years."

He gave her a look she disliked intensely, a look that closed her out, a look that said, "You know nothing about my life and that's the way it will stay."

She closed her eyes against the hurt, against the tears. Oh, that wall he'd built around himself. She wanted to rip at it, beat at it with her fists.

Within that circle of numbness, she watched him grab up a suitcase, reach for her elbow, felt him escort her out of the room.

"At least there is one thing you've spared me," he said, in that odd tone he used when he teetered between amused tolerance and seriousness. "You haven't said I told you so."

"I don't know what you mean."

"If I had stayed that twenty-four hours you asked for, I'd have been there when you needed me. I'm sorry I wasn't." After articulating that little tidbit that tossed her back into the sea of love and confusion, he escorted her out of the room.

If she hadn't been impressed by his living quarters, she'd be darned if she'd be impressed by his jet, with its jade velvet easy chairs and its brass-framed cabinets. No way. She sat in the comfortable easy chair and leaned back as if she'd done it a hundred times before. "This is nice." So cool.

"Liz." He looked as if he were trying to keep a straight face.

"What?"

"This is just like riding on a commercial airline. You have to strap in for takeoff." He undid his belt, stood over her, and was sliding his hands down alongside her hips on each side of the teal velvet before she could move.

"I can do it." She tried to move where his hands weren't, but it was impossible. His fingers slid along her hips, making her forget everything except the way he felt, touching her, and the way he smelled, clean, spicy, the way he looked, darkly intent, achingly beautiful. Wanting and love rose up, filled her heart.

His dark eyes met hers, roved over her face. Without changing expression, hardly moving, he lifted her palm and kissed the hollow. "You're a lovely woman. Inside and out. You make me want to bury myself in you. Especially when you look at me like that." He brushed a thumb over her bottom lip. "I think we have a problem, sweet Liz. What do you think?" He returned his attention to her abdomen, where the belt lay. He smoothed his fingers over her belly, taking his time bringing the clip together, watching her face all the while.

"I think I want a different flight attendant. One without such a forward manner."

A dark brow lifted. "Do you really?"

"No."

He laughed and snapped the buckle with a click. "Why is it you always say what I least expect? Maybe that's why I'm never bored around you." He dropped a kiss on her forehead and left her sitting there, reeling, aching, loving him desperately.

It was twilight when they walked into the hospital. Boyd had been moved. He was out of intensive care, installed in a private room—an excellent sign, Rachel told Liz. It also enabled Rachel to spend most of her time at Boyd's bedside, even though he'd slept most of the day. But when Travis hustled into his father's room, Boyd opened an eye and said, "What...are you...doing...here? Didn't want you to..." He closed his eyes, obviously frustrated by trying to think of a word.

They'd been adversaries for as long as Travis could remember, but hurt sliced deep at seeing Boyd like this, his gift of speech impaired, his hands blue-veined and fragile on the white hospital sheet. A fallen warrior, painfully conscious of how incapacitated his wounds had left him.

"I came to make sure you weren't flirting with the nurses." Travis's wonderful mouth lifted, and his hand closed over his father's. As she watched them, Liz's heart swelled with love and pride for them both.

Boyd blinked his eyes and tried to shake his head, stretched out his other hand for Rachel. "No chance... She's been...eagle eye on me."

"You bet I have." Rachel's smile was brave, but her eyes were wet.

"You go...back. Work to do...there."

He tried to be fierce, that fallen warrior. Travis squeezed the chilly hand that lay unmoving under his. If he had stayed—

Travis couldn't think like that, not now. He had to reassure his father. "I'm going to stay as long as you need me. I can still keep in touch with the office by computer, e-mail and the fax machine. No problem."

He might have been standing there listing the wonders of modern communication like an idiot, but he was really asking for forgiveness, and Boyd knew it as well as Travis did. Travis requested mercy from his father with his eyes, with his voice, with the warm hand placed on his father's cold one.

His face raw with feeling, Boyd blinked once. That quickly, Travis was forgiven. "Stay...then. Your...home... too." Boyd's eyes moved to Rachel, as if he needed her approval of his decision.

"Travis can do whatever he wants, but I won't be there to cook for him." Rachel's voice trembled, but her head was high. She was as proud of Travis and Boyd, and as happy to see them reconciled, as she was, Liz knew. "So you see, my dear, you're asking the wrong woman. Liz will have to feed and water your son, as well as the rest of your crew. I'm staying here with you."

A tear slipped from Boyd's eye, and he gripped Rachel's hand tighter. "Should...have...married you...long ago. Shouldn't have listened...to you. Damn fool." A spasm of pain crossed his face.

"Are you all right?" Rachel cried.

Boyd blinked his eyes. "All right...as any fool...can be."

Rachel brought Boyd's hand up to her lips and kissed it—a reward for his courage.

Across the bed, Travis's dark eyes found Liz's. In understanding, she nodded, turned to go.

Gently Travis withdrew from his father. "We're going to leave you now, Dad, get back to the ranch and see what needs to be done. You're in excellent hands."

Boyd's eyes flashed to Rachel's face, his heart in them. "The...best."

In the car, in the passenger seat next to Liz, his nose filled with the scent of her, an earthy scent of clean woman, an evocative blended perfume, Travis tried to banish from his mind the picture of his father lying on that hospital bed, his eyes on Rachel as if she were his lifeline.

He couldn't do it.

His father had wealth, land, political power. None of it meant a damn now. The only thing that meant anything to Boyd McCallister at this moment was that precious human being who was willing to share his pain and trouble, the woman who stood by his bed, as fierce as an Amazon warrior, warding off despair, holding his hand and looking at him with enough love in her eyes to sustain life in both of them.

The sight of Rachel and his father tied together by a bond that had endured over time, distance, and a disparity in life-styles that should have destroyed their love long ago was burned into Travis's brain. He didn't like it. He wanted to forget it. It made him uncomfortable. It made him wonder if he'd tied life all up and put it in the wrong package.

His dad would survive and be stronger than he had been. Boyd knew for a certainty that he had Rachel, that her love didn't depend on his tall physique or his ability to ride, or on his silken words of love. Rachel loved his father for himself, the man he was without all the trappings. No wonder Boyd had stayed faithful to Rachel all these years. Maybe loving one woman would almost be worth the risk...for that.

No. It worked for his father, but that didn't mean it would work for him.

"You're very quiet. Are you...worried about your father?"

How patient Liz had been with him, letting him sit in his solitary silence for most of the ride home. She was like her mother. A quality woman. "No, I'm not worried. He's in very good hands."

"Yes, his doctor is excellent—"

"I wasn't talking about the doctor. I meant your mother."

There was that little silence that told him Liz was thinking. "You approve of their...relationship?"

He felt a flicker of impatience. It wasn't like her to be tentative. She wasn't looking at him. She was driving the car, concentrating on the road, but he felt her sensitivity.

"I was just sitting here envying the hell out of him."

She was relieved, he could see it in her face, in the slight relaxation of her grip on the steering wheel. For some reason, he was irritated.

"I'm glad you don't object."

"Why would I object? I told your mother at Diana's wedding that I thought she should have married Dad a long time ago." He turned to look at her, let his eyes feast on the long, tangled hair, the lovely symmetry of her profile. "What kind of a jerk do you think I am? Never mind, don't answer that. Just because I don't want marriage for myself doesn't mean I think everybody should avoid matrimony."

She smiled, and his heart lifted. He said, "Sometimes you know me better than any person on earth does. And sometimes you don't know me at all."

She said, "I don't suppose any person can know any other person absolutely. You always did expect perfection. From yourself, as well as everyone else."

He liked it better when the mood was light and they were teasing each other. "And you went and retrieved me from Chicago just so I could come back here and crack the whip. Not very smart of you, woman."

"My goodness, that's true. I forgot that you'd be cracking the whip on me, too."

"Never. I'm smarter than to take my life in my hands like that."

She smiled. It was a faint one, but it was enough of a lift of the lips to please him. Then she was serious again. "You won't try to crack the whip over Harv, will you?"

"Does that worry you?"

"I don't—I don't want trouble. It wouldn't be good for your father. Harv can be...prickly. You may have to be more tolerant with him than you are with your employees in the city."

"The man works for my father. That makes him my minion, for the time being."

"He's just been made foreman. He wouldn't like to be ordered around in front of the other men."

"In other words, you're telling me he's going to give me a bad time and I'd better be prepared."

"I'm not saying that you should expect trouble. I'm just saying that Harv does have a talent for goading people and getting under their skin—"

"He isn't the only one. There's a certain red-haired young woman who has a God-given talent for being a thorn in a man's side."

Determined not to be goaded herself, she said, "You'd do well to brace yourself for more of the same. I'm not going to keep quiet if I think you're doing something wrong."

"I've already tried bracing myself. Maybe I'll have to come up with something more...productive." With that provocative statement, he put his head back on the seat and closed his eyes, leaving her to deal with the aftermath of those softly spoken words, the sparking under her skin and the fire in her veins.

At the ranch, Liz didn't expect him to stash his cases in the bedroom in double-quick time and come strolling into the kitchen to say, "Your first order of business must be getting those yahoos fed their supper. What can I do to help?''

Surprised, she said, "You don't need to, really. I can manage alone."

"I'm certain you can. But why should you, when I'm here?"

There were several good reasons why she should send him on his way. Those reasons had to do with the jut of his hips as she tied the kitchen towel around them, the turned-over shirt collar that her fingers ached to smooth down, the tilt of his head over the cutting board as he shredded the lettuce into finer strips than she would have, the look of complete concentration on his face, his dark hair shining under the fluorescent light, his hands long-fingered and sensual on the knife. He gave the task his complete concentration. The way he would make love.

Self-conscious, Liz turned around too quickly to head for the refrigerator. She bumped into him, smelled soap, felt shoulder muscles. Heat pummelling her skin, she side-stepped. He dodged in the same direction. On purpose, she deduced from the slow, sweet smile that curved his lips. He caught her arms. "Relax, Liz. We're going to be working together a lot in the next few days. I won't bite. Unless you ask me to."

His hands were warm on her upper arms. She tilted a face up to him that was cool, but her eyes blazed. She couldn't go on with him like this, him teasing her with sexual innuendos and repulsing her when push came to shove. "It will be a lot easier to get on with a job if you don't touch me."

His face went blank and smooth as ice, as he released her at once.

Travis wanted to be angry with Liz, but he couldn't. She was right, he did touch her entirely too much for a man who was determined not to be involved with her. He turned back and lifted the knife, and it felt heavy and cold in his hands. He had a thought, not a comforting one. *The apple didn't fall far from the tree. Like father, like son.* Was Liz *his* lifeline? Was that why he couldn't keep his hands off of her?

She gave him crisp orders: Put the ingredients in the bread machine and start it, would you open the refrigerator door so I can put in this gelatin salad for tomorrow, these potatoes need to be peeled. She readied the pan of browning onions for the potatoes, he chopped them up and poured them in. She sent him out on the back stoop to husk the ear corn, he rinsed off the excess silk and dropped the ears in the boiling water. He picked up the utensil to turn the hamburgers frying in the skillet, she said she'd already turned them. He gestured with the saltshaker, she shook her head—and tried desperately to ignore the wonderful way his mouth tilted as he set it down.

An hour later, when they piled the contents of the hearty meal on trays and began ferrying the food to the bunkhouse, Travis leading the way, Liz told herself she *would* survive his being here.

The air was cooler, twilight just beginning, turning the prairie to rose and gold. Away from the intimacy of the kitchen, she would stop thinking about him.

Travis walked into the light ahead of her, a silhouetted man painted against the sky. That exceptional backside moved with smooth precision. That didn't mean she wondered what it would be like to walk with her hand in his back pocket and feel that muscle moving under her fingers. He had a subtle fluidity, he seemed to glide over the ground with a grace that seduced the eye. That didn't mean hers were enchanted. His bloused shirt was begging to be tugged out of his trousers, and then there would be all that warm bare skin undergirded by smooth, sleek muscles. That didn't mean her hands were itching to explore, not a bit.

In a pig's eye.

She was in trouble. Travis had come to stay—and there was no one to act as a buffer—not Rachel, or Boyd, or Diana. They were essentially alone on the ranch. Liz would have to use every ounce of her determination to keep that cool wall of impersonality that she'd patched together in the kitchen shored up. If Travis made another move toward her, spoke to her in that wonderfully evocative way he had in Sioux Falls, she'd fall into his arms. That would be heaven. Falling out again would be hellish.

The cowboys lounged around the bunkhouse table, which was already set with dishes and silverware. When Liz appeared in the doorway, Harv raised his arm and stared at his watch deliberately. Liz flushed. It was twenty minutes after six, according to the clock that hung on the wall. Rachel served the men their supper at six o'clock on the dot, winter and summer. Jim had often bragged that they could set their watch by her.

"Sorry I'm late, guys." Liz fastened on a bright smile and moved forward with her food tray, knowing their interest would be caught by the aroma of browned onions and potatoes, and the piled-up hamburger sandwiches.

Harv lounged in the chair at the head of the table, the chair that had been Jim's for as long as Liz could remember. She had a pang of regret and loss for the big, bluff, gentle giant who had been her friend for so long. He was on his way to Las Vegas with his beloved Callie, looking forward to a well-deserved vacation.

As her mother had always done, Liz set the two main serving dishes down in front of the foreman and turned to where Travis stood waiting with the second tray.

"Well, look who's acting as mother's helper with his apron on," said Harv.

Liz was defensive instantly. "It's not an apron. It's a towel. And you should be glad he's wearing it," she said militantly to Harv. "You'd still be waiting for this food an hour from now if he hadn't helped me."

Gently, Travis pushed Liz aside and leaned over Harv to set his burden on the table. "What is it about my *apron* you don't like?" His voice was low and controlled—like the first growl of a lion.

"Oh, I like the *apron* just fine. It's what's in it I don't care for. Gives the rest of us guys a bad name." A pause, the bright blue eyes looking Travis up and down. "That is, if you really are…a guy."

Liz's green eyes caught Travis's, seared to his soul. He recalled a convention where a man had stood up and said Travis's speech was based on an erroneous premise, a board meeting where a woman had accused him of jeopardizing the company with his youthful and impetuous schemes, a day on the beach when he'd restrained a young man who was verbally abusing his girlfriend.

He wasn't a macho cowboy. He didn't care a fig for the opinion of the men watching him. The only eyes on his face that mattered were Liz's.

"I'd give you a chance to reconsider that statement," Travis drawled, "but unfortunately, I don't have time. I have to do the dishes."

Chapter Eight

In the silence, golden beams from the setting sun captured dust motes in suspension. Then Liz laughed. She couldn't help it. Love for Travis and admiration for his droll sense of humor filled her anxious heart.

Len relaxed and grinned and looked his young age again. Tom Callahan's high forehead wrinkled with puzzlement. He was plain-spoken, responsible, and his life had three boundaries—the ranch, the television news, and the alimony checks he sent every month to his wife like clockwork. He didn't understand jokes. March Huddleston did. A crusty old cowboy whose skin was as dark and wrinkled as the hardtack he loved to eat, he slapped his thigh and chortled, his laughter louder than Liz's. Craig Seaton had knocked around in the world, and liked being settled on the ranch. He sat silent, his arms folded over his chest, his eyes cutting to Harv.

Travis's gaze was drawn to Liz, to her smile, to her

gorgeous sea-green eyes, sparkling with admiration that warmed his heart and other essential parts of his body.

They were in this together.

Harv wasn't amused, or appeased. Nor was he going to surrender. "So you're doing dishes."

"Yes," said Travis, evenly, "but as it happens, so are you." His gaze swung around to the other men. "And so is every other man jack who puts his feet under this table. Liz is going to have enough to do without cleaning up after a bunch of able-bodied *men* like you. As of tonight, we're instituting a new system for meal cleanup. Len, it will be your job to draw off a couple of pails of hot water from the bathroom. When everyone is finished eating, we'll set up shop here, and you men can clean up after yourselves."

"I'll be damned if I'll do my own dishes," Harv declared. "I work hard all day—"

"If you want to eat," Travis said slowly, carefully enunciating each word, "you'll clean up after yourself."

Liz stepped forward, ready to intervene, but Travis flashed her a warning look. She stayed where she was.

"Sit down at the table, Liz," Travis said, his voice warmer, lower, kinder. "I know you must be as hungry as I am."

"Actually, I was looking forward to eating something," she said as she sank into a chair.

"I'm starving." Len said the words with such heartfelt sincerity that Liz, March and Travis smiled.

"Pass Len one of those hamburgers before he expires," Liz directed, in an unconscious imitation of Rachel. "And get those potatoes circulating around the table before they get cold."

Dew glistened in wet, silvery beads over the prairie when Travis came out of the big house the next morning, a little before five-thirty. The sky was the faint blue of dawn. The cool air was sweet now, all the more to be savored, for the promise of heat was there in the slow rising of the sun. He'd had about three hours' sleep the night before. Perhaps that was why he seemed to feel the morning through his senses so acutely, feel as if the birds were singing at the top of their lungs in the trees. Or perhaps he had simply forgotten how beautiful dawn on the ranch could be.

He caught up with Lester outside the corral. Harv was already mounted on his roan. Travis said, "I'll need a horse."

Harv was in full cowboy regalia, his boots dew-wet, his hat band sweat-stained, his red bandanna crisp, his blue shirt matching his eyes exactly. He tilted his hat back on his head, settled into his saddle and gave Travis a long look that was supposed to intimidate him. It didn't. "What for?"

Travis had long experience in dealing with rude, obstinate men. Patiently he said, "I'm going to be working with you this morning."

"With or without your apron?"

Travis hung on to his patience, kept his face smooth, his hands relaxed. Harv was a young fool, but he was Boyd's young fool. Lester's attitude was not Travis's concern. "We're wasting time. I thought I'd give you the courtesy of picking my horse, since I don't know whose horse is whose these days. I can see you don't believe in courtesy. Now if you'll excuse me—"

March Huddleston came riding up on his black mare, Sassy. "He giving you a hard time, Travis?"

"I'm trying to find out which horse is available to ride," Travis said easily.

"There is a matter of safety here." Harv was all cool efficiency now that another member of his crew was present. "If we have to call in the emergency crew to pick him up when he falls off a horse, I'm responsible."

March snorted and spat and shot back, "He was riding while you was still drinking your mother's milk. 'Sides, we can use another hand. Makes less work for the rest of us. You can use the bay, Travis. I'll get him for ya."

March reined his horse around and headed for the cluster of horses.

"If anything happens to you, you're responsible for yourself." Harv squinted up into the sun.

"I've been responsible for myself for a long time," Travis said. "I think I can handle it."

"We've got work to do. We can't be playing nursemaid to you because you've decided you want to come out and play."

"I'll keep that in mind," Travis murmured.

"You do that," said Harv, and turned his horse to ride away, leaving Travis standing there looking after him with a faint smile on his lips, thinking that Harv could do with a little training in the concept of win-win.

Dust swirled in the corral, and a heat haze hung over the prairie. It was almost noon, and the sun was a burning presence in the sky, making the men pull off their hats and wipe their brows. Seated on the back of her gray gelding, thinking that every year it somehow always managed to be hotter than blazes during the two days of calf branding, Liz tipped up her hat and pulled her red bandanna from around her neck to swipe at her forehead.

She plopped her hat back on her head and twisted in the saddle, scanning the prairie for Travis. She'd thought he'd stay in the house and work on his computer, which he had, sometime during the night, installed in Boyd's study. Travis hadn't been on the back of a horse since the day they lost Andrew. And so, in that early-morning hour when she caught sight of Travis mounted on the big bay gelding, helping with the easier task of rounding up the cattle and herding them into the larger corral where the rest of the crew would begin the more difficult work of cutting out the calves, her heart had nearly stopped in her breast.

Now, in the heat of the noonday sun, when Travis rode toward her, he looked just as delectable, just as comfortable in the saddle, as he had this morning—even though he had to be feeling it in his rear end and thighs. With elegant ease, he reined his big bay horse up next to hers.

"Hot enough for you?" he murmured, that maddening smile tipping his mouth at the corners.

"What would you do if I said no?"

"Turn up that old sun another notch, sweetheart, if that's what you wanted. Some guys promise a woman the moon, but my specialty is the sun. Want a drink?" He pulled a battered canteen from behind his saddle.

She wouldn't put any heavy meaning on his light words. She knew better. "My gosh. Where did you get that?" She took it, put it to her mouth, drank. The water was cool, only slightly musty-tasting. "This thing must be a hundred years old. I remember it from forever. Where did you find it?"

"In the bottom of my closet."

"And I just drank from it? Will I die right on the spot, or will it be a slow, tortured death?"

"It'll take a while. Like the next hundred years." A tip of the hat, a flash of white teeth against his tanned face, and he refastened his canteen and rode away.

Nice straight back, nice narrow hips. Darn, the man was maddening. She could have sworn he was a dyed-in-the-wool never-sentimental kind of guy. Obviously, she'd been mistaken. That was the canteen both she and Andrew had teased him about once. Was it possible Travis was starting to heal just a little? At the thought, her spirits soared.

A Hereford calf with the biggest eyes and the longest eyelashes in the world skidded to a stop just short of Liz's gelding.

"You're next in the dentist chair, young fella. It's a shame, too, you with those beautiful brown eyes. They remind me of somebody else I know."

Heaven help her. There Travis was, riding easy in the saddle, not more than twenty feet away from her on the other side of the corral. If he read lips, she was dead.

Pull yourself together, Grant. There's work to be done here. No mooning over the boss's son. Just because he looks like the ultimate cowboy, with his body elegantly adjusting to each step of the horse, is no reason for you to lose your head. Your heart's already gone, that's true, but—

The calf didn't want to leave his mama, and his mama seconded the motion with a mooing protest. Mama, seasoned by several spring brandings, was smart enough to maneuver her baby to keep him close.

Liz's horse, Gray Smoke, knew this old cow for what she was, a stubborn bovine. Cow and horse were about to butt heads when a rope came singing through the air and circled the cow's neck. Travis had seen Liz's trouble, and he wasn't about to let her leg get squeezed in the confrontation.

It was later, after Liz had successfully guided the calf into the pen, when Len reined his Appaloosa up next to hers. "I didn't know he could do that."

"There's a lot of things you don't know."

"Liz, if you're planning on preparing dinner, you'd better quit here and go back to the house." Travis's voice.

Harv swung the branding table around, released the calf he'd been working on to Len, who clipped on an ear tag. While Len warily hitched up his jeans, Harv took off his hat and fixed his piercing blue eyes on Liz. Slowly his gaze shifted to Travis seated on his horse beside her. "She stays here. We need her."

It seemed to Liz that Harv had been waiting for this moment, planning for it. She wanted to put her hand out on Travis's arm, to— She didn't know what—show support, restrain him? Stop the world so he wouldn't be hurt?

"I'll take her place." Seated in the saddle with such easy assurance in the burning heat, Travis looked as cool as pond water. If he had ever required another person's support in the world, it didn't show at that moment. He was the consummate corporate man, nerveless, in control. Liz folded her hands over Smoke's reins.

"We need somebody who knows how to cut calves, not some damn city boy who'll end up keeping us out here till midnight."

The air seemed grittier, the sun hotter, in that second of silence. "I don't think I'll slow you down that much," Travis drawled.

"You can't do squat," Harv said, and spit on the ground. "This ain't no dish brigade."

March Huddleston turned his bearded face up to the sky, as if he had a sudden intense interest in the wispy drift of cirrus clouds. Len took a long time wiping his neck with his bandanna.

"Nor is it a contest of machismo—or a battle of wits," said Travis evenly.

"Ha!" March snatched his hat off and slapped it on his thigh. "If it was—" his narrow-eyed gaze swung to Harv, and one hand swiped back his hair "—you'd lose, Harvey, hands down."

"Shut up, old man," said Harv, his eyes on Travis.

Travis's mouth tightened. Harv had closed the noose by being disrespectful to the man who'd put Travis up on his first pony. "It's always been my policy to refrain from putting an employee down in front of his crew. But you force me to remind you that in my father's absence, I am acting chief here. As such, what I say goes."

"You don't have to remind me of a damn thing. I remember you with an apron tied around your waist very well."

A pleasant smile lifting his lips, Travis said, "I'd still be the boss, even if my choice of attire was little pink panties."

March guffawed, and Len laughed with him.

"Cute," Harv said. "Real cute." His face was flushed with anger, and his blue eyes were brilliant. "Let's see if you can work your horse as well as you work your mouth."

Silence fell like a pall on the corral. Travis's horse moved nervously under him. "Go on, Liz," Travis said evenly, his eyes on Harv. "You're not needed here."

She went—but once inside the blessedly cool house, she took up a station at the front window, her fingers nervously pushing aside the lace curtain to give her a view of the corral.

Dust curls spiraled. In that melee of men and cows, the crew on horseback might have looked unrecognizable to any other set of eyes, but Liz's gaze homed in on Travis like a guided missile. He sat taller in the saddle, wore his hat tipped just a little lower. And he was cutting out a calf like an old pro.

Pride. It coursed through her, made her feel as if she

were watching her child go off to his first day of school. Of course, Travis had once been a good cowboy, as good as any on the planet, but it had been so long ago, and just because he sat a horse well, that didn't mean he'd stay in the saddle during the intricate twists and turns it took to cut out a fleet-of-foot young calf. If it had taken him too long to corral a calf, or worse, if his horse had turned too sharply and Travis had fallen off in front of the crew, she would never have forgiven herself.

Staying on board a well-trained cutting horse must be like riding a bicycle; Travis's muscled body obviously remembered the skill very well. Scooter was an excellent cow horse, ten years old, and smarter than most cowboys. So was Travis. They made a good team.

When Travis had corralled his first calf and had the second one herded into the gate before the branding crew was ready for either one, Liz sighed with relief and turned away from the window.

Weary. Liz felt tired right down to her bones, weary from shepherding cantankerous cattle, placating irascible males, and preparing their supper, though she'd kept it simple and hearty—steaks, potatoes baked in the automatic oven, green-bean casserole and sweet-potato pie heavy with brown sugar and dotted with pecans.

After the evening meal was over and the men washed the dishes and stacked them according to Travis's instructions, Liz climbed up the three steps into the little house that she and her mother called home.

Dust lay in a fine gray film over the dark end tables in the living room, a testament to Rachel's absence. The house was too hot, too closed, too filled with the whispery pad of Liz's stocking feet on the bare wooden floors as she went about opening windows.

The first drift of cool evening air feathering over her

arms accompanied a slow, languorous tune playing on the radio that made her imagine a moon shaded by a wisp of a cloud, trees sighing while two lovers strolled beneath, whispering love words that only they understood.

Snap out of it, Liz.

A carefree fantasy stroll on a summer night with a man was a foolish romantic dream that would never come true for her. Her life was her work on the ranch, her responsibilities. What she needed most in the world just now was to call the hospital to find out how Boyd was doing and have a good visit with a female of the species, preferably the one she called Mother.

"Oh, sweetheart, I tried to call earlier. Boyd is so much better. His doctors and nurses can hardly believe how much progress he's made in twenty-four hours. He's on some new medication that is marvelous." Rachel sounded giddy with relief, her voice fizzing with joy.

He's also got your love, and that's the best medication in the world.

The lace doily under the lamp glowed with rainbow colors, evoked Rachel's presence. The lace vibrated with colors, bright red, purple, yellow, green. The doily shone with an assertive joyousness, like her mother. Liz's finger traced the intricate patterns of delicate thread. Her mother's positive thinking lent joy and grace to those around her. And strength.

"I'm so glad Boyd is better. Tell him we're all praying for him."

"How are things going? Did they get started at the branding?"

"Everything's going fine."

"You sound tired, dear. I think you need some sleep."

"Not a bit. Travis has organized mealtime to make my job easier. Will you be— Are you coming home soon?"

"It will be a few more days until the doctor can make a decision about where Boyd should be. I have a motel room, and I went back there this afternoon to get a shower and change my clothes."

"I'm so glad Boyd is better. When the branding is done, I know Travis will want to make the trip to the city to see him again."

"Tell Travis not to worry. If I can assure Boyd that everything is going smoothly at the ranch, that will be excellent medicine for him."

More assurances that everything was fine, more lies—of course Liz wasn't exhausted—more commands that Rachel mustn't worry about her daughter, she must stay until she could come home with Boyd.

"I love you, baby. You're the best daughter on earth."

"I love you, too, Mom." Liz fought to keep her voice even, so that her mother wouldn't sense the rush of emotion that brought stinging tears to Liz's eyes.

Change. She'd hated change as a child, hating being wrenched out of her life to come to the ranch. There would be more change now. Her mother would marry Boyd and go to live in the big house. It was what they should do, must do, if Liz had anything to say about it, she thought fiercely. One female Grant pining after a male McCallister was enough around here.

But after Rachel claimed her happiness, what would Liz do?

She couldn't stay. She would have to forget about Travis and her dream of loving him forever and get on with her life.

She would have to leave the ranch. That was the only way she'd ever forget Travis.

How much it hurt, that thought.

She would miss the ranch, the peace, the satisfaction of

working outdoors. She'd miss her mother and Boyd. She'd miss the thought of Travis. That was all she'd had, but at least it had been something. She'd miss...

Blaze!

She hadn't seen him for two days. This, after she'd promised faithfully that she'd never forget him, never leave him.

Some friend she was.

The stable was dusky-dark, steamy from the heat of the day, redolent with scents of straw and manure. The tack room gave off the aroma of leather. A corn knife with an eighteen-inch blade dangled on the door, rattled against the wood as she walked by. "I'll bet you thought I deserted you—"

A horse's neigh of pain and despair seared the night quiet.

Chills of fear danced over her skin. "Blaze?"

A bang, a rattle, legs thumping against a stall wall, another cry that took the chill down to her bones.

Two ropes tied to each side of the stall were looped tightly around Blaze's neck, and his wild eyes told her of his fright, his struggle, his pain. Sweat gleamed on his hide. As if he hated to have her see him brought so low, he went into a panic of straining and pulling, this way, that way, until at last he subsided, his breathing labored.

The knife. She ran to the tack room door, fumbled with the thong that held it suspended on the nail. It wouldn't give. Angry to the point of tears, she grabbed hold of the handle and jerked. The nail came flying out of the door, but she didn't care. The knife was hers.

"Easy, Blaze. Easy. We'll have you out of there in no time. I'll let you out in the corral for a run. You'd like that, wouldn't you? A nice long run in the cool evening air—"

The knife was heavy. She lifted it, sliced through one rope. "Just one more rope to cut and you'll be free, my love—"

Hard, unfamiliar hands snatched her up, twisted her around, lifted her off her feet. Harv's brilliant blue eyes flashed in the stable with male arrogance, triumphant possessiveness. "You sure can talk sweet love words, baby. How about saying something nice to me?"

Instinct told her not to resist him. Not yet. "Put me down and I might consider it."

Holding her close, he let her down slowly over his body, watching her face as her hips and breasts glided over his chest.

She gritted her teeth together to keep from crying out at the forced intimacy. She had her feet on the ground now, but he held her in an unbreakable grip. "Now that's much better."

Blaze protested Harv's presence, neighing, struggling, gasping for breath. The horse was in more danger now than ever, since Liz had freed him on one side but not the other.

She must not lose her head. She must think of Blaze and not herself, keep her anger under control and her wits about her. "Let me cut Blaze loose first. He's going to hurt himself—"

"Serve him right if he did. He needs to be punished. He's been a naughty boy."

"What did he do?" She wanted to kick and scratch and claw, and she would, but not just yet.

"He wouldn't let me ride him. He doesn't like me. We'll see if he likes me any better when I take him out of those ropes."

"He'll eat you alive."

"I wouldn't like that." Harv flashed a smile that was

meant to impress her. "I wouldn't like that a bit. Now, if you wanted to eat me alive, that would be a different story. I'd like to tell you just where to start.... Ooh, look at those green eyes sparkle. You'd like to use that knife on me, wouldn't you?"

"I'd like to hit you on the head with it."

Harv laughed. "If the little boss was half as fierce as you are, he'd be a real man, not the citified sissy he is—"

"Let her go."

Travis's voice was low, and his dark form was nearly invisible in the stable doorway.

"Who's gonna make me?"

"Do it. Now."

Slowly Harv let Liz go. The instant she was released, Liz turned back to Blaze, raised the knife and sliced through the second rope.

"You shouldn't have done that," Harv said to Liz, but his eyes were on Travis.

"My very thought," Travis murmured. "Don't touch her again, Lester. Stay away from her...and the horse."

"Like I said, who's gonna make me? A little apron-wearing male pretender like you?"

"Call me any name you like. I don't give a damn about your opinion of me."

"And I don't give a damn about your orders." His hand shot out, circled around Liz's waist. She cried out and kicked at his shins. He yelped, but he tightened his hold, dragging her up to his side. "McCallister, here's a little lesson for you. Time you learned a man's got to reach out and take what he wants. See how easy it is?"

"I'm a firm believer in speaking to a man in a language he understands. It's obvious you and I haven't been communicating well." With a lightning swiftness, almost in one movement, Travis pulled Liz out of Harv's arms and put a hard fist in his stomach. When Harv doubled over with a cry of pain, Travis gave him a clip under the chin that sent him staggering back against the stable wall.

Coolly Travis watched as Harv sagged against the wall, his eyes glazed, his breathing ragged and heavy.

"Perhaps we understand each other a little better now." He held out a hand, and Liz slid hers into it and stepped to his side.

"What needs to be done for that horse, Elizabeth?"

At Travis's side, she stood with him, watching Harv. "He needs to be let out into the corral, where he can be exercised safely, in the dark. Then he needs a good rubdown and some water and feed." She shot a heated, furious look at Harv. "He probably hasn't had anything since the last time I fed him."

There was banked fury in the way Harv collected himself, the way he stood braced against the wall, staring at Liz and Travis. His voice was heavy with belligerence when he said to Travis, "Well, you got it all your way, haven't you? If I hit you back, I lose my job."

"This has nothing to do with your job. This is personal, between you and me. If you want to go outside and continue this, just say so."

Harv's chest heaved with his hard breathing. Liz held hers.

"Or we can make it another time," Travis said, in an even, cool voice. "It makes no difference to me—as long as you learned something from our little...training session."

"I wouldn't have touched her if I'd known she was your private property." Harv made a big show of brushing the hay off his chest.

"She isn't my 'private property.' She belongs to herself. It's a concept you need to come to grips with, Lester."

"Dress it up in whatever fancy language you want to, I don't care. You sure you won't change your mind in the morning and throw me out on my backside? Or brag to my crew how you blindsided me?"

"There's another thing you need to learn. When an enemy offers you amnesty, take it and run."

Harv grimaced, as if Travis had spoken in a foreign language.

Liz leaned over and retrieved his black Stetson from the floor. "Here's your hat, what's your hurry?"

He scowled at her, grabbed his hat and stomped out the door.

"An old country saying," Liz said to Travis, needing to smile, feeling such relief that she wanted to shout with it.

"I'm familiar with the phrase."

"It means the sooner I see your backside going down the road, the happier I'll be."

"I know what you meant. Liz, stop trying to distract me. He didn't…hurt you, did he? If I thought he had, he would have crawled out of here on two broken legs."

She put her head down, took a deep breath, lifted her chin. "No, he didn't hurt me. Thank you, Travis."

"Were you really going to hit him on the head with that corn knife?"

"What do you think?"

"I think you'd do almost anything to protect someone you loved. I'm glad you didn't think of putting it between his ribs."

"I'm not the violent type. I'm a pacifist. But just in case—" her eyes sparkled with mischief "—want to show me how to do that one-two punch? Was that right-left, or left-right?"

"I'm not showing you anything. You're lethal enough as it is."

That brought more sparks to her eyes, and showers of fireworks to her heart. "Travis, I—"

"Let's see to your horse, hmmm?"

She didn't know what he was thinking. He'd acted as a champion for a horse he hated, and he didn't seem to regret it. He was courteous when he helped her guide a panicked, shaky Blaze to the corral, patient as he stood at her side when she released Blaze to freedom, silent as he watched Blaze cavort like a child in the moonlight. He stood back, watching, not touching her, not involving himself with her or with Blaze.

Her heart ached with yearning for him. How could she not want him? He was all the things she had admired all her life, a man of quiet strength and beauty, his face darkly chiseled by the brilliant moon.

They were beautiful together in the moonlight, the horse and the woman. The sight of them made Travis think that this was why strong men wrote poetry. The stallion pranced and bobbed around the woman, all masculine power and grace and high-spirited relief, his coat shining in the soft light. Moonbeams gathered in Liz's hair, caressed her smooth cheeks, made her eyes dark pools. How graceful she was, feminine and trusting, stretching out her hand for the horse to eat an apple from.

Then, in that moment of silence and moonglow, she turned to him. "Thank you for staying."

"You're welcome. I enjoy watching love, even if I can't believe in it."

His eyes caught hers in the moonlight. She felt as if he were drinking in the sight of her, his gaze moving slowly over her face, her throat, her hair. His voice low, he said,

"I'd better say good-night, before I lose my head and tell you how beautiful you are and how much I—admire you."

In that heart-beating silence, she said, "You don't mean that. I'm not...beautiful."

He shook his head, but he didn't move.

She took a step closer to him. She could feel herself breathing, feel her chest moving up and down, hear the pound of Blaze's hooves on the soft earth, feel the soft night breeze, the cool moonlight. He was so close, she could reach out her hand and touch him.

"Travis, I need you. I need you to make love to me. Now. Tonight."

"You've got moonlight in your eyes, Liz. It's making you crazy. I guess the moon made me a little crazy, too."

A rueful smile on his mouth, he turned with that easy grace he had and left her standing in the night-shaded corral, her hand out, Blaze's warm lips nuzzling her neck.

Chapter Nine

The moon fanned silver banners through the trees and turned Liz's bed into a silver bower. Resplendent moonbeams poured over her shredded dreams. Leaves rustled in the cottonwoods, mocking her with whispers of love.

I guess the moon made me a little crazy, too.

They hurt, those words. For Travis had said them and walked away.

He'd spoken those empty love words and left her standing alone in the corral, heated and aching and wanting him so much that her body burned. He'd left her with visions of his sweet, familiar mouth tasting her, his hard body pressed to hers.

She'd wanted him as an innocent girl, but she hadn't known then how hungry desire could resonate through a woman's body.

She kicked off the sheet, her skin burning. Cool air drifted over her, offering no surcease.

You could have followed him.

She'd had one small opportunity to jump off the edge of the world and tell Travis the truth, that she no longer cared what the family thought or even what he thought, that all she could think of was being in his arms. Loving him.

Standing there in the corral with his face etched in light and shadow, he'd looked...lonely. Why hadn't she gone after him?

Too proud, too afraid. Too cowardly.

Had his words meant anything at all?

You didn't have the courage to find out.

The earth turned, the endless night became a morning brilliant with birdsong. Restlessly Liz tossed back the sheet and slipped into a blouse and jeans cooled by the night air. She crossed the yard to saddle up for another day's work, breathing in the sweet, hot air, her blood racing with excitement. What would he say to her this morning?

For a man who'd never wanted to be a cowboy, Travis rode toward her with all the panache of the consummate Western man. He looked very natural mounted on the big bay, his white hat less than pristine and tilted over his forehead, his dark blue bandanna fluttering. His beauty always delivered a shock to her nervous system, and all the more so this morning, after a night spent thinking only of him. Her mouth went dry, her heart into double time.

If she hadn't been watching him so closely, she would have missed his greeting. He flicked a gloved hand to his hat brim, wheeled his horse around and left her sitting on her horse, both of them eating his dust before she could raise a hand in reply.

It hurt terribly. She gripped the reins tighter and turned her horse around, heading away from the rest of the crew. She might as well have been Harv; Travis had greeted him in exactly the same way. The warmth stinging in her cheeks was all she had to remind her of his soft words spoken under the moon.

She didn't want to think that he spent the rest of the day avoiding her, but it did seem odd that he found so many straying calves in the opposite corner of the prairie from wherever she was.

She could tolerate perspiration and dust and calves bawling. She couldn't tolerate the way she was feeling. She must, *must*, give up all those hopeless dreams of him and accept reality. She must treat him as impersonally as he treated her.

In her heart, she knew that wasn't possible. There was only one way to achieve a permanent cure. She would have to go away.

The rest of the day, she ruthlessly pushed aside thoughts of Travis by throwing her heart, body and soul into her work. For the most part, she was successful in keeping her gaze off of him—except for those few times her concentration lapsed and her eyes sought him hungrily. Crazy, maybe, to think of ballet at the sight of Travis and his horse working. Impossible to think of anything else. The bay was easy and graceful, accomplishing the sudden twists and turns required of a good cutting horse. Travis matched the horse's grace, his balance in the saddle impeccable. By the end of the day, however, Liz's sharp eyes saw how much more carefully he sat on his horse.

"Well, of course, Travis is probably feeling it in his rear end. He hasn't been on a horse in years," Rachel said on the phone to Liz that evening. They had already exchanged news of ranch and hospital, and Rachel had told Liz that Boyd was talking almost normally and there was some feeling in his hand again. Now they were calmly discussing Travis's behind, Liz thought, eyes rolled to the ceiling, in the typical straightforward style of her mother.

"No doubt he's got the beginning of saddle sores. Go upstairs and get that bag balm I keep in the medicine cabinet. It's the best thing in the world for saddle sores. Take it to him tonight, so he'll feel the good of it tomorrow."

There was a picture. Liz knocking on Travis's door and saying to him, 'I really didn't want to bother you, but Mother insisted you take this bag balm for your saddle sores.'

This was *not* possible. "Mother, I don't think—"

"Travis is family, Elizabeth. He's also a man. He needs to be taken care of. Heaven knows he won't do it himself."

"But I—"

"Never mind your buts. It's Travis's we have to think of. When I call you tomorrow night, I want you to tell me that you did as I asked."

That was it. The Oracle, albeit a blunt one, had spoken. It was difficult to concentrate on the phone conversation after that, her heart thumped so loudly in her chest. The quickened beat made her whole body throb while she listened to assurances from her mother that Boyd would be home soon.

"Travis called just before you did. He said things were going well at the ranch, too."

"At least we got our stories together."

That made her mother laugh. "As if you two would story to me." A little space of silence. "Liz, everything *is* all right between you and Travis?"

"Of course. Everything's fine."

Later, when Liz had hung up the phone, she thought she must never forget how perceptive her mother was.

If she took at least five minutes to turn around and another eighteen to walk upstairs and another fifteen to find the bag balm, maybe those two squares of light shining from Travis's bedroom would go out and she'd be able to say, "Oops, too late, Travis has gone to bed, can't go."

Fat chance. Those lights were still burning at three o'clock in the morning. They're not likely to go out at nine this evening.

Stupid to worry about it. She'd just march up to the door of Mr. Smoothly Sophisticated CEO from Chicago who lives in a building where the geraniums were bigger than trees and say, in a bright, singsong Debbie Reynolds voice, "Here's bag balm for your saddle sores."

She went in the kitchen to think, ended up with her face buried in a tea towel.

She'd have tea. It would take a long time to brew. She'd have coffee, start up the big pot. She'd have cocoa. She'd have all three, one at a time.

Don't be such a coward. You're a grown woman, for heaven's sake. You know you're perfectly safe with him.

Yes, I'm safe with him, but is he safe with me?

Why hadn't she thought of that line with her mother?

Suppose he really does have saddle sores. Untreated, they'd give him permanent scars. It would be a shame to have scars on that nice rear end.

Think of it as a trip to the dentist. Just go and get it over with.

Two at a time up the stairs, before she could stop and think, a hunt through the medicine cabinet that, darn it all, turned up the bag balm.

She had to have something to carry it in. Her makeup bag. The tartan one.

She upended it, making lipstick, blush and eyeshadow fall out and roll on the counter.

Her hair looked wild. So what was new? She caught up

a comb, ran it once through her long tresses, bunched up her hair and tamed it with a silver clasp.

Change clothes?

Why would she need to?

Middle button undone on her blouse. Swell. Knock at his door with bag balm, and a button conveniently undone. Are you going to volunteer to apply it, too?

She was going to volunteer for a job in Zaire.

Before she lost her courage altogether, she raced down the stairs. She had her hand on the doorknob when she realized the medication still sat on the bathroom counter.

Another trip upstairs made her breathless when she closed the front door behind her, and her heart pounded in a syncopated beat that rocked her whole body.

Outside, a cricket chirped merrily. What did he know? He should go get chased by a pheasant.

The moon drifted through the clouds. They might get rain tomorrow. A deluge. With a little luck, maybe she'd drown.

She put her hand up to knock at the front door, took it down. She'd never knocked on the door of this house before. But Travis had never been alone in this house before.

She knocked so hard she had to rub her knuckles afterward.

Nothing. No sound, no movement. She knocked again.

One more time, and I can leave. Oh, joyous thought.

Under the raised hand, the door opened.

She almost dropped the bag balm. Backlit, his feet bare and lean and elegant, his equally bare chest muscled and darkly furred. He was centerfold material, the stuff of female fantasy. His jeans looked as if he'd just pulled them on, the waist snap undone. His fingers combed back unruly dark hair. Male dishabille, good enough to eat.

Her breath caught in her throat. Along with her heart.

His brow furrowed. "Liz? Why didn't you come in through the kitchen?"

As confused as he, she blurted out the truth. "I don't know." She felt like such a fool. "I'm intruding. I shouldn't have come."

He frowned with impatience, shook his head. "I was just doing some work, sending some stuff to Chicago. I was in the middle of it when I heard your knock. Was there something you wanted?"

"No, I— That is, Mom suggested— We were talking and— I thought— No, it was her idea—"

He leaned back against the door, arms folded, those beautiful, furred pectoral muscles far too well displayed. They turned her brain to mush. She wanted to touch them, wanted to feel the strength beneath that silken hair. All she could say was "What...are you doing?"

"At the rate you're going, I'll take root here before you finish a sentence. I thought I'd get comfortable. Or would you like to come in while you're deciding whether it was your idea or your mother's that brought you knocking at my door?"

"It was Mom's idea."

It was so imperceptible she almost missed it, that cooling of his smile. "Well. Mystery settled." His tone was cooler, too. Her answer hadn't pleased him. Had he wanted it to be her idea to come calling? Surely not.

"I was just getting ready to take a break. You can tell me what your mother wanted over a cup of coffee, if you like."

The thought of blurting out the reason for her errand on his doorstep made her say, "Yes...that sounds good."

He stepped back and allowed her to pass by him, but when she started for the kitchen, he grabbed her elbow. "Uh-uh. Wrong way. I've got everything set up in my bedroom, including the coffeepot. I thought it would be easier for you to clean the house if I kept my mess contained in one room."

His eyes caught, held, hers. In the soft lamplight, their dark gleam was no longer banked, as it had been when he stood with his arms folded in the door. Those brown eyes glowed with a new aliveness, awareness, teasing. "Afraid to come into my parlor?"

Darn that betraying warmth, she felt it everywhere. She brought her chin up a notch. "Of course not. Don't be ridiculous. We've got all that straightened out between us."

"Yes, indeed," he murmured, his mouth twitching as he turned on those long, bare feet and led the way to his bedroom.

It might have been a room to sleep in, but it looked as if several reams of paper had exploded over every flat surface. She couldn't even see the bed, there were so many aqua-bound tomes scattered over it, and his desk was buried under manila files. He'd appropriated another table for a computer, a fax machine and a telephone, and there wasn't a bare space showing on that surface, either.

"You look very...busy."

"The express-mail company is so happy with our business, they'll probably send me a fruitcake at Christmastime."

"You hate fruitcake."

"It was a joke, Liz," he said, smiling that indulgent smile.

"I knew that. Is this what they mean when they say 'paperwork'?"

"I like things documented in hard copy, and I'm not a neat worker. I drive Hilda to distraction. Now you can see why I set up shop in here, rather than appropriating Dad's office." He scooped a clutch of manila envelopes off the chair in front of the desk and gestured at it. "Sit down."

She sat.

"Now, to what do I owe the pleasure of this visit?"

He stood leaning back on the corner of the desk, crossing his long legs at the ankle, his arms braced to hold him in place. In the lamplight, he was so masculine and so beautiful that he robbed her of every shred of coherent thought.

"I was afraid— Mom and I thought—" Oh, cripes, Liz, pull yourself together. Stop dithering and hiding behind your mother's name and just spit it out. "I brought you some medication. Bag balm."

He raised an eyebrow. "Bag balm? The stuff we used to use on cow's udders when we were milking?"

"It's very good for saddle sores."

In the silence of that room, she heard the tick of a clock while he thought it over. His lips tilted up in a smile. "And I tried so hard not to let them show."

"Travis, please. I don't know whether you have them or not. I just thought you might have been hurting, because it's been so long since you've ridden and—"

"Relax, Liz, I was just teasing you. I'm not used to playing soldier to your Florence Nightingale."

Studying his smoothly muscled arms, she said breathlessly, "There's liniment in there, too, and some witch hazel." She tried to keep a cool, impersonal face, but it was difficult when his maddening smile still lifted his mouth and he wore that air of indulgent amusement. "Don't put the witch hazel on any place you have broken skin. It stings."

"I'll try and remember that." He said it very soberly, very carefully, but she knew darn well it took all his control to keep from smiling.

The fax machine began to rattle.

"Well, I'd better go. You're busy—" She pushed herself halfway out of the chair, but she didn't get very far. He pushed her down again, his hands warm and gentle on her shoulders.

"Relax. It's automatic. I don't have to do anything to it."

"Oh." She felt him release his hold on her, knew it was shameless to wish he hadn't. Did he have to stand so close, yet so far away, with that wonderful masculine body half-naked? She was only human, and as susceptible to beauty as the next woman. She couldn't think. Well, there was one part of her body that was active, but it wasn't her brain.

"You can't go until you've had your coffee." His voice was smooth as silk, not a bit of tension in it.

"I've changed my mind. I don't want coffee." Hers had a betraying catch.

"What do you want, Liz?"

He had such consummate control that she couldn't tell what was going through his mind. With any other man, she would have known it was a come-on, but Travis's face wore that cool no-way-am-I-going-to-let-you-know-what-I'm-thinking look. She longed to match his sophistication, but he was playing a game she had never played, with rules she couldn't fathom. "I don't want anything. Mom wanted me to bring—" That maddening spark of amusement gleamed in his eyes. "Well, you know what Mom wanted me to bring, and I've brought it, so I'll be going now—"

He leaned over her, his long-fingered hands gripping the arm of her chair, making her his captive. That quickly, he took possession of her mind, heart and soul. She sat looking up at him, all eyes and heart. "What are you doing?"

"Getting your attention."

"You have it."

"Good. Listen to me, Liz. Don't come over here again."

The words were softly spoken, but they stung just the same. She'd never have guessed that was what he was going to say. "Why not?"

"When you were a kid, I might have had to explain it to you. You're not a kid now."

Flushed, her feathers ruffled, she moved to stand up. He pushed her down again, his hands warm and hard on her shoulders—and released her instantly. While her face was clear, vulnerable in the lamplight, his was shadowed.

He settled back on the desk, his arms folded over his chest. "Shall I spell it out for you, then? Shall I tell you how I'd like to take you down on that bed and unbutton the rest of those buttons?"

Her hands went instantly to the idiotic button that wouldn't stay closed. "I don't want you to tell me a thing. You've already said too much."

"I haven't even begun. If you were any other woman, I would have suspected an invitation. But I know you. I know you think you're safe with me." In the silence that followed, he straightened off the desk. "You aren't."

She rose to her feet, trembling. "I have nothing to fear from you. This is what you love, your machines and your papers and your books. I could never compete with them." She swept a hand around.

He wanted to tell her that standing there the way she was, trembling, yet fiery with courage and determination, she was beyond lovely. And he wanted her desperately. "This is what I'm good at," he said in a cool, emotionless tone.

"No, you're good at something else. You're very good

at building walls to keep people out. I'm awfully tired of butting my head against your brick outposts.''

"Maybe it's time you stopped trying,'' he said, in that slow, smooth drawl.

Furious, she twisted around to the bed and began snatching up ledgers, picking up the pieces of his life and stacking them in her arms. He stood with his arms folded across his chest, his smile faintly indulgent, letting her play out the game her way. A book fell out of her arms and thumped on the floor, the quarterly profits from two years ago. Blandly he stepped around her, retrieved it and tucked it under her chin.

"I don't need your help!'' she cried.

"As you wish.''

Her arms piled high, she twisted around to Travis. He said with a droll, tongue-in-cheek delivery, "Now that you have the bed cleared off, is there something you'd like to use it for?''

"I didn't clear the bed, I gathered up the substance of your life so you could hold it in your arms.'' Her cheeks glowed with rosy anger, and her eyes snapped green fire at him. With one quick thrust, she shoved the books into his arms. "Love these,'' she said. "They will never die and leave you.'' Liz whirled around and walked out of the room, leaving Travis standing there with his hands full and his heart empty.

He stood for a moment, waiting for the slam of the front door. It didn't come. He strolled to his bedside, opened his arms and let the ledgers that held the work of his life fall onto the bed.

He stood for a moment in the softly lit room, fighting against the feeling that she had seen into his soul. Travis was an old hand at tamping down emotion, and even more expert at dealing with the bitter aftertaste of a confrontation, but he felt overwhelmed by an emptiness he didn't understand. Stupid to feel this way, as if he'd lost the only person in the world he'd ever really cared about. She'd gotten angry and she'd gone away, and that was fine. They couldn't go on playing with fire. For if they did, one of them would get burned, and it would surely be her.

He'd cut off an arm before he'd hurt her.

From the look on her face when she gave him that final pronouncement, it appeared that she'd truly given up on him this time. That was what he wanted. Exactly what he wanted.

Now if he could just get rid of this idiotic ache that seemed to rise up from the bottom of his soul and consume him, he'd be able to concentrate. There was work to do, the most pressing task to get the presentation for the board ready in a readable, logical form so that Hilda could present it.

A half hour later, he pushed away from the computer keyboard in disgust. He'd write a line, delete a line, try again. It still wasn't going together. He wasn't concentrating on his work. Liz's face kept floating in his vision, the hurt, the determination, the beauty.

Never before had anything, or anyone, interfered with his work.

He lunged out of the chair, went to the coffee carafe and filled his mug before heading out of his room.

In the kitchen, his long-fingered hands wrapped around his cup, he prowled about restlessly, conscious of the cool tile under his bare feet, opening cupboards, forgetting what he was looking for, remembering when he saw the flowered sugar bowl centered in the lace doily on the table. Scowling, he doctored his coffee, stirring it absently. His feet chilly, he leaned back in the corner of the cupboard the way Liz had that first night.

He wished he could reel time back and start all over again. He'd done it wrong right from the beginning.

No, he hadn't done anything wrong. He'd done it all right. She was safe. He would go away soon, and she would still be safe. That was all that mattered.

In her little house Liz paced the length of the kitchen and back again. She would not go back and apologize. He deserved everything she'd said to him, and more.

If he had saddle sores all the way up his back, she wouldn't feel sorry for him. He was mule-stubborn, insensitive, harebrained, addlepated, single-minded, shortsighted...and what was more, he didn't know a thing about her *or* himself. If he thought she wanted him, he was wrong, wrong, wrong. She wouldn't have him if he was served up on a platter with an apple in his mouth. He could go back to Chicago tomorrow, for all she cared. Why stop at Chicago? Why not Timbuktu, Xanadu—? A sound shattered the quiet, the piercing scream of a horse in pain. Blaze!

Her heart vibrating with fear, Liz dashed outside. The yard was cool, dark and moonlit, oddly peaceful and quiet. Unmindful of the dark, she sprinted across the yard. She was halfway up the corral fence, her hands grasping, her feet scrabbling, when Harv yelled at her, "Liz! Stay where you are."

He was in a saddle on Blaze's back, his legs clamped tight around Blaze's belly. In her bewildered panic, Liz had the incongruous thought that she couldn't imagine how Harv had gotten close enough to saddle Blaze. Harv wore no hat—it lay in the dirt, trampled more than once by Blaze's hooves, by the look of it. Didn't the idiot realize the same would happen to him?

Liz's body went tight with fear.

Light and shadow played over man and horse, giving them an awful beauty. Harv had the reins in a death grip, and there was an unholy smile on his face. It was then that she saw the wicked crop he was wielding. Welling drops of blood showed exactly where Blaze had been hit repeatedly.

A hot fury like nothing she'd ever known burned through Liz, nearly choking her. "Get over and get off on the other side of the fence before he kills you."

Harv twisted his head around. His teeth flashed in the moonlight. He was enjoying himself. "This white devil is going to learn who's boss around here if I have to kill him to prove it."

She'd never before in her life wanted to physically hurt another human being. *"Get off that horse."*

Blaze heard her voice. His cry was high and harsh, and he reared high, exposing his whole chest. Harv clung to the saddle like a burr, even when Blaze came down and danced sideways. The horse's rebellion earned him another crack of the whip across his neck.

"Stop that!" Liz cried desperately.

"No way. I'm going to teach this horse the lesson he needs."

Blaze went still suddenly, his breathing harsh and fast.

"There, you see. He can be trained—"

Blaze shot straight up in the air, came down on all fours. While Harv struggled to recover his balance, Blaze reared again, a huge, crazed horse in full spate, bathed in the terrible softness of the moonlight. Still halfway off the ground, Blaze twisted in a killing sidewinder. Harv flew out of the saddle and tumbled into the dust two feet away from Blaze.

Her heart in her throat, Liz scrambled over the fence.

* * *

The fax machine chattered, stopped. There was an eerie quiet in the house. Something, some residue of country wisdom, made Travis stand and listen.

His curtain fluttered at his open window. A horse screamed in terrible triumph.

Travis's blood ran cold. He raced to his closet, dragged shoes out, stuffed his feet in them. His mind churning as fast as his feet moved, he sprinted out the front door, heading for the corral.

There was dust in the air, he could smell it. The vapor lamp illuminated the yard, the moon shone down over the corral. Inside the enclosure, Blaze reared and bucked. He was out of control, furious with fear and pain, his white coat shining like a beacon.

A dark figure lay crumpled in the corral. Harv wasn't moving or speaking, and his leg was turned out at an impossible angle. He was unconscious. Dead-center in the corral, her slender body interposed between Harv and the horse who wanted to kill him, stood Liz, tall, poised, cool, her only weapon in the battle her low, soothing voice. She had her hand raised to Blaze, as if offering him a treat. Blaze had his ears laid back against his head and his teeth bared.

Travis's heart stopped. He was powerless. If he did what he ached to do, shouted to her to get out of the way and climbed over the corral to push her aside, he risked arousing the stallion to new fury and endangering Liz even more.

"It's all right, baby. It's all right, sweetheart."

There she stood, her hair shining in the moonlight, only her slender, feminine body, her crooning voice and her stunning courage keeping the furious horse at bay, distracting him from the determination to trample the man he hated to death.

Travis could stand it no longer. In the lowest, most controlled tone he could manage, he said, "Come out of there, Liz. Now."

She didn't seem surprised by his presence. She must have heard him on the corral fence. "If you want to help, try to get Harv out the back gate. I think his leg is broken." In the same low tone, she crooned, "It's all right, Blaze. No one is going to hurt you again."

Not true, thought Travis. If that horse harms Liz, he'll be breathing his last.

Travis moved stealthily off the corral fence, aware of the rasp of the wood against his fingers, the vagrant breeze on the back of his neck. Every sense he had was heightened. Slowly he started the circular trip, the endless trip, around the outside of the corral.

Blaze spotted him, jerked his head up and down in response.

"Easy, sweetheart," Liz said soothingly. "That's just Travis. You like him, he pays for the hay you eat."

She actually was making a joke, he thought, his admiration for her soaring to new heights.

"You like all that nice hay, don't you? And the apples I bring you. Then you like Travis. He provides all your food. He's your friend, just as I'm your friend. He won't hurt you, and neither will I. I just want to take you inside the stable and put something on your wounds to stop them from stinging. They hurt, don't they, baby?"

Even while Travis crept along on the outside, his ears, mind and heart were attuned to every nuance of that low voice. If he heard even the slightest bit of fear or panic in it, he was going to be up and over that corral fence like lightning.

He reached the back gate, and told Liz he had.

In the exact same tone in which she'd been talking to

Blaze, Liz said to Travis, "If you lift the gate a little, it won't squeak."

Blaze bobbed his head, snorted, and pranced away from Liz. He made a little circle in the north corner of the corral, reins dangling. He seemed to have lost interest in Harv's motionless body, lying supine in the dust. All his attention and energy were directed toward Liz.

The contrast between her slender, feminine vulnerability and the stallion's male aggression made Travis's throat tight. He had to get her out. He came through the gate and took two steps toward Blaze.

"No." Liz warned him away. "Don't try anything. Let me handle him. He's used to me."

"From the look in his eyes," Travis said, in the same pleasant, soothing tone she was using, "I'd say he's ready to kill anybody who touches him."

"He won't kill me. Don't interfere with me, Travis."

He had little choice but to do as she asked. He could feel his breathing moving his chest, feel his muscles screaming with the need to toss Liz over his shoulder and dump her on the other side of the corral, where she would be safe. That same residue of country wisdom that had brought him out here told him to obey Liz to the letter. He wasn't the cowboy. She was.

"Stay where you are."

"Whatever you say."

Crooning sweetly, Liz took two cautious steps toward Blaze. He was farther away from Harv now, and for that she was grateful. It occurred to her that she was risking Travis's life, as well, asking him to help Harv. The thought lent new urgency to her anxiety, anxiety that she must control.

"Sweetheart, I don't have a treat for you, but I'll certainly get you something when you're safely back in the stable.''

His ears came forward, as if he understood the word *treat*. Liz felt a ripple of relief at that first sign that Blaze's tension was easing. She took another step toward him. He bobbed his head, executed a couple of mincing sideways steps, but made no move to run past her. He seemed to be wearying of the effort it took to resist her. He was more relaxed, his adrenaline flow was ebbing, and he seemed to be feeling the effects of his battle with Harv and his strenuous bucking and rearing.

She knew that if she was too anxiously worried about Travis's safety and conveyed her state of nerves to Blaze, he'd flare out of control again. But she couldn't keep herself from reaching for the rein on the right side of Blaze's head. When she caught it, she trembled with relief. "I have him. Tell me where you are," Liz said to Travis.

"Standing next to Harv."

"Can you move him?"

In the silence, she felt her own breath pause while she listened for the slight sound of Travis's denim whispering as he kelt down to Harv.

"I have him under the arms."

"Try moving him just a little. If he cries out in pain—"

Travis gritted his teeth, thinking that if Harv regained consciousness and made any kind of sound, they'd both be in very deep trouble.

"Sweetheart," Liz said to Blaze. "I'm going to reach for the other rein. It will be all right."

Blaze whinnied furiously and jerked his head back, pulling the first rein out of her grasp.

She stifled a gasp of dismay. "I've lost him."

Travis stilled where he was, Harv heavy in his arms.

Liz clamped her teeth together in frustration. With

Harv's weight on him, Travis was more exposed and vulnerable than she. Blood pulsed in her veins, filling her with panic. She couldn't think, couldn't speak. She had foolishly endangered Travis by letting him come into the corral, and now she'd lost her hold on the rein.

"Talk to him again," Travis ordered in that low tone. "Your voice is magic."

Travis's calm courage brought her out of her state of terror, infused her with renewed determination. She began crooning nonsense to Blaze once again, her voice so loving, low and sweet that the horse allowed her to approach him. She grasped the first rein. He bobbed his head, but she already had the leather wrapped around her wrist. She reached for the second rein, nearly cried with relief when it was safely in her possession.

"I have both reins," she told Travis, her voice breaking. "Can you move him out through the gate now?"

"I'll try."

Liz held Blaze, saw him tremble. She went on talking to him, promising him the moon and the stars if he would just stand quietly. She told him how brave he was and what a strong horse he was and how glad she was that he didn't hurt the man—she didn't dare use Harv's name— and how he would certainly be eating lots of apples in his old age.

The creak of the stable gate—blessed, blessed sound— told her Travis had dragged Harv to safety.

After that, the sights and sounds blurred together in her mind, leading Blaze to his stall, running to get a blanket to cover Harv, calling the ambulance crew, the anxious waiting until the red lights came flashing into the yard, watching the crew check over Harv, now conscious and very much in pain, and ferry him into the ambulance, the installation of Blaze in his stall, seeing to his wounds and giving him water, the trip to the hospital with Travis behind the wheel of Boyd's BMW, Travis's grim face when he strode back into the waiting room toward Liz after he talked to Harv and to the doctor at the local clinic.

"He'll live. He has a slight concussion and a cracked rib on his right side, and his right leg is broken in two places, but both of them are clean breaks. They've already set the leg, and they're in the process of putting him in a cast. I told Harv I'd instructed the desk to send me the clinic's bill, and his check with severance pay would be delivered to him tomorrow."

"Was that all you told him?"

His eyes flashed darkly over her. Her hands felt icy, her cheeks were burning. He seemed to know she was on the edge of shock and needed stimulation. He reached for her hands, gathered them up in his own warm ones.

"No, it wasn't all," he said bluntly. "I told him if he ever came on the place again, I'd break his other leg." A timed pause. "In two places."

She laughed. She couldn't help it. It was nervous laughter, tension-breaking laughter, relieved laughter.

There was tension of another kind in the car on the way home. Travis was quiet, his darkly beautiful face pensive in the lights of the dash as she rode beside him. She didn't know what he was thinking.

At the ranch, he got out of the car, while she opened her door and put suddenly shaky legs on the ground. He was at her side instantly, grasping her elbow, steadying her. He didn't say a word as he walked her to her door.

"Will you be all right?" He looked so gravely concerned, so dear, so beautiful. She thought about how he had listened to her out there in the corral—and trusted her.

She wanted to say yes, she meant to say yes, but she shook her head, gave him a brave half laugh, half sob that went straight to his heart. "You won't shoot Blaze, will you?"

He made a sound of exasperated tenderness. "Woman, you are impossible. That horse put you through hell."

"So have you, and nobody's shot you yet."

On a choked laugh, he pulled her into his arms.

Chapter Ten

"Are you all right?" Liz asked Travis in that moon-scented night. His dark head stayed bowed, his face buried in her hair. His skin smelled clean, soapy, fragrant with his own special scent. Liz felt as if she were drowning in him.

"No." His soft laughter feathered through her hair, tickled her ear. "I doubt if I'll ever be quite all right again."

His voice was so close that the words seemed to be vibrating in her chest. His arms were warm and his body was hard and male. Very definitely male. He had lowered the wall. She didn't know why or how, she only knew that he had. And he was giving her a glimpse of heaven.

"You won't destroy Blaze, will you?"

"What a single-minded woman." He sounded caught between amusement and resignation. "No," he said, "I won't shoot your horse."

"He's not my horse—" She lifted away from him, her

heart anxious to make him see that she wasn't trying to usurp ownership of Blaze—or claim anything else that didn't belong to her.

"Yes," he said, "he is." To Travis, it seemed that, on this night, everything belonged to her, this woman with the flame-red hair and the cream-sweet skin. Even his soul. But he knew what she was thinking. She was thinking about Andrew. And so was he. He closed his eyes, waiting for the pain. It didn't come, not now, not standing locked in the arms of this beautiful, strong, courageous woman. She made him want to speak of Andrew. She made him want to bring his brother's presence into this moon-bright night. This woman who'd had the courage to save a man's life, and now was fighting for the life of Andrew's horse, made it seem as if anything were possible on this night. Even his absolution from guilt. He said, "Do you know why we call him Blaze?"

"No, I don't."

"Dad told Andrew he could name the horse. Andrew had read a book about a horse named Blaze, and that was the name he wanted. I explained to my little brother that the horse should be black with a white spot in his forehead to be called Blaze. Andrew didn't care. He just shook his head and said that was what he wanted to call his horse. I can remember the way his face looked yet. Stubborn little cuss." He smiled, remembering. And watched Liz's lovely mouth curve up in an answering smile.

He wanted, needed, to tell her the truth. "I haven't been able to talk about Andrew. Not until...you."

"I know that you've blamed yourself for not stopping him, but it wasn't your fault," she said quickly, "and you must remember that. Feeling guilty has made it hard for you to talk about him. We must always remember him and speak of the things he said and did," she said softly, "so that his spirit will live on. If you let go of your guilt, you'll be better able to keep his memory alive.''

As if in agreement, the wind sighed in the trees, whispered secrets and wandered away, leaving the air calm and still. All that was left for Liz in the night air was love. Her love, and Travis's, for Andrew. Her love for the man who held her so tenderly, who cared so much for Andrew that he had tortured himself for being the brother who was still alive.

She didn't know if her words had begun the process of healing for Travis. She didn't need to know. The recesses of his heart did not belong to her. They must remain his and his alone. She only knew that he was listening to her with his heart. That was all she could ask of him.

No, there was more she could ask of him. And of herself. The night was honest. So must she be. She could not speak of her love, but she could show him.

She became like the wind, pliable, seeking, her slender body yielding to his, wanting to heal him, give him everything, all that she was.

His warm hands captured her cheeks, and she felt the weight of each of his fingers, the tips speared into her hair, the slight rasp of his palm. He murmured, "I don't have the words to tell you the things I want to say. I want to tell you that you're the most amazing woman I've ever known, but it doesn't seem…enough.''

"Oh, it's enough.'' Her voice was husky with a breathless laugh.

"I want…more. I want more from myself…for you. You deserve the best of me.''

Liz felt a sensation entirely new to her, a sense of her power meeting his, so that their strengths entwined. She knew with glorious surety that she was the perfect complement for him. For the first time in his life, Travis seemed to recognize it, too. The heat burning inside her compelled her to press her hips against his and issue the age-old invitation to the ultimate intimacy. "I've always had the best of you, your consideration, your caring. But I...want more. I suppose a lady shouldn't admit that she wants a certain man terribly to make love with her, but I've wanted to be with you for so long—"

"Oh, sweetheart, most ladies wouldn't be so honest. But most ladies don't have your intestinal fortitude." His voice was a low rasp of sound, an agonized reaching for control.

She didn't want his control. "Do you like ladies with intestinal fortitude?"

"I never knew how much I liked a certain one until just now."

She met his eyes, let her love shine from hers with bright, clear truth. She offered all that she was, knowing that if he didn't accept her now, he never would, and her heart would be truly broken.

He made a sound, a low groan filled with amusement, reluctance, desire. When she was thinking that she couldn't breathe and she might possibly die if he put her out of his arms, the moon disappeared behind his dark head and his warm mouth settled on hers.

He wouldn't make love to her. But one small kiss would be harmless, there in that quiet, star-glittered night. He simply wanted to prolong the moment of profound intimacy by touching his mouth to hers—and perhaps give her a tender reward for her courage. One kiss, to taste the laughter on her mouth and keep that whole sky of stars shining in her eyes.

Travis's mouth was heaven, warm and strong. Tender, too, and far too restrained. A fierce wildness rose in Liz. She took his mouth with blatant eagerness and clutched him close, told him with her mouth and her body that she didn't want his consideration, that she had waited too long for him and she didn't want to wait any longer.

For that agonizing instant, he seemed stunned by her response. Thoroughly impatient now, wanting him to understand quite clearly that there would be no turning back this time, she tugged his shirt from the back of his pants and slid her hands between his waistband and his bare back.

The touch of her fingers on his naked skin tossed Travis over the edge. Hunger exploded in him, and he kissed her with passion unleashed, his body moving to shelter her inside his arms, his leg finding a home between her thighs.

Travis was tormented by a thousand sensations, the scent of her hair, the softness of her breasts, the provocative curve of her hips tucked against his. When she lifted her head and her eyes met his, he felt the electric excitement coursing through her. His own level of excitement soared, as if he'd suddenly touched a thousand volts of power.

"Would you like to come in for coffee?"

Coffee. He didn't know whether to laugh or hug her tighter. Surely he hadn't misunderstood her invitation. He nuzzled his face in her hair to hide the smile on his lips from her, but the humor lurked in his voice. "If I came in for coffee, your clothes would be scattered all over the floor and you'd find out what it was like to lay on top of the kitchen table naked."

"Well, we can't have such disregard for order and neatness. What would you suggest as an alternative?" She met his boldness with green eyes sparkling and alive with desire, her body tingling with excitement at the sheer fun of talking about sex with him.

"We could save a lot of time by starting upstairs," he said. He lifted away from her and smiled. He was giving her the tiny breather she'd hoped to gain by offering him coffee, and she loved him all the more for understanding.

"And keep the house much neater, too."

"I'm a great believer in neatness," he said.

"I know. Anybody who rearranges his sock drawer every Sunday night—"

"That is the last straw, woman. Expect retribution very soon." The husky words were tantalizing.

"Promises, promises." She marveled at her ability to reciprocate his sexual teasing with words that were just as provocative.

He turned her around and gave her a playful pat on the rear, guiding her up the steps of the porch toward the front door, his arm comfortably around her waist. "I'll have you know I don't rearrange my sock drawer every Sunday. I'm cutting down. Once a month is my limit now."

"There. A reformed man. I always knew I liked you."

"I never realized what a gift you were giving me until tonight."

She rewarded his serious, vulnerable words with a kiss.

This time, he forgot restraint. He took her mouth with precise and rhythmic intensity, just as he had that night on the street in Sioux Falls. She shifted her weight slightly to absorb his passion, and he caught her closer, taking what he wanted to take, what she needed to give.

"Sweetheart, if you don't move very soon, there will be clothes all over the porch."

Smiling, the excitement fizzing through her like lightning, she turned to open the door and invite him in.

Liz tried to hang on to the humor, the tenderness, the intimacy, but suddenly she was alone with him in the darkness and his hand was heavy and warm on her waist, just below her breast, and she knew that soon her clothes would be gone, and he would be touching her bare body, exploring her as she had often dreamed he would do. This was not a dream, this was reality, and Travis was an experienced man, while she...

Walking ahead of Travis into her room took all the courage she had. He was as quiet as she was. Was he thinking that he'd been moonstruck, that he really didn't want to make love to the little country girl he'd known all his life?

Travis reached for the chain on the lamp beside her bed and pulled it. Into the light sprang the bedroom of a girl, not a woman. She who hated change made her dolls comfortable on her pillows during the day while she was working. There was a bride doll without the veil, torn off by a ten-year-old impatient to see her face, a gypsy with a green-and-red skirt embroidered in black, a teddy bear who had no fur left on his chest.

"I suppose I'd better move these." She snatched up the bride doll. Tenderly Travis plucked it from her hand. "You can change your mind, Liz."

"Maybe I can, but I'm not going to. And don't you dare be scared off by a couple of dolls."

His smile was a flash of white against the tanned skin of his face. "I'll try not to let them get the best of me." He turned around and set her bride doll on the rocking chair near the bed.

She wrapped her arms around his waist, pulling him against her, his back against her breasts.

He covered her hands with his. "Not quite so brave after all?"

"Scared I won't be good enough."

He turned around in her arms, caught her chin and tilted her face up to his. "It isn't a contest. It's just you and me, being together for the first time, recognizing what we should have known long ago, that we need to be together. All right?"

Her throat full, she nodded.

He smiled at her then, and his arms enclosed her, and he carried her down on the bed with him.

The weight of him, and the hardness of his body, told Liz of Travis's need, but his hands were tender, and so was his mouth. When he lifted away from their first kiss on the bed, with their bodies touching, he gazed down at her. Close. It was wonderful to be close to him, to feel every part of his body, to see his face so near her own. The soft light in the room clung to the beautiful planes of his cheek and jaw.

She had wondered forever what it would be like to be with Travis. Now she saw that it was simple. There was no awkwardness in the slow undoing of her buttons. It might have been what she was born for, to watch his face darken with desire as he spread the cloth apart and looked at her bra-covered breasts. Cool air rushed over her skin. Did he like what he saw? Needing assurance, she reached up to trace the bones of his cheek, threaded her hand back through his dark hair. It felt silken and heavy under her fingers.

"Am I...all right?"

"Not quite yet."

"What's wrong with me?"

His mouth tipped up in a beautifully sensual smile. "You're wearing too many clothes." He said the words with a low intensity that was like music to her ears.

"I'm sorry I don't have on something lacy—"

He leaned over and stopped her words with his mouth, and his hands deftly found and unclasped the front catch. "You don't need lace. You don't need anything to look beautiful. Your body is superb. Lift up, sweetheart."

And then he drew her clothes away, and she lay bare before him, with her heart throbbing in her chest. He leaned forward and kissed her gently on the breast and put his hand on her breastbone, as if he knew what she was feeling and wanted to absorb her quickening beat of life. She lost her heart even more to him for touching her so sweetly, so gently. Then he cupped her breast, and she lost all thought of sweetness and gentleness. She wanted to rise wildly on the lift of her feelings, she wanted to soar. He was helping her fly, murmuring love words that made no sense and yet seemed vivid and haunting, halting her restless seeking for that unnameable place and showing her what it would be like if he took her there with his mouth, his hands. Then the rest of her clothes were gone and so were his, and he gave her the freedom to touch. She took it, discovering the beauty of his muscle and skin and bone, beauty that she had long memorized with her eyes and now had the luxury to explore. She felt like a child who'd been given the moon. She heard him breathing, felt the wisp of a breeze on her bare skin, felt the heat growing, the flames fanned by his mouth on her breast, his hand inside her. Sweet and intimate and hot and glowing, his touch was, making her ache and want. She reached for him and found his silky smoothness. His eyes flared darkly, and she was filled with pleasure to see her effect on him.

The ache and the need spiraled higher, and she moved restlessly in his arms.

It felt so fresh and new to him, as if he'd never held a woman in his arms before, never been caught in a room with light and shadow and cool and heat, never been suspended on the knife edge between need and satiation. Perhaps he never had. Not like this. Not with such a completeness, a feeling of aching want and content mixed together. He touched her breast, explored the rosy tip, leaned forward to savor it with his mouth, felt her writhe at the pleasure from his double onslaught of lips and hands.

It was then, with this lovely, strong woman on the brink of surrender to him that he remembered. He pulled away from her and rolled over on his back, an arm flung up over his forehead.

"What is it?"

He shook his head. "I've been a stupid idiot." He thought of the irony of it, and his mouth turned up in a rueful smile. He'd been so sure when he returned home the second time from Chicago that he was in control of himself and that this wouldn't happen that he was unprepared. "Sweetheart, I am so sorry—"

"It's all right." She rose with a grace that he had to admire, her slender body as curvaceous as Venus's, and went to the small nightstand beside her bed, where she withdrew a small package and returned to place it in his hand.

"I want you to know that these aren't—this isn't something I keep on hand. I bought these the day after Boyd told me you were coming home for the wedding. I didn't think anything would happen between us, but in case it did, I wanted to be prepared."

"You country women are smart, as well as beautiful." He pulled her down into his arms and kissed her.

"We do know a little something about breeding."

"You also know something about good breeding." He rolled her over onto her back, caught up a toe, pressed it to his mouth, made her shiver with electric shock, with laughter. He explored her knee with his mouth, the inside of her thigh. Then he spread her legs and knelt between her bare thighs, his eyes watching hers as he unfolded the condom from the package.

"Help me," he said.

She shook her head, her courage failing her. His eyes dark with challenge, he took her hand and guided her trembling fingers to him. Silently, without self-consciousness, he showed her how to sheathe him. When she had finished, he gathered up her shaky and newly experienced hand and brought it to his mouth. Gently he kissed her wrist. Then his tongue came out, and he made her palm warm and moist. While her head was reeling with the intimacy and the flare of feeling in every part of her body, he knelt to her and parted her legs and made that most intimate part of her as moist and wet as he had made her palm.

With his slow, knowledgeable and willing mouth, he tortured her, making her burn and ache and need and want.

Travis felt her turning to flame under his mouth, and the fire rose in him. He was going up in flames with her.

When her hands clasped his shoulders, tugging him toward her, he could bear the sweet torture no longer. He began to sheathe himself in her body—and even while her sweet tightness made his body ache to take more, he encountered the barrier he had never expected to feel.

"Liz, sweetheart, love—" He held himself in tortured abeyance.

"No," she whispered. "No. Please. You mustn't stop now."

He held her close, wishing there was some way he could lessen her discomfort and knowing the only way was to be quick. He thrust deeply into her, finding the center of her, that molten core that would be his ultimate satiety, his soul and heart knowing that he had been a fool to think he would find her otherwise than this. Her gift to him was complete.

The thought of her keeping herself for him nearly sent him over the edge into climax. He exerted iron control, gritting his teeth to keep from acting like an unschooled boy. But his heart swelled within him, even as he lifted himself away from her a bit to brush a strand of that fiery hair away from her cheek, and the fierce possessiveness he felt for her overwhelmed him as he looked down into those shining green eyes. *Mine.*

"You should have told me." He tapped her lightly on her nose in loving censure, thinking that he had never seen a more beautifully serene face in his life.

"Why? If you didn't make love to me, there was no need. And if you did, you'd find out."

"Practical," he murmured.

"Sneaky," she said, and her smile went straight to his soul.

"This is how it feels, then," she said.

He examined her face for signs of discomfort and self-consciousness. He found neither. He saw only a woman who appeared shamelessly pleased with herself. And with him. "Yes," he said.

A soft look of love crossed her face, a look that enchanted him.

She said, "I like the way it feels." And she wiggled a bit, making him like the way it felt even better.

His mouth curved. "Do you indeed?"

"Do you like the way it feels?"

"Yes, ma'am."

His tone was deeply sensual. Liz luxuriated in the feel of him, the sound of him.

When she reached up and traced the curve of his mouth with her fingertip, she made Travis think of wanting to love her again and again. He decided he must be the most possessive man on this side of the moon. For even though he was fitted snugly inside her, all he could think of was how long he could make it last without causing her discomfort, and how soon he could be with her again.

He knew these were thoughts he shouldn't be having, but her finger had gone on exploring his mouth, his nose, his ear, and there was a subtle movement in her hips that indicated she was discovering the full range of her feminine power. He let her glory in her newfound skill, murmuring to her that she was to have the freedom to touch him anywhere and everywhere she liked.

An impish light in her eyes, she dropped her hands to his buttocks. "You never did tell me if you had need of that bag balm."

"See for yourself."

She explored, finding a curve of smooth skin covering a muscle-hard flank.

"I guess you didn't need it. Oh, well, it's the thought that counts." She gave him a saucy grin.

"Indeed," he murmured dryly into her ear. Her light touch was torture. Her butterfly fingers seemed to be everywhere, on his spine, his shoulder blades, learning his backside much too intimately. He swallowed once and reached behind to capture that teasing hand, bringing it up to his mouth to tongue lightly between her fingers, administering his own torture. Then he found another way to tease her, withdrawing himself from her and then returning to probe delicately in the most sensitive, feminine place. She closed her eyes, reveling in the sensuous pleasure of giving her body up to him to do with as he would.

Her surrender ignited the fire deep inside him, and he could no longer tease. He thrust deeply, taking her again and yet again, watching her face, watching her lift her chin in ecstatic pleasure. Time stopped for him, and for her. They were caught together in the ancient art of giving and receiving, until at last he knew her release was inevitable and he loosened his control to drop over the edge with her.

She recovered from her drowsy satiety to find him leaning over her with a cool cloth in his hand. She might have been embarrassed to have him act as her servant, but he wore that serious look of concentration as he cleansed her legs and toweled her dry that made her feel self-consciousness would somehow be out of place. And so she lay there and let him tend to her, thinking that this man was worthy of all the love she had held in her heart for him.

"Are you hurting?" He looked gravely serious, attentive.

"I...feel different. Not hurting exactly, just...sensitive."

Without changing his expression, he dropped a kiss on her knee and turned around to stroll back to the bathroom.

He was splendid in his nudity, the more so to Liz because she had touched and explored that taut body and knew of the delights and pleasures it held.

When he returned, he reached down for the sheet and covered her while he looked soberly down at her. She caught his hand. "Stay with me."

He looked as if he wanted to say no. "For a while," he said.

He lay down beside her, knowing he shouldn't, knowing that soon, very soon, he would want her again.

Liz wondered if it would always be this way with him, that Travis would try to put boundaries on what he was feeling. Those boundaries had dropped for a little while, she knew they had. Perhaps they would again.

She felt oddly hesitant and shy about touching him again, but when he turned toward her and pulled her into his arms, she snuggled up against him, his arm around her, her bare breasts against his chest, her hand on the smooth, rounded jut of his hipbone. *Mine,* she thought. *I've waited so long, and I'm so glad I did.*

Travis felt the light pressure of her slender fingers on his hipbone and gazed at his lover. Her eyes were closed, those dark auburn lashes curved against her cheek. Her hair was beautifully mussed, lying around her head in a cloud of rich, silken red and gold. He wondered at the courage and strength of this woman, the resilience of her. He drew the sheet down a bit, just to look at her. His eyes were hungry for her, and his body, though sated, remembered how it was to be with her...and began to grow hungry again. Still, he wouldn't disturb her. She looked so peaceful....

She might look peaceful, with that angelic face and those closed eyes, but her hand had wandered and found him. Her light touch sent a jolt of pleasure through him.

With one quick movement, he pulled her over on top of him, only meaning to startle her a little and take his revenge against those marauding fingers. Those green eyes flashed open, and devil lights danced in them. Her smooth, beautiful breasts lay crushed against his bare chest, exactly where he liked them.

"You need to be taken in hand, lady."

Travis's eyes held the slumberous look of a man caught between satiety and desire. His dark eyes captured the lamplight, absorbed it.

"And you think you're the man for the job."

"Yes."

"No equivocation, no hesitation. I like that in a man."

"What else do you like in a man?"

"Action," she said, those devilish eyes playing over his face with supreme confidence.

He smoothed back the hair that hung like a red-gold curtain around her face. "Sweetheart, I need to be careful with you. This was your first time. I don't want to hurt you—"

"You won't hurt me. You could never hurt me. Please, Travis. Make love with me again."

And so he demonstrated that he was, indeed, a man of action.

He asked, "Will you take a shower with me?"

Another first for her, but one she couldn't refuse. "Yes," she said throatily.

Shyness overtook her as he held out his hand to pull her out of bed. She tried to tell herself as she walked ahead of him that there was nothing left about her body for him to learn, yet to stand in the brightly lit bathroom and have him lovingly wrap her hair in a towel with the same sober concentration she'd seen on his face when he was cleansing her gave her such a jolt of pleasure that she had to duck her head to hide her face from him. And, of course, the towel promptly unfolded from her head. He simply rewrapped the towel. Then, as if he knew what she was feeling, he kissed her. She found herself kissing him back, standing on tiptoe, drowning in the feeling of pressing her bare breasts against his chest, reveling in the fit of their bare hips locked together.

"Careful, sweetheart."

She drew away at once. "Did I hurt you?"

His curved mouth and the state of his body told her what she had done.

"Oh," she said.

"Oh, indeed."

"You— It seems easy for you to...again..." She stumbled to a stop, thinking there were things she didn't know how to say to him.

"Yes, as long as you stand there looking like Aphrodite rising from the sea, *it's* very easy for me."

The shower had been installed inside the claw-footed bathtub, in a circular ring. He drew back the curtain and held her hand while she climbed inside, then followed her in.

He turned on the water. The shower curtain clung to her backside. "It wasn't meant for two," she said, a little breathlessly.

"All the better to wash you with, my dear. Stand closer."

She hesitated. The shower curtain clung again.

His eyes on hers, he picked up the soap and pulled her close, soaping her while he held her in his arms.

The slippery soapiness of his hands on her skin made her more intensely aware than ever of her breasts, her nipples, her thighs. Nothing escaped his tender ministrations.

He tipped the soap into her hand. "Your turn."

She couldn't refuse a new way to explore his body. She was buffeted by a surfeit of sensation, soap and curly hair and skin and hard muscle and bone. And it came to her then that she must remember everything, every minute of sweet revelation, for soon her day in the sun would be over and she would step out into the cold.

His attention to her continued as he toweled her off and unwrapped her hair. He picked up her brush from the counter, and again looking like a sober servant dedicated to his job, ran the brush through her hair. It spun out and clung to him, and Liz thought, every part of me loves and needs him.

Back in the bedroom, he pulled the chain on the lamp to fill the room with starshine and lay down on the bed with her and tucked her under his arm.

Liz was sure she wouldn't sleep a wink locked so close to Travis's bare body, her own tingling with a thousand sensations of water and soap and love. Surely she would stay awake and remember, remember. Travis had already slipped into sleep, his breathing slow and even, when she heard the clock chime three times. It would be lovely to close her eyes, just close her eyes for a little bit....

She awoke to a room full of sunshine and warmth and a bed with tousled sheets and only her own bare body inside them. Eyes closed, she stretched to full torsion, feeling the slide of the cotton against her sensitized breasts. This was what it felt like to be loved by Travis....

"Good morning." His low, deep voice brought her eyes flashing open. Travis stood beside the bed, fully dressed in dark jeans that were already dusty and a blue work shirt with the sleeves rolled halfway up, his blue bandanna tied around his brown throat. He held hat and gloves in his hand, and his dark hair was mussed. "I trust it is a good morning," he said, with a faint amusement touching his voice, curving his lips.

"It's an excellent morning. Why didn't you wake me?"

He tucked his gloves in the crown of his hat and tossed it on her nightstand. "I thought you needed your sleep. You had a rather...busy night." Those brown eyes raked her face. "You seem to have weathered it with no ill effects."

"I feel wonderful," she said, and blushed.

He'd sworn he wasn't going to touch her. He'd check on her and see that she was all right and then he'd go. But Travis found himself sitting down on the bed and reaching out with his hand to trace the curve of her lovely cheek. "You look wonderful," he said.

"Thank you."

"You're welcome." He smiled at her. When she flashed her uninhibited, glorious smile back at him, he felt his body tighten instantly, as if last night had prepared him, and now there was no thought needed, his body had glimpsed paradise and wanted more.

Fool.

He collected himself and stood up. Her face lost its sunshine.

He heard himself ask, "Is anything wrong?"

Her chin came up. He braced himself.

She said, "Perhaps I should ask you if you're suffering any ill effects?" Her pride shone in her eyes, in the way she hitched herself up in bed and covered her breasts with the sheet.

His eyes locked on hers, he leaned forward, drew down the sheet and kissed her on the rosy tip of her breast. Her sharp intake of breath gave him inordinate pleasure. "Not a one," he said, doing his best to look blithely unconcerned about the turmoil he knew he'd caused in her, pulling the sheet up over her and raising his head to meet her eyes again.

"You need taking in hand," she said.

"Are you woman enough to do it?" he asked, one eyebrow arched in mock arrogance.

"Yes." Boldly she reached up and caught the end of his blue bandanna. "I want another kiss, cowboy."

"I'm not a cowboy, but since I seem to be the only one in the room, I'll be glad to oblige the lady."

He leaned forward to brush her mouth lightly, but she guessed his intent and pulled harder, bringing him down on the bed and more under her control. She kissed him eagerly, her hands cupping the back of his head.

"Two can play at this game," he murmured, and pushed her back against the pillows. "You are something else, do you know that? I swore I wasn't going to touch you this morning."

"It's not nice to swear."

"But you are nice." He rubbed a finger over the round curve of her bare shoulder. "Very nice. If I told you exactly how nice, you'd be unbearable to live with. I couldn't do that to Rachel.''

"So considerate." She captured a lock of that straight, dark hair and tugged.

"Ouch," he said, in exaggerated reaction. "And here I came upstairs to tell you that the coffee's made, and I'd bring you some if you wanted it."

"Umm, sexual prowess, and at home in the kitchen, too. You'd make some woman a wonderful—" she slammed to a halt, her eyes catching the look in his "—cook."

If he noticed her near faux pas, he gave no sign of it. She moved closer for another kiss. What she got was a light tap on the thigh. He said, "If you plan on getting out of bed before noon, you'd better get at it."

The familiar sound of a car's tires crunching over the gravel in the yard was entirely unexpected. "Who just came in?"

Travis lifted the lace curtain with a strong brown hand. "It looks like your mother and my father have come home from the hospital."

Liz screamed and tossed the covers back, while he turned, leaned back against the wall and gave her that maddening, poised smile. She snatched up her bra and turned her back to him, but couldn't hook the front hook with her trembling fingers.

"Here," he said easily, coming around to face her and catching the sides of her bra in his capable hands. "Allow me."

He fastened her bra deftly, then stood with his arms folded, exuding that infuriating calmness, while she pawed frantically through her drawer for panties.

"You need to do some rearranging of your own," he drawled.

She found a pair, slipped into them. "You're so help-ful," she said.

"I try to be. I'm just not appreciated." He went to the closet, found a blouse, helped her slide her arms into it and carefully closed each button for her. "Relax. We'll both emerge from the house fully dressed. That is, if you can calm down."

He leaned forward and brushed a kiss on her lips, which didn't help to calm her at all. He said, "Will you be upset having your mother see us together?"

"No, of course not, it's just that—"

He gave her a light tap on her mouth with one fingertip, stopping her words. "Never mind. If you don't get so ex-cited that you walk out of the house with your bottom as bare as a baby's, we might just pull this off. Give me a head start, hmm?"

Fully dressed, Liz stood at the window of her room with one hand on the lace curtain and watched him stroll across the yard to greet Rachel. He was the picture of a cool, insouciant male. He even had a coffee cup in his hand.

Liz shook her head, marveling at his poise, and tried to regain her own as she bounded down the stairs, two at a time.

They were in the kitchen of the big house, Rachel, Travis leaning back against the counter in the place Liz thought of as her own, and Boyd, seated in a wheelchair. Travis's father looked uncharacteristically pale, but he was smiling. He held a coffee cup in his hand, too.

Her mother's eyes and face betrayed the tension she had endured. The lines in her forehead seemed etched a little deeper, as did the ones around her mouth. But she looked happy to be back in her element, bustling around the kitchen to get the cream for Boyd's coffee out of the re-frigerator, while she urged Travis to have a cinnamon roll.

Rachel glanced up, saw Liz, came forward to enfold her daughter in her arms. "It's so good to be home," she whispered in Liz's ear.

"It's good to have you home."

Liz went to Boyd, leaned over and kissed his cheek. "You look fine. Are you sure you didn't go to the hospital just to ask those pretty nurses to vote for you in the next election?"

Boyd laughed. "We were just telling Travis that he's in for another wedding," he said, his eyes on Rachel.

Liz's eyes flashed to Travis's face, caught the slight nod of his head, the tug of a smile on his mouth.

"What did Travis say?" Liz asked.

"He said he didn't think his heart would take it. I assured him it would be a small affair, nothing like we put on for Diana."

"So who is the lucky lady?" Liz asked, knowing he wanted to tell her as if it were a surprise.

Boyd's eyebrows flew up in mock surprise. "Why, your mother, of course. Who else? Now, my son, that leaves you as the only single member of this family. When are you going to get busy?"

Travis made an elaborate show of looking at his watch. "You just beat Rachel's top time of one minute and fifteen seconds in getting to the discussion of my marital status, Dad. You came in at slightly under a minute."

"Continuity, son. Continuity and family. Those are the things that really matter in a man's life. That's what this little trip to the hospital taught me." There was a pause. Boyd looked down at his hands. Liz watched him, breath held. He said, "I'm not going to be running for office next year. I'll leave that to the younger men who think it's important." He reached for Rachel. She came to him, tears shining in her eyes. "I found out what was important to me. Not a minute too soon, either."

Liz watched Travis carefully for some sign of displeasure, but she saw none. Travis had on the cool, noncommittal face that he wore so well, his arms folded over his chest, his body relaxed.

"How are things going here?" Boyd asked Travis, his hand still holding tightly to Rachel's.

"We're haying this morning." No betraying flick of a teasing eye did he send Liz's way. "I've put Craig Seaton in charge, as we discussed. He seems to be handling everything well." Travis straightened away from the counter. "Now that you're home and Seaton appears to have things in hand, I'll be going back to Chicago in a day or two."

Liz felt Rachel's anxious gaze on her, but she held her smile in place.

"You must do what you think best, son. I've kept you from your work long enough."

"You'll let me know when you've set the date for your wedding."

"Of course we will," Rachel said warmly.

"If you'll excuse me, then—" Catching her eye for one small, electric moment, Travis dipped his head and went out the kitchen door, closing the screen quietly behind him.

Chapter Eleven

There was only that one small electric moment, one sizzle of lightning, one shared lovers' look between his brown eyes and her green ones in the kitchen, where so many momentous moments in Liz's life seemed to have taken place. Then there was nothing.

The next day, they were both working with the haying crew, she driving the tractor and watching the bales of green hay tumbling into the wagon, while he, bare-chested in the heat, wielded the hay hook and arranged the bales on the wagon. The whole time, Travis treated her with a generic politeness that made her skin prickle more fiercely than the pesky stems of dried hay that would trickle down under her collar to the small of her back.

Liz kept thinking of that moment in the kitchen, remembering how his gaze, a lover's look, had brought a tingle to her arms, and a stinging longing to her body. Today, his hair was damp, brown and satiny, a result of being slicked back quickly under the outdoor tap. She wanted to touch him with a violent longing. And couldn't.

All during that sweltering summer day, that one electric moment in time seemed to be all she was meant to have. Her heart ached for Travis to talk to her, to look at her, and she could think of nothing else, no matter how hard she worked in the evening, helping her mother prepare the supper meal, peeling potatoes by the pound, her face steamy from the heat of stovetop and oven.

But it was not to be. Not once during the supper meal did he look her way.

She knew the truth then. He was leaving, and he didn't want to hurt her by giving her false hopes and making her believe that he had come to care for her.

There must be a way to love Travis and let him go. She'd thought she could do that.

She realized now that letting Travis walk out of her life would be more difficult than she had ever dreamed.

That night in bed, Liz acknowledged the heartbreaking truth, that there was nothing to keep Travis on the ranch, no flood, no famine, no disaster with Blaze. Soon, very soon, the day after next, he would be gone. And she would be left to deal with a heart and body that had known the delights of his loving.

She wrestled the sheets aside. She felt it like a fire inside her, the need to be with him again, to feel his arms around her, to feel the soft warmth of his breath on her face, see his eyes glow in the lamplight, so darkly brown and burnished with passion, the way they had been when he entered her, when she belonged to him and he to her.

She would miss him so desperately when he left. And yet there were questions in her mind. Suppose the impossible happened and he asked her to come with him. Would she have the courage to leap off the edge of the world?

How could she? She didn't belong in his world. Her trip to the city to retrieve him had shown her that.

Silly to think about what *might* happen. The question hadn't come up yet. And it never would.

Travis ripped the sheet of paper out of the printer. He'd looked forward to these nights when the ranch quieted and he was able to work. Not anymore. Now his thoughts were on that little house sheltered under the cottonwood trees at the opposite end of the yard.

He remembered the bed tucked under the eaves, the sweet body he'd tasted there. What was he going to do about Elizabeth Annabell Grant?

He knew what he wanted to do about her. He wanted to go to her and bury himself in her softness, re-create the wild excitement and the sweet contentment that only she could give. He wanted her now, and he'd still want her a hundred years from now. He knew that, knew it with every fiber of his being. But he couldn't have her, mustn't have her. He hadn't done well with people who put their lives in his keeping.

He turned back to his computer, wishing to hell that he could concentrate on the work that needed to be done.

On the second evening, when the day's work was done and Travis strolled into the bunkhouse behind the rest of the crew, the smell of sun-dried hay clinging to his clothes, his face deeply tanned, the dark hairs on the backs of his arms showing tips of sun-streaked gold, Liz had the misfortune to follow in behind him. She headed for the trestle table, concentrating all her effort on balancing a tray full of serving dishes of creamed peas and potatoes and a platter of ear corn, while her unwilling arms and knees went to jelly. But her eyes *would* cling to the dark, curling hairs dampened with perspiration at the nape of Travis's neck, examine the movement of his lean hips under blue denim.

The tray teetered, putting the corn in dire danger of tumbling to the floor. Travis, alerted by the sound of clinking dishes, reached for the tray, his mouth lifting in a smile. Just when she thought her heart would stop at the sheer beauty of his dark face, he turned and set the tray easily on the table.

"Thanks," she said, in a breathless tone, to his back.

"You're welcome." He smiled at her.

It was a polite smile, nothing more. But the sound of his voice set up tremors deep within her.

Travis inserted himself in the bench seat with that lazy grace that was his and accepted the roll plate that was being handed around. Liz remembered where those hands had been, what they had done, she remembered how those long legs had tangled with hers, she remembered how the muscles in his back had felt like sheathed steel under her fingers. With a hot face, she seated herself at the table, quite sure she wouldn't be able to eat a thing. Aware of March's quick quizzical glance, which switched to unconcern in a flash of an eye, and her mother's curious glance, Liz said, "Please pass the corn."

March choked on his food. "Mr. Seaton's an expert on corn—corny jokes that is—he'll git it for you."

The joke of course, went over Craig's head, yet he knew that March was teasing him. He flushed, but reached for the dish of ear corn and good-naturedly smiled at Liz.

"If Craig is an expert on corn, you must be an expert on ham," Travis told March, sober-faced.

March laughed and slapped his leg. "Reckon I deserved that."

It was when they had returned to the kitchen and were finishing the cleaning up that her mother said with a studied nonchalance, "You haven't had a chance to have a good visit with Boyd. Go along now and have a little chat with him before he gets tired and has to go to bed." Liz opened her mouth to protest that there was more food to put away and she should stay until the work was done, but her mother anticipated her. "Go on now. Scoot."

It wasn't a strange request—she'd always liked Boyd and had a good relationship with him—but there was something about the expression on her mother's face...

Boyd wasn't an invalid, he'd been moving about the house cautiously, but he tired easily, and he was sitting in his favorite chair in the living room, his cane on the floor beside him. Behind him, the fireplace opening had been shielded by a wicker screen, and the philodendrons her mother loved grew in profusion in front of it. On the mantel sat the trophies Andrew had won for showing his prize calves at the fair, seven of them.

"He won the first one when he was eleven," Boyd said, his eyes following Liz's to that row of shiny cups. "He had an eye for prize-winning cattle."

"And horses," Liz said.

"He was a good lad."

"He had a good father."

His eyes glistened, but he reached for control. "I sense that some healing has been going on here while I was doing my own in the hospital. I'm talking about Travis, young woman."

As if she needed to study the trophies more closely, she went to the fireplace, putting Boyd at her right side. She didn't know what he was going to say. Too late, she remembered where Travis had acquired his astuteness. "I hope so, sir."

She turned, her hand dropping from the mantel in an unconsciously graceful gesture.

"I think you might have had something to do with that."

"Travis told me the story of how Blaze got his name. We talked about Andrew, about how...determined he was."

Boyd smiled. "How diplomatic you are. I think you mean stubborn. He certainly was...determined. Your mother had her hands full with him. But she managed. She always did." Boyd gazed past her, to a place behind her, his face thoughtful. "I never imagined the day would be so long in coming when Travis would forgive me—and himself. But now it has, thanks in no small measure, I'm sure, to you, young lady."

"I didn't do anything, really...."

Boyd held up his hand. "Travis told me how you saved Lester's life. I'm eternally grateful to you for that. Young fool! He certainly pulled the wool over my eyes. That doesn't happen too often."

"I'm sure it doesn't," she murmured.

He shook his head. "And I'm an old fool. I didn't ask you to come to see me to talk about Andrew or even our impetuous young scalawag, Lester. I wanted to reassure myself that you have no qualms about my marrying your mother."

Tears sprang to her eyes. She went to Boyd and knelt down in front of him, her hands on the arm of his chair. "Of course I don't mind. Mother has loved you for so long—"

"More fool she," Boyd said, and his eyes were full, too, but he was smiling. "How much time I've wasted, young Miss Liz. How I wish I could take back those years. I should have made your mother my bride long ago. It took waking up in the hospital to make me realize that life is finite and I'd wasted a great deal of mine."

"I know that Mom put you off—"

"That's no excuse. I shouldn't have listened to her. I should have grabbed her by that head of red hair and dragged her off to the church."

Liz smiled at him with all the fondness that was in her heart for him. "I hope when you set the day, you'll use a more sedate method of getting her to the altar."

"I have your approval, then?" He looked oddly young, boyish, and very much like Travis.

"My approval and my love. I give it with all my heart." Liz leaned forward and kissed him. Boyd caught her to him and held her in hands that were strong and firm.

"Travis. Just the fellow I wanted to see." Rachel caught him as he was padding through the kitchen in his stocking feet, boots in hand.

He felt for a moment like he was eighteen again and trying to sneak in after a late date. Rachel always heard him with those eagle ears of hers.

She arranged the tea towel on the bar opposite the stove, taking her time to carefully display the embroidered design, a faceless little girl in a red paisley sunbonnet hanging clothes on the line. Travis knew he should prepare himself for whatever Rachel was going to toss at him, but it was hard to prepare for a meeting when the agenda was known only to one's opponent.

"Sit down. I'd like to talk to you for a minute."

Those were words that had struck fear in his heart when he was sixteen and had been out the night before, driving too fast. He had nothing to feel guilty about now, but, absurdly, he did. A thousand possible topics of conversation Rachel might want to discuss sprang to his mind. He probably deserved to be brought up short on every one of them.

"Can I get you a cup of coffee?"

She was stalling deliberately, all the while looking as innocent as Saint Joan. He told her no, he was quite full still from the wonderful supper she'd cooked.

Travis fought the urge to run his hand through his hair and sat with one arm on the table, his eyes on Rachel. Over the years, he'd learned to keep his head about him when confronted by irascible heads of boards, but Rachel had once been his surrogate mother, and he'd always had ambiguous feelings about her. He'd been eleven when she arrived on that snowy January night, and he'd been too old to accept her as a mother substitute. And yet, as that terrible year went on, Rachel had earned his respect. When he was a teenager, he'd been convinced she could read his mind. He'd long since given up that childish suspicion, but still, as far back as he could remember, no member of his family had ever pulled the wool over her eyes. He supposed she knew exactly what had happened in that bedroom under the eaves. The only thing he didn't know was what she intended to say to him about it.

Right now, she seemed inordinately interested in removing her apron and hanging it beside the tea towel. She was tall, slender, and curvaceous in her jeans, and when she turned around to him, her cheeks were soft and faintly pink. Good bones and good breeding. No wonder his father had been smitten for so many years. Liz would be just as stunning when she reached middle age. It jolted him a little to think that some South Dakota dude might become just as taken with Liz and carry her off to his little house on the prairie.

Rachel settled into the chair across the table from Travis, giving him a straight look with green eyes just a shade lighter than Liz's. He knew in his gut that Rachel in a mood to be straightforward was trouble.

"No one has really asked you how you would feel having a stepmother, and I thought perhaps I should."

That certainly wasn't one of the things he'd expected her to say. Travis relaxed back in his chair, his breathing more even. "I thought you knew that you have my complete blessing."

She looked down at the table, as if studying the crocheted doily that sat under the sugar bowl. Her fingers found the starched strands of the doily, played with them. "I wanted you to have a chance to register a protest, if you thought you should, when we were safely out of Boyd's presence."

Travis picked up that restless hand that was worrying the doily and brought it to his mouth. "I couldn't be happier for you both. As for the stepmother bit, well, I don't think I'll need help tying my shoes." His smile was warm and intimate and seemed to bring a deeper pink to her cheeks. "And I'd appreciate it if you didn't yell at me to pick up my room. Particularly right now, when it's a little disordered."

Her smile was beautiful to behold. "I'll try to remember that. Rules for stepmothering an adult child. No yelling about picking up your room."

He kept her hand clasped in his on the table. "It's long overdue, you know, your wedding to my father."

"I do know that." The green eyes looked at him with a passionate intensity that nearly overwhelmed him with their resemblance to Liz's. "I've wasted so much time, been so foolish. I so much regret those wasted years." She rose then, with sudden abruptness, and ripped off a paper towel from the suspended roll, ran water over it and began to rub a spot on the counter that Travis couldn't see. She looked up suddenly, those green eyes darker than they had been a minute ago. "I don't want my daughter making the same mistake I did. That's why I've told her I'm glad she's made the decision to leave the ranch.''

He was an old, practiced hand at keeping his poise, but it took all the effort he had to say in a normal tone, ''Liz is leaving? When does she plan to go?''

''As soon as she can find another position.''

''She hasn't found anything yet?''

''No. But she's sent out a few applications. I do hope she won't go too far away. But she's talking about North Dakota. So cold there in the winter. Or Wyoming.''

''I...didn't realize she was thinking of leaving. Has she been...unhappy?'' He couldn't imagine the ranch without Liz. She had always been here. No matter where he went, no matter how long he stayed away, whenever he returned, she had always been here.

''Not unhappy, exactly. Just feeling that she needs to get on with her life.''

How vigorously Rachel scrubbed, how carefully she kept her back to him. He closed his eyes against the sudden sharp and unexpected pain. He told himself that Liz's leaving was for the best, that it certainly simplified his life. Why was it he suddenly felt he didn't want his life simplified? He wanted her here, where she had always been, where he'd thought she would always be, safe, warm, welcoming when he came home. The one thing in his life he could depend on. But, of course, there was nothing in life a man could really depend on.

''She must do what she thinks best,'' he said in a cool tone.

''Yes, that's what we all do in the end. I knew you'd understand,'' Rachel said, and turned her back to scrub furiously at the cupboard.

While he sat there thinking the conversation must be at an end, Rachel turned around to him again. ''Your father and I decided not to wait for Diana's return to get married. We've planned a small ceremony here at the house on Friday. We've made our plans quickly and quietly, to avoid any publicity. We would like you and Liz to be here. Could you possibly stay until then?''

He didn't want to stay. He wanted to escape, to go back to the city, where he was safe from feeling buffeted by the storms of emotion, where he could forget that Liz had walked out of his life. "I suppose I could manage to put off leaving until after your wedding."

"Thank you, Travis." She came to him and pulled him up in her arms to brush her mouth against his cheek. "You've always been such a good boy."

His mouth tilted up in a smile. "Yes, ma'am."

Rachel listened for Travis's bedroom door to close. Then she went in to Boyd, where he sat in his chair in the twilight, looking out over his ranch. In a soft voice, she asked, "Well? How did it go?"

Boyd shrugged. "I did my best. You had the toughest assignment. How do you think you did?"

Rachel sighed. "I told him she was going away. Whether it will do any good to believe he is going to lose her, I don't know. Nothing ever quite works the way it should with that hard-headed son of yours. He's determined to make up his own mind about things."

"You're sure he loves her?"

"I know he does. He's loved her for years, just as she has loved him. He simply doesn't understand himself well enough to know that Liz is what he needs most in his life. He did agree to stay for our wedding."

"Well, my boy is hardheaded, but he isn't stupid. He'll figure it out."

"But when, my darling? When he's sixty-three?"

Boyd held out his hand to Rachel, and she came and caught it up in hers and knelt down beside him.

"Let's hope he's not that much like his father. We McCallisters are hardly worth all the trouble we cause you Grant women, are we?"

"You're worth every minute of it, and don't you forget it."

He looked down at the lamplight playing on her red hair. There were a few silver strands in it now. He reached out to touch those silken strands. All he needed in the world was here, right in his hands.

Liz couldn't sleep. The house was too hot, the will-o'-the-wisp breeze too fleeting to cool her warm body. And it was much too quiet. Her mother had moved into Diana's old bedroom in the big house to be near Boyd, and so Liz stayed alone in the little house she'd shared with her mother for so long, and slept in the bed that was haunted by memories of Travis, loving her.

Tomorrow he would be gone.

Around midnight, Liz rose from her bed for the fourth time to check the lights at the windows in Travis's bedroom, all the while telling herself she was a fool. She couldn't go to him, and he wouldn't come to her.

She closed her eyes to shut out the wanting, the needing, but when she opened them again, the ache was still there, gathering strength.

The lights in Travis's bedroom winked out.

She stood for a moment, trying to visualize him lying down in his bed. Did he think of her, want her even a tiny bit as much as she wanted him? The open window brought the scent of the ranch, the faint smell of dust mingled with the rich, deep aroma of new-mown hay. Blaze whinnied his lonesome-horse cry. A mare in the far corral answered.

"You, too, Blaze?" Her lips curved in a smile, and Liz let the curtain drop and went to lay back down on the bed, her cotton shirt nightgown riding at midthigh.

The soft tap at her front door brought her flying up out of bed. She hadn't been expecting it, and yet, and yet…

She flew down the stairs, her bare feet barely touching the risers. She'd left the screen door open to let in the breezes, and it was Travis who was stepping in, Travis who caught her in his arms.

"I couldn't stay away any longer," he murmured softly, opening her world from emptiness to joy.

He'd taken a shower, she could smell the scent of soap on him. He was clean as a breeze from the mountains, his skin warmly fragrant with good grooming, his jaw newly shaven and smooth. She wanted to melt into him. She whispered. "Why would you ever try? I thought if you left without our being together again, I might just die."

He kissed her, taking her mouth into his with the expertise she had come to know was his.

When he lifted his head, she couldn't fight the melting feeling in her feminine core. Nor did she want to. She was alive with the need to lie down with him, feel the sweet weight of his body covering hers. He had taught her much that first night, and she had learned well. Most particularly, she had learned that with surrender comes triumph.

"Sweetheart—" his hands slid up her back under her loose nightshirt "—if you'd rather not be stretched out here in the hallway, I suggest you turn your beautiful little rear end around and get it up those stairs."

There was no lamplight in her room, only starshine. There was no hesitancy in her acceptance of him this time, only his body taking hers down on the bed, his mouth seeking hers hungrily. His hand slid under the loose cotton and followed the smooth path of her slender body up under her nightshirt to find her breast and claim it boldly, possessively. Her hands were equally possessive, making quick work of stripping away his shirt and unzipping his jeans. He caught her arms, lifted them, and her shirt was gone. She helped him out of his jeans and his briefs. He encouraged her to take what was hers, and so she touched him, wondering once again at the silkiness of him, the sleekness of him, the moisture that his ardor had already brought forth. The look of dark pleasure on his face filled her with excitement, with joy. And then he laid her back gently and took possession of her with his hand, and when she gasped with delight, he kissed her lips and thrust his tongue into her yielding mouth and showed her such pleasure as she had known only with him. And when she cried out for him and told him how much she wanted him, he sheathed himself to protect her and gave her what she needed. Exactly what she needed.

They lay beside each other, sated. Yet, after a soft, quiet time of murmuring and kissing, and reveling in the miracle of their intimacy, they discovered the strength and the need to love yet again.

They showered together, laughing, teasing, she turning the spray on his back, he catching her hips and holding her still for his soapy-faced kiss.

When they returned to her shadowy room, his mood changed. Looking as serious as she had ever seen him look, Travis leaned over to snatch up her nightshirt from the floor. In the evocative darkness scented with their clean bodies, he slipped the cool cotton over her head.

"Your mother tells me you're leaving the ranch."

She sat down on the bed, unable to take her eyes off him while he moved with consummate ease to dress himself, turning away from her to slide his legs into his briefs and jeans. When he turned back, she lifted her chin with characteristic pride. "Yes."

He sat down on the bed beside her, his body warm next to hers. "I don't want you to go."

Had he purposely chosen this time to say these words to her, when he was a dark silhouette in her room outlined against the faint light coming in from the window, his shadowy face not giving her a single clue about his feelings?

"Why not?" Her voice sounded husky to her ears.

"Why not?" He sounded impatient. "Because I want you to be here when I come home again—"

"When will that be?"

"I'm not sure. Thanksgiving, perhaps—"

"And you want me sitting here waiting for you, so you'll have two turkeys to enjoy."

There was a long silence. Then he said in a cool tone, "I take it you think that's a bad idea."

She sprang up from the bed, clasped her arms across her chest and stood looking out the window into a South Dakota night that held warmth and crickets and heartache. "Why go through this charade of caring about what I do or where I go, Travis? Just go your way, back to Chicago, and I'll go mine, and we'll forget we ever spent this time together."

"You can do that? Just dismiss what we've had together and go on with your life?"

She twisted around toward him, wishing he could see the light of fire in her eye. "It's what you expected to happen, isn't it?"

"No. I expected to call you and talk to you. I expected to see you again when I come home for the holidays—"

"Oh, I see. You want me to sit here and be the little

raisin in your fruitcake of life. Oh, I forgot. You don't like fruitcake.''

He didn't react to her sarcasm. "Do you think I want you out there wandering around in the world, running into guys like Lester and having God knows what happen to you—''

"I'm not your responsibility!" she cried. "I'm the lady the footloose cowboy took to bed when he had a few minutes off between branding and the hay field.''

"I'm no cowboy," he said.

"No, you aren't. A cowboy would have had the decency to confine his kissing to his horse before he rode off into the sunset.''

He didn't need a light in the room to see the fire blazing in her eyes. "I never wanted to hurt you.''

"You didn't hurt me. You haven't touched me. I'm a free woman, free to go anywhere and love any man I please.''

His jaw was set, and so were his shoulders. "No, you're not. You belong here, with your family and my family and Blaze—''

"No," she said. "I don't belong here. I never did.''

"Liz." He clasped her shoulders. "Please...don't go. Please...stay.''

She shook her head. He felt her resistance under his hands. "I...can't.''

He dropped his hands. "I didn't know you were so stubborn," he said.

Coolly she tilted up her chin. "It runs in the family.''

"I'd better go," he said.

"Yes.''

He turned and walked silently out the door. She sank onto the bed, shivering and cold, very cold. Her body was cold, her heart was cold. It was very late, almost three-thirty in the morning. It didn't matter. She wouldn't sleep the rest of the night, anyway.

A little before six, she slipped out of the house. Dressed in her jeans, her shirt and her boots, her eyes determinedly directed away from the big house, where Travis was, her mind blessedly numb, she headed for the stable.

Blaze was as ready for his morning run as she was ready to share it with him. He greeted her with a loud whinny of ecstatic energy and bobbed his head as she came into his stall to feed him the bit of apple she'd brought. While he munched, she tossed his blanket on him and then the saddle, making sure she waited until he had to take a breath, so that the cinch was tight.

He was a little fractious as they headed out into the dewy morning filled with birdsong, going west, toward the part of the sky that held remnants of the night. The sun was rising at Liz's back, golden streamers of light playing over the dew-sparkled prairie. Blaze, bless his heart, commanded all her attention, with those little mincing sidesteps he took, the quick bobs of the head that were his little tests to see if she was alert. He was like a mischievous schoolchild who needed to be watched every minute.

Keeping a light but firm hand on the reins, she guided him out of the corral. When the gate creaked shut behind her, she let him have his head.

"Go," she said, and Blaze went, running like the wind, stretching his legs to full strength like the Thoroughbred racehorse he was.

Still in his clothes, Travis finally lay down on the bed about five-thirty in the morning, but he couldn't sleep. A half hour later, when he heard the sound of hoofbeats in the yard, he sprang out of bed and went to the window. He saw Liz then, mounted on Blaze, her hair flying under

her ha   addle. He kept
watchi   d and they dis-
appear

An   ble, looking at
Blaze   n the blue devil
she'd   so long on that
horse

Tr   Seaton stacking
bales

Se   e barn, his face
half-   swiped a sleeve
over   ler.''

''   orning ride more
than

S   aybe. Maybe not.
Couldn't say for sure. Never   .'' With that, he
went back to his work of tossing bales around.

''Thank you so much for your succinct and incisive report,'' Travis said under his breath.

He emerged from the barn into a warming sun, but there
was an icy chill around his heart. His gut instinct told him
something was wrong.

Rachel was in the kitchen, preparing pancakes for the
on-the-dot-of-seven breakfast. ''Have you seen Liz?''

She gave him a quizzical look. ''No, I haven't. I was
expecting her to help me this morning, too, after she came
back from riding Blaze.''

His anxiety level went several notches higher. He didn't
like the look of things. He didn't like it one little bit.

He checked with his father, he checked with March.
Neither one of them had seen Liz—or Blaze—this morning. When he returned to the kitchen, Rachel offered him
coffee. He took a cup and went out to the porch with it,
pacing, the coffee nearly forgotten in his hand.

In the living room, Boyd, shaved and showered, came hobbling out to the living room on his cane. "What is he doing out there?" Boyd asked Rachel.

"I think," Rachel said, "he is worrying about Liz."

Boyd started toward the door. Rachel caught his arm. "Let him alone, dearest. It will do him good to discover that he can't control everything quite as well as he thinks he can."

Boyd looked down into her face. "Are you sure he'll be all right?"

"Quite sure. Come into the kitchen and have some coffee, and let's talk about how interesting life will be with all our children and grandchildren keeping us on our toes. Diana sounded so happy when she called last night. I'm glad your children have accepted me so well, Boyd."

"Why not? They've thought of you as their mother for years. Now it's just a matter of putting it on the record."

She smiled at the political reference. "The pancakes are your favorite this morning. Blueberry."

"I knew I loved you, woman."

"I'm afraid to say that yours is a cupboard love, my friend."

Boyd glanced again out the window at his son. "I hate to see him suffering."

"A little suffering is good for him. Builds his character," said Rachel, smiling.

Travis stared off into the ever lightening sky. *If that woman doesn't appear on the horizon soon, I'm going to go out there and drag her home by that long red mane of hers.*

He saw the little dust motes rising on the horizon first. Then Blaze trotted into the yard, his saddle empty, his reins dangling and his left ear bleeding. Someone had taken a potshot at him.

Chapter Twelve

The world reeled. Travis flung his coffee cup aside and, one hand on the rail, leaped off the porch. At the sound of the pottery clattering and the sight of a man flying through the air, Blaze shied and reared.

Travis's brain clicked on. Watch it. Don't spook Blaze. You need him. If Liz is out lying in the road somewhere, that horse is the only creature on God's earth who knows where she is. Keep your wits about you, man.

"Whoa, boy, whoa." Travis tamped down sharply on his worry for Liz and approached the stallion as he had seen Liz do that night, thanking a munificent God that he had at least a little insight into how to calm Blaze, feeling his throat fill at the sudden memory of her courage and beauty.

"Careful." March Huddleston came up behind him, his gravelly voice issuing the warning. "Hard telling what that horse will do when he gits riled up."

"Stay back," Travis ordered. "Let me do this. Whoa, boy, whoa. Easy, old man." Travis was aware as never before of the big horse's power and muscled heat. If, in his excitement to escape whoever had shot at him, Blaze had hurt Liz, he'd be going to the glue factory. And if some maniac had shot Liz as he seemed to have the horse, he was another candidate to become paste. "Let's see what's wrong with your ear."

Blaze shied and minced away, but he was a curious horse, and he wouldn't leave until he saw whether Travis did have anything interesting in his hand.

"Got any apples in the bunkhouse?" Travis said in a low tone to March.

"One. I'll git it for ya."

Travis went on talking to the horse soothingly, keeping his hand out of reach just enough that the horse was forced to step closer. It seemed to Travis like an eternity before March returned and handed him the apple, neatly cut in four sections.

"I opened it up for ya, so he could get a good whiff of it."

"Thanks, March. I'm glad you thought of that." Travis opened his palm, exposing the apple, the sharp drift of fruit sugar hitting his nose. "Here it is, boy. Here's your treat. Come and get it."

Blaze was wary, but he had a good nose, too, and he loved apples. He pranced forward, his eyes never leaving Travis's face. Travis stayed still, crooning. Blaze danced back, skittered sideways, bobbed his head, pawed the earth and stepped forward again. That apple was too enticing. He was inches away from Travis's hand.

"I got to give you credit," March said to Travis's back, keeping his voice low and even. "You're a cool one."

Out of the corner of his eye, Travis saw Craig Seaton

emerge from the barn. Len Hollister hustled out of the bunkhouse to see what was happening.

Travis didn't have the courage March was crediting him with. He wasn't facing a Blaze in a spate of hatred, as Liz had. "Tell everybody to stand still. I don't want this horse spooked again."

"You heared him," March growled. "Everybody stays put."

"Come on, Blaze. Come and see what's in my hand."

His voice was low and irresistible. The stallion danced forward, bobbed his head and snatched away the apple. Travis was just as quick, catching up one of his reins. Quickly he held out his hand, with another section of the apple. "Don't run away boy. There's more where that one came from." He captured the other rein.

"Whatcha gonna do now?" March asked. "You ain't never rode this hellion before." March moved forward, his brow creased. "You ain't been on the back of a horse as temperamental as this one is for a long time."

"He's the only one who knows where Liz is."

Craig Seaton came to life and remembered his position. "He's a one-woman horse, Travis, and his ear's been nicked. You're taking your life in your hands, you climb on his back. I can't be responsible—"

It was quite a speech for Seaton, and if Travis had had more time, he'd have appreciated that the man was conscientious enough to worry about him. "You're not responsible for me." Travis gathered up the reins and stuck his foot in Blaze's stirrup. Blaze reacted by twisting around in a circle. Then he started bucking. With one leg in the saddle, Travis clung to the pummel like a burr. Blaze had another trick to discourage a rider he didn't like. He trotted to the corral fence and tried to rub Travis off. Travis gritted his teeth and hung on, as determined to climb aboard as Blaze was to keep him out of the saddle. Distracted by his ride by the fence Blaze lowered his guard. Travis took advantage of his moment of inattention and swung his right leg over, succeeding in seating himself in the saddle. When Travis took a firm but light grip on the reins and urged him forward, Blaze obeyed, looking dazed.

"Gee," Len Hollister breathed. "I didn't know he could ride like that. I thought he was...just a sissy town boy."

March said, "There's so dang much you don't know about what goes on around here you shouldn't even be opening your mouth." He squinted up at Travis, took his hat off, ran a hand through his thinning sandy hair. To Travis, March said, "You be careful, you hear?"

"I hear," said Travis, and he reined Blaze around to the direction from which the horse had come.

"I didn't know he was such a good cowboy," Len Hollister said, his eyes wide as he watched Travis guide the big horse down the road.

"Like I said," March growled, "dang awful lot you don't know. Best thing to do is keep your eyes open and your mouth shut until you get that rotten condition of yours remedied."

"What rotten condition?"

"Stupidity."

Out on the trail, Travis leaned over Blaze's back. "Okay, boy, let's go. Take me to her."

Sick in his heart, frightened out of his mind, Travis clamped his legs around Blaze's belly and urged him faster over the road. *Where was Liz?* Had she been hit, as Blaze had been, and was she hurt more severely than the horse? His gut felt wrung inside out. If anything had happened to her, he'd track down the murdering idiot who'd taken a shot at her if it took him the rest of his life.

He hadn't prayed in years. He wasn't sure he knew how.

But the words were a litany in his mind. *Please let her be all right.*

The wind and Blaze's furious pace whipped the hat off his head. He didn't care. He had to find her.

He saw her bandanna first. It fluttered from the stem of a silk pod weed. She lay a little ways away, on her side, her feet drawn up, her head back.

Something, some powerfully benevolent spirit, reminded him to tether Blaze on the fence before he went to Liz.

Kneeling down beside her, his heart thumping unmercifully in his chest, Travis ran his hand over her, checking for broken bones or a sign of bleeding from a gunshot wound. There was neither. Liz was warm and breathing and all in one piece. She'd obviously fallen off Blaze's back and been knocked unconscious. His soul spilling over with gratitude that she wasn't seriously injured, Travis gathered Liz into his arms and said her name with all the heartfelt emotion of his relief.

She opened her eyes. He thought he had never seen such a beautiful sight as those green depths staring up at him. There was puzzlement, and then lightning-quick comprehension. "I heard a shot. Blaze. Is he—"

"He's fine. What about you?"

"I took a spill. It was my own fault. I was leaning forward to look at Blaze's ear, and while I was forward in the saddle, there was another shot and it spooked him and he reared. I was caught off guard. Ouch! That hurts."

"I'm sorry, love." His fingers probed her head tenderly, and he found the lump. He didn't want to tell her, but he was sure that when she leaned forward to see about Blaze, she had saved her own life.

"Good thing I landed on my head. Hardest part of my

body," she said, with a rueful smile that tore at his soul. "What are you doing out here?"

"Oh," he said, choking on his laughter and his love for her, "I just happened to be in the neighborhood."

She put up a slender hand to touch his forehead. "You weren't worried about me, were you?"

"No, of course not. Why would I worry about you? I'm just the cowboy who kisses the girl and then rides off into the sunset without giving her another thought." He plucked her fingers off his face and brought them to his mouth to kiss.

Travis looked so beautiful, his face dark and hard with concern for her, his tenderness betrayed in the black depths of his eyes. Her senses already heightened by the touch of his mouth on her skin, Liz felt as if she would burst with love for him. She said, "You wouldn't want this to become a habit."

He lifted dark lashes that were utterly beautiful. "What? Kissing your hand? Or worrying about you?"

"Worrying about me," she said breathlessly.

"It's been a habit to worry about you for so long that I can't remember when I started."

"I'm...sorry I frightened you," she said. "I'm really all right."

He caught her up in his arms and stood up with her to carry her over to Blaze. "Travis, put me down. I said I'm all right...."

"Yes, you are definitely all right. You are also all mine. Which means I can indulge myself if I want to take care of you."

She examined his face, afraid to believe her ears. Was he merely talking this way because he'd been afraid for her safety? "Does that mean you belong to me, too?"

"If you'll have me," he said.

The temptation was strong to take advantage. She couldn't do it. If he regretted his words after the shock wore off, she would be devastated. "I'll think about it," she told him.

"And do you take this woman to be your lawful wedded wife?"

"I do," said Boyd, standing tall and proud beside Rachel.

"The ring, please."

Travis handed the minister the ring. How devastatingly handsome he looked, his tall, lithe body neatly clothed in a dark gray pinstripe suit. When he looked at his father, Travis's face was beautiful. That was the only word for that classically chiseled, exquisitely planed countenance. If Liz hadn't fallen in love with him years ago, she'd certainly have fallen in love with him today.

Liz stood beside her mother, trying to hold her mother's bouquet without trembling. Liz felt more nervous than Rachel appeared to be. Her mother was the picture of serene confidence.

There were only the four of them in front of the fireplace, with the men who worked on the ranch gathered behind them, March looking strange with his shaven chin, a betraying bit of blood where he'd nicked himself, his hair slicked back, Len Hollister blushing with self-consciousness, and Craig Seaton not quite knowing how to hold his hands as he stood there in his best brown suit.

The ceremony was over quickly. Rachel had given the minister strict instructions that he was not to draw out the proceedings. Boyd had insisted he would stand up with his bride without a cane and, of course, Rachel was concerned about his tiring.

After the papers were signed and Liz and Travis had

scrawled their signatures as witnesses, Rachel took her place behind the table and served her groom the first piece of the wedding cake. Rachel had baked the delicious carrot cake, a favorite of Boyd's, herself.

Liz took pictures of her mother feeding Boyd, enjoying the look of proud love on Boyd's face, the rapt happiness on her mother's. Travis had a camera in his hand, and was shooting his share of candid shots of the happy couple, as well.

When Rachel and Boyd had finished the ritual sharing of the sweet and had sipped their first champagne as man and wife, their arms linked, Rachel kissed her husband and then put her champagne flute down with an air of determination. She wanted a picture of Travis and Liz together, she said, and she meant to take it herself.

Liz acquiesced, knowing that her mother would not listen to a protest. Travis stepped to Liz's side and slid his arm around her waist. What was he thinking? She couldn't tell. His face was as enigmatic as she'd ever seen it.

His hand was warm at her waist. Warm and familiar. She hoped the camera would lie just this once. For if it recorded the love she had in her heart for Travis at this moment, it would be caught in time for all the world to see.

The moment the picture was over, Travis stepped away from her. Liz had a sudden vision of looking through a photo album years from now, when Travis was gone from her life. She would sit gazing at the only picture she had of the two of them together, and she would remember this day and think that she had been right to put Travis off. For he had made no move toward her since that day he picked her up and rode with her on Blaze's back into the yard, like the prince returning with his bride.

It had been an illusion of love under the stress of her

accident. Now that he knew she was all right, Travis would go back to Chicago and live his life, and she would live hers. She supposed she'd see him at holidays, but by then, they'd both be married to other people and they'd consider this time they had together as an experience that was simply a part of life, the way people did with lovers who'd been in their lives briefly.

When Boyd and Rachel left for an overnight trip to Sioux Falls to stay in a luxury hotel, the house was quiet, unbearably quiet. Liz washed the glass plate that Rachel had used for the wedding cake, hung up the dish towel and went into the living room. There was a piece of bright green ribbon on the floor, a streamer from her mother's bouquet. Liz rescued the ribbon and tucked it in the pocket of the silky chiffon dress she'd worn to be yet another woman's bridesmaid and went out of the house to seek the solitude of her own little home.

Dressed down in jeans and boots, Liz was mucking out Blaze's stall when Travis finally tracked her down in the heated twilight.

"You changed your clothes," he said.

She stopped, looked up at him with a glance full of worlds of things she wasn't going to say, and went back to work. "I hate it when the chiffon gets caught in the shovel."

"Me, too," he said.

She stopped shoveling, propped her hand on the fork handle and studied him. He could see she wanted to smile, but she was darned if she was going to. "Did you want something, or did you come out here to practice being clever before you go back to the city?"

"I'm not sure. I was hoping to find you in a better mood." He tilted his head to one side. "I don't think I've ever seen you so grouchy before."

"Well, having your mother get married before you do will do that to a lady."

"Ah," he said. "Perhaps she has better taste in men than you do."

"Obviously." She bent over to shovel a few more scoopfuls of straw out the door into the wheelbarrow. He stood there, thinking it would be a prudent thing to let her vent a little more of her energy, one hand propped up against the stud of the opposite stall.

She shifted the wheelbarrow for a trip out the door. "You're in my way."

"You know," he said, his tone droll, "somehow, when I imagined asking the woman of my dreams to marry me, this wasn't the scene I pictured."

The handles of the wheelbarrow in her grip, she was caught in flight. "I thought you were never going to get married."

"I thought I was never going to get married, too."

"You don't want the responsibility."

"That also was true."

She heard the "was," but she was afraid to believe in it. "You're a coward," she said coolly, without accusation.

He thought about that for a moment. "I'd like it better if we stopped at my not wanting responsibility."

She picked up the wheelbarrow and pushed it past him. "Where's Blaze?" he asked.

"He had a date with a mare."

"And you let him go?"

"He's a big boy." She trundled her load outside and went to dump the straw on the compost pile in the corral.

"So everybody's got somebody but you and me," he said to her back in the warm sun.

"Pretty much. I heard you had Sheriff Hanson put out an all-points bulletin for Harv."

"I plan to press charges." He paused. "I found the tree I think he was sitting in."

"He had to be pretty determined to climb a tree with a broken leg."

"Lester was never short of determination when it came to justifying himself. At least he had sense enough to stop shooting before he actually hit you."

"I don't want to talk about him any more."

"Well, we've found something we agree on. Liz." He took the pitchfork out of her hand and tossed it on the ground.

"Yes, Travis?"

She was determined not to cooperate, he could see that. He supposed her pique might be just a little justified. He'd wanted to wait until Rachel and Boyd were safely married and on their way. He hadn't wanted anything to interfere with their happiness. He'd thought she would understand. Obviously, she hadn't. Perhaps with good reason. She wasn't as sure of him as he was of her. But she would be. He would see to it.

"Are you going to come here so I can kiss you, or are you going to go on playing dumb?" He grabbed her hand and pulled her toward him. She resisted just enough to make him exert some effort.

"I never was very good at playing dumb."

"That's very true. Sometimes you frighten me with your insights."

"But not enough to frighten you away."

"No." He smoothed back her hair, his smile fond and possessive. "I'll have to live in the city," he said. "I have a business to run. It will be hard for you to live away from the ranch. I know that. Do you think we can work out some way to mesh our lives?"

She was versatile, his Liz. And smart. She didn't bat an eye. "We could stay the summer here, to satisfy me. Then we'd move to the city for the winter months. You know things are slow here on the ranch in the wintertime." She faced him, her head back, her eyes glistening with courage, with love.

"We might confuse the children. They might have to wake up and ask, if this is June, are they in South Dakota?" He wasn't seriously objecting, he was teasing her.

"But they'll have the best of two different worlds. Think of how well-rounded they'll be. I can't wait to see them. Can we start a family right away?"

"Maybe we could hold off just a little bit?" He raised a dark eyebrow. "After all, you're not so very old."

"Thank you very much, Mr. McCallister." She gave him a light tap on the cheek. "But you are past thirty, my friend. Your biological clock is ticking. How long can we afford to wait?"

"Cruel, woman, cruel, to remind me of my advanced age."

"Travis." She was serious now. "You do…want children, don't you?"

"Only if they all look like you. So. Are you going to be mine, lovely Miss Liz?"

"You're sure you want me?"

She wasn't being coy. She was asking him if he really had changed. "Dammit, woman, when I saw you lying on the ground, I thought I had lost you forever. You know I want you. I've always wanted you. I don't give a damn where I live, as long as you're there with me, in my bed."

"Like I said," she murmured, raising her face to his, "we'll have such well-rounded children."

* * *

Mrs. Prudence Welsh lived directly across from the church in the little prairie town, and her eleven-year-old daughter Chelsey loved to watch the brides going in and out of the church on their special day. But at the end of this ceremony, the little girl saw something she'd never seen before.

"Mama, come quick. There's a bride out on the lawn of the church and she's turning cartwheels. Look, Mama, her white dress is flying all around her."

"Yes, honey, it's that Grant girl. You know, she always was a little different, working like a man on that ranch. I guess we can't expect decorum from a gal like her, even on her wedding day."

Wistfully, Chelsey said, "She looks happy to me. If being different is what it takes to be happy, I'd like to be different like that."

A week later, in Travis's luxurious bedroom in his condo, Travis watched his wife getting ready for the reception to be held in their honor, with so much pride and love in his heart that he thought his face must betray every bit of it. Liz looked so beautiful in her long sleek gown of lemon yellow. The only thing he didn't like was that she had insisted on wearing her hair up. He supposed she did look more sophisticated. Hair up or down, she was heart-stoppingly beautiful. He knew one thing for sure—he was extremely glad she'd be wearing his ring when she stepped out into that pack of wolves.

Liz turned around to him. "I don't know what you're thinking, my dear, but I hope it isn't something about me. You look very fierce."

"I was thinking what I would do to any gentleman who makes a pass at my beautiful wife."

"I'm not beautiful...."

"Of course you are." He dropped a kiss on her nape, making her breath catch. "Let's skip this party and go back to bed."

"Travis, please. How can I concentrate on remembering the things Hilda told me about everybody if you keep talking about going to bed?"

"I'm practicing the displacement theory," he said. "Thinking about making love to me is supposed to keep you from being nervous about meeting my friends."

"I'm not nervous. I'm terrified."

"Don't be. You're lovely and smart and I love you. What else do you need?"

"Osgood Feathers's approval," she said, the light of amusement dancing in her eyes.

"He'll tell you you're stunning. Because you are."

Later, when she handed that worthy gentleman his favorite drink—gin and tonic, heavy on the tonic—he said to her, "My dear, you are simply enchanting. I'm so glad Travis has found someone like you to share his life. You can't imagine the things that poor man has had to put up with. Women crashing in on him at the office, making astounding statements. Quite shocking. There was one quite brazen young woman, red-haired, I believe—" He stopped speaking and directed a startled glance at Liz's hair, done up in a chignon, with a diamond glittering in her red-gold tresses.

"I say, is it you, then?"

"I'm very much afraid it is."

He looked quite abashed. "I think I've rather put my foot in it."

"Not at all. You're quite right about my husband needing to tighten the security at his office. I'll speak to him about it, shall I?"

Later, as they were getting ready for bed, Travis pulled

Liz into his arms. "What did you say to Osgood at dinner? You quite had him enthralled."

"I was describing how we artificially inseminate our cattle herd. He was most interested."

Travis put his head back and laughed. "I guess I don't need to worry about you having trouble coming up with interesting topics of conversation."

"You don't need to worry about me at all," she murmured, pulling him down on the bed and stripping his shirt from his trousers. "We'll find something much more interesting than worrying to do."

Chelsey Welsh was fourteen, and her room was filled with posters of rock stars and movie stars these days. But she still loved to watch the little church across the way. It was to be a christening on this day. She knew the signs, lots of cars pulled up close to the church and a lady getting out of the car with a baby held tenderly in her arms. This lady was tall, with dark hair, and so was her husband. The baby was a boy, she knew, because his blanket was blue.

"Yes, that's Diana McCallister. I've forgotten what her married name is," Chelsey's mother said. "She's come home from her place in Boston to get her little boy baptized. I heard Boyd McCallister talking about it in the store the other day. Walking around proud as an old peacock, he was. Second grandchild, he said. Then he started telling me about how his son has a little girl who's two. There she is. Doesn't she look cute in her little bonnet— Oh, oh. There goes her hat. Why, what's that? It looks as if her father is teaching her to turn cartwheels. Why, I never heard of such behavior on a Sunday morning, and right on the church lawn, too. I must speak to Pastor about this."

"Oh, Mama, lighten up. They're just having fun, playing together. I wish I'd had a daddy to play with me like that. Papa is always working.''

''Just not dignified. Now look there. My word, if it isn't that Grant girl. And she's turning cartwheels, too. What *is* this world coming to?''

''As long as there are babies around, Mama, I think the world is coming to something really good.''

* * * * *

This summer, the legend
continues in Jacobsville

Diana Palmer

A LONG, TALL
TEXAN SUMMER

Three **BRAND-NEW** short stories

This summer, Silhouette brings readers a special
collection for Diana Palmer's LONG, TALL TEXANS
fans. Diana has rounded up three **BRAND-NEW**
stories of love Texas-style, all set in Jacobsville,
Texas. Featuring the men you've grown to love from
this wonderful town, this collection is a must-have
for all fans!

*They grow 'em tall in the saddle in Texas—and
they've got love and marriage on their minds!*

Don't miss this collection of original Long, Tall Texans
stories...available in June at your favorite retail outlet.

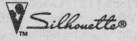

LTTST

Silhouette

SPECIAL EDITION ™

FROM BUD TO BLOSSOM

Through the eyes of love, a plain Jane can become a princess...an ugly duckling a lovely swan! Enchanting stories of the transforming power of love, written by four wonderful writers!

Beginning in July 1997:

MAIL-ORDER MATTY
by Emilie Richards (SE#1113, July)

Matty Stewart eagerly married her secret crush when he needed a mother for his baby girl. But when the infant's custody was threatened, would their relationship survive?

And don't miss these upcoming titles:

IT COULD HAPPEN TO YOU
by Gina Wilkins (SE#1119, August)
Kim Berry was afraid of her own shadow, but when she fell for daredevil Zach McCain, it was time to stop running from life—and romance!

MRS. RIGHT by Carole Halston (SE#1125, September)
Single dad Jeremy Wells vowed never to open his heart again, but could the perfect woman show him the healing power of love?

THE KNIGHT, THE WAITRESS AND THE TODDLER
by Arlene James (SE#1131, October)
Lonely Edward White was unexpectedly transformed into a white knight when he helped—and fell for— waitress Laurel Miller and her adorable child!

And the Winner Is...
You!

...when you pick up these great titles
from our new promotion at your
favorite retail outlet this June!

Diana Palmer
The Case of the Mesmerizing Boss

Betty Neels
The Convenient Wife

Annette Broadrick
Irresistible

Emma Darcy
A Wedding to Remember

Rachel Lee
Lost Warriors

Marie Ferrarella
Father Goose

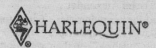 

COMING NEXT MONTH

#1111 THE 200% WIFE—Jennifer Greene
That Special Woman!/Stanford Sisters
Abby Stanford always gave 200% to her family, her job…even to making cookies! And when she met Gar Cameron she knew that if he married her, she'd be the *perfect* wife. But Gar didn't want perfection…. He just wanted to love Abby 200%!

#1112 FORGOTTEN FIANCÉE—Lucy Gordon
Amnesiac Justin Hallwood felt inexplicitly drawn to beautiful Sarah Conroy and her toddler son. Would he regain his memory in time to start anew with the woman and child who were so deeply a part of his past?

#1113 MAIL-ORDER MATTY—Emilie Richards
Matty Stewart married her secret crush, Damon Quinn, for the good of his baby girl. But when the infant's custody became uncertain, they had to decide whether love alone could keep them together….

#1114 THE READY-MADE FAMILY—Laurie Paige
Harrison Stone felt trapped when he realized bewitching Isadora Chavez had duped him into marriage to safeguard her younger brother's future. Could this newfound family learn to trust in their hearts—and embrace honest-to-goodness happiness?

#1115 SUBSTITUTE BRIDE—Trisha Alexander
Rachel Carlton had secretly yearned for her twin sister's fiancé for years—and impulsively posed as David Hanson's bride! Now she needed to captivate her unsuspecting "husband" on their week-long honeymoon before the truth came out!

#1116 NOTHING SHORT OF A MIRACLE—Patricia Thayer
Widowed nurse Cari Hallen needed to believe in life—and love—again, and single father Nick Malone needed to open his heart to hope again, too. But it would take nothing short of a miracle to join these two unlikely people together….

Silhouette

SPECIAL EDITION

That's My Baby!

April 1997 **WHAT TO DO ABOUT BABY**
by Martha Hix (SE #1093)
When a handsome lawyer showed up on Carolyn Grant's doorstep with a toddler in tow, she didn't know what to think. Suddenly, she had a little sister she'd never known about...and a *very* persistent man intent on making Caro his own....

June 1997 **HIS DAUGHTER'S LAUGHTER**
by Janis Reams Hudson (SE #1105)
Carly Baker came to widower Tyler Barnett's ranch to help his fragile daughter—and connected emotionally with the caring father and tenderhearted girl. But when Tyler's interfering in-laws began stirring up trouble, would Carly be forced to give up the man and child she loved?

And in August, be sure to check out...

ALISSA'S MIRACLE
by
Ginna Gray (SE#1117)

He'd told her that he could never have a child, and lovely widow Alissa Kirkpatrick was so in love with enigmatic Dirk Matheson that she agreed to a childless marriage. Until the pregnancy test proved positive....

THAT'S MY BABY!
Sometimes, bringing up baby can bring surprises...and showers of love.

Look us up on-line at: http://www.romance.net

TMBA-A

New York Times Bestselling Authors

JENNIFER BLAKE
JANET DAILEY
ELIZABETH GAGE

Three *New York Times* bestselling authors bring you three very sensuous, contemporary love stories—all centered around one magical night!

It is a warm, spring night and masquerading as legendary lovers, the elite of New Orleans society have come to celebrate the twenty-fifth anniversary of the Duchaise masquerade ball. But amidst the beauty, music and revelry, some of the world's most legendary lovers are in trouble....

Come midnight at this year's Duchaise ball, passion and scandal will be...

Unmasked

Revealed at your favorite retail outlet in July 1997.